She knew what it was that coiled within her. Desire. The wanting and needing to touch this man, to kiss him. To do more than that with him.

Desire was a new experience for Jett. And it pounced upon her with an aggression that startled her. She wasn't sure how to handle it. She'd not known desire for another person. Not in Daemonia. Though the desire for things, safety and control had always resided inside her. And certainly she was no virgin who hadn't a clue what to do with herself regarding a man and sex. She had done things to survive.

No regrets, her darkness whispered.

No, of course not.

But now? Now she was free. And she wanted to explore the exciting feeling that warmed her from ear tips to toes. And everywhere in between.

Michele Hauf is a *USA TODAY* bestselling author who has been writing romance, action-adventure and fantasy stories for more than twenty years. France, musketeers, vampires and faeries usually feature in her stories. And if Michele followed the adage "write what you know," all her stories would have snow in them. Fortunately, she steps beyond her comfort zone and writes about countries and creatures she has never seen. Find her on Facebook, Twitter and at michelehauf.com.

Books by Michele Hauf

Harlequin Nocturne

The Saint-Pierre Series

In the Company of Vampires

Visit the Author Profile page
at Harlequin.com for more titles.

TEMPTING
THE DARK

———

MICHELE HAUF

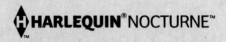

Recycling programs
for this product may
not exist in your area.

ISBN-13: 978-1-335-62962-3

Tempting the Dark

Copyright © 2018 by Michele Hauf

Printed in U.S.A.

Dear Reader,

The hero of *Tempting the Dark* was introduced in *An American Witch in Paris*. The heroine of that story wasn't overly impressed by him, but I was. And I knew as I was writing that story that Savin Thorne needed to tell his own strange and wicked tale.

He was a great mystery to me, and sometimes a writer will never learn everything about their protagonist. But the journey from page one to the end was filled with danger, discovery and surprises. Savin is a true hero, even if a little forced to be one, or if it's simply that he doesn't recognize his own heroics. The best heroes are never aware of their true greatness. That's what makes it a joy to discover them on the page, right along with everyone else.

I hope you enjoy this story!

Michele Hauf

Chapter 1

Savin Thorne stood before the weird, wavery, silver-blue vibrations that undulated in the midnight sky twenty feet above the lavender field. He waited. Twenty minutes had passed since he arrived in the beat-up pickup truck he barely kept alive with oil changes and the occasional battery jump. He'd gotten a call from Edamite Thrash regarding a disturbance in this countryside location, north of Paris.

He knew this area. It was too familiar. His family once lived not half a kilometer away. Yet when driving past the old neighborhood, he'd noted his childhood home had been torn down. Construction on a golf course was under way. Just as well. The bad memory from his childhood still clung to his bones.

To his right, Edamite Thrash, a corax demon, stood

with his eyes closed, his senses focused to whatever the hell was going on.

Savin could feel the undulations in the air and earth prickle through his veins. A heebie-jeebies sensation. The demon within him stirred. Savin tended to think of the nameless, incorporeal demon inside him as "the Other," for no other reason than it had been a childhood decision. She was upset by whatever was irritating the air. And when she stirred, Savin grew anxious.

Ed had been getting instinctual warnings about this disturbance for days, and tonight those dire feelings had alerted him enough to call Savin.

Savin reckoned demons back to Daemonia. The bad ones who had no reason or right to tread the mortal realm. The evil ones who had harmed mortals in this realm. Sometimes even the good ones who pushed the boundaries of secrecy and might have been seen by humans or who were trying to tell the truth about their species.

Savin wasn't demon. He wasn't even paranormal. He was one hundred percent human. Except for the part about him hosting an incorporeal demon for the past twenty years. That tended to screw with a man's mental place in this world. But most days he felt he was winning the part about just trying to stay sane.

A sudden whining trill vibrated the air. Pushing up the sleeves of his thermal shirt to expose the protective sigils on the undersides of his forearms, Savin planted his combat boots and faced the sky that flickered in silver and red.

Ed hissed, "Savin, did you hear that?"

"I did. I'm ready."

Behind them, hefting a fifty-pound sack of sea salt

out from the back of a white hearse, Certainly Jones, a dark witch, prepped for his role in whatever might come charging at them.

"Hurry up, Jones!" Ed called. "It's happening!"

With that announcement, the sky cracked before them. A black seam opened from ground to clouds. From within, a brilliant amber flame burst and roiled. A whoosh of darkness exploded out from the seam.

Savin cursed. That could be nothing but demons. An invasion? He felt the dark and malevolent beings, incorporeal and corporeal, as they flooded into this realm. Cool, hissing brushes across his skin. Wicked alien vocals. The gnashing of fangs and rows of deadly teeth. Tails scything the air. Claws clattering for flesh. And the ones he could not see vibrated a distinctive hum in his veins.

The protection sigils he wore tattooed on his body kept those invisible incorporeal demons from entering his system. As did the bitch demon he'd been serving as shelter to for twenty years. But that didn't mean he was impervious to an external attack by a corporeal demon. He was strong but did not hold a weapon.

The only weapons he required were his stubbornness and his innate ability to see and deflect most demons with a few choice warding incantations.

In the inky darkness, there was no way to count their numbers as they spread across the field and whisked through the air above the men's heads. Standing center of the freshly laid salt circle, Certainly Jones began to recite a spell. Ed swung above his head a black bone lariat bespelled to choke and annihilate demons.

For his part, Savin could recite a general reckoning spell that would reach about a hundred-foot circumference about him and send those demons back to Daemonia. So he began the chant composed of a demonic language he hated knowing.

"There are hundreds," Ed said as a curse as he avoided the salt circle with a jump. "We'll never get them all. Savin?"

He couldn't speak now, for to do so would shatter the foundation of the spell. Raising his arms, palms facing inward—but not touching—and exposing the demonic sigils on the underside of his forearms, Savin expanded his chest and shouted the last few words. And as he did so, the power of those spoken words formed a staticky choker between his fingers. He spread his arms out wide, stretching the choker in a brilliant lash of gold sparks. Then, with a shove forward, he cast the net.

Demons shrieked, squealed and yowled as they were caught by the sticky, sparkling net. Like a fisherman hauling up his catch, only in reverse, it wrapped up dozens, perhaps a hundred or more demons, and wrangled them back through the rift in the sky.

"I expel you to Daemonia!" Savin recited, then immediately prepared to begin again.

"That took care of at least half!" Ed called. "But some are getting away. Jones! How's it going getting that damned door to Daemonia closed?"

"Soon!" shouted the witch.

Savin's net, filled with yet more demons, wrangled another gang and whipped them back through the rift.

The dark witch, a tall, slender man dressed in black, stretched out his tattooed arms. Using specific tattoos as spells, he shouted out a command that gripped the serrated rift in the sky and vised it suddenly closed.

The night grew intensely dark. Not even a nocturnal

creature might see anything for the few moments following the closure of the rift to the Place of All Demons.

Savin dropped his arms and shook out his entire body like a prizefighter loosening up his muscles. He felt the air stir as a few creatures dashed above his head. None dared come too close, or try a talon against his skin. They could sense his innate warning.

No demon dared approach a reckoner.

Ed tugged out his cell phone from an inner suit-coat pocket, and the small electronic light glowed about his face and tattooed neck. The thorns on his knuckles glinted like obsidian as he punched in a number. "I'm calling the troops in Paris. We'll head to town. Certainly, will that seal hold?"

"For a while," the witch said. "But I'm not sure how it was opened in the first place. Had to be from within Daemonia. Which is not cool. Something wicked powerful opened it up."

The witch cast his gaze about the field. Dark shadows flitted through the sky, black on black, as the demons that had avoided Savin's net dispersed. The cool, acrid taste of sulfur littered the air.

Savin thought he heard someone walking across the loose gravel back by his truck. He swung around, squinting his gaze. He didn't see motion. Could have been a demon. More likely a raccoon.

"The energy out here is quieting," he stated. For the hum in his veins had settled. "I think we're good for now. But Ed will have to post a guard out here."

The corax demon nodded to Savin and gave him a thumbs-up even as he spoke on the phone to organize scouts.

Savin slapped a hand across Certainly's back. "Good going, witch."

"I can say the same for you. You took care of more than half of them. I don't know anyone capable of such a skill."

"Wish I could be proud of that skill, but…" Savin let that one hang as he strode back to the parked cars with the witch.

His system suddenly shivered. Savin did not panic. He knew it was the Other expressing her thanks. Or maybe it was resentment for what he had done tonight. He'd never mastered the art of interpreting her messages. So long as she kept quiet ninety percent of the time, he couldn't complain. Some days he felt as if he owed her for what she had done to help him. Other days he felt that debt had long been paid.

"I'm off," Ed said as he headed to his car. "I'll post a guard out here day and night. Thanks, Savin. I'll get back to the both of you with whatever comes up in Paris. If my troops find any of the escapees, we'll gather them for a mass reckoning. Okay with you?"

"I love a good mass demon bash," Savin said. But his heart could not quite get behind his sarcasm. "Check in with me when you need my help again." He fist-bumped Ed and the dark witch, then climbed into his truck and fired up the engine.

Alone and with the windows rolled up, Savin exhaled and closed his eyes. His muscles ached from scalp to shoulders and back, down to his calves and even the tops of his feet. It took a lot of energy to reckon a single demon back to Daemonia. What he'd just done? Whew! He needed to get home, tilt back some whiskey, then crash. A renewal process that worked for him.

But first. His system would not stop shaking until he fed the demon within.

Reaching over in the dark quiet and opening the glove compartment, he drew out a small black tin. Inside on the red velvet lay a syringe and a vial of morphine that he kept stocked and always carried with him. He juiced up the syringe and, tightening his fist, injected the officious substance into his vein. A rush of heat dashed up his arm. A brilliance of colors flashed behind his eyelids. He released his fist and gritted his teeth.

And the shivers stopped.

"Happy?" he muttered to the demon inside him.

He always thought to hear a female chuckle after shooting up. He knew it wasn't real. She had no voice.

Thank the gods he no longer got high from this crap. The Other greedily sucked it all up before it could permeate his system. A strange thing to be thankful for, but he recognized a boon when he saw it.

Flicking on the radio, he nodded as Rob Zombie's "American Witch" blasted through the speakers. Thrash metal. Appropriate for his mood.

Savin was the last of the threesome to pull out of the field. He turned left instead of right, as the other two had. Left would take him over the Seine and toward the left-bank suburbs of Paris. He lived near the multilaned Périphérique in the fourteenth arrondissement. Driving slowly down the loose gravel, he nodded to the thumping bass beat, hands slapping out a drum solo on the steering wheel.

When the truck's headlights flashed on something that moved alongside the road, Savin swore and slammed on the brakes.

"What in all Beneath?"

Was it a demon walking the grassy shoulder of the road? He'd *felt* more incorporeal demons move over him during the escape from the rift than actually witnessed real corporeal creatures with bodies. But anything was possible. And yet...

Savin turned down the radio volume. Leaning forward, he peered through the dusty windshield. The figure wasn't clawed or winged or even deformed. "A woman?"

She glanced toward the truck. The headlights beamed over her bedraggled condition. Long, dark, tangled hair and palest skin. She clutched her dirtied hands against her chest as if to hold on to the thin black fabric that barely covered her limbs from breasts to above her knees. Her legs were dirty and her feet almost black.

She couldn't be a resident from the area. Out for a midnight walk looking like that? Or had she been attacked? Savin hadn't passed any cars in the area, which ruled out a date-gone-bad scenario. That left one other possibility. She had come from Daemonia. Maybe? Corporeal demons could wear a human sheen, making them virtually undetectable to the common man.

But not to Savin's demon radar.

Shifting into Park, Savin spoke a protective spell that would cover him from head to toe. He was no witch, but any human could invoke protection with the proper mind-set. The demon within him shivered but did not protest, thanks to the morphine. He shoved open the door and jumped out. His boots crushed the gravel as he stalked around to the other side of the hood.

"Where in hell did you come from?" he called. Daemonia wasn't hell, but it was damned close.

The woman's body trembled. Her dark eyes searched

his. They were not red. Tears spilled down her cheeks. She looked as though she'd been attacked or ravaged. But demons were tricky and knew how to put on a convincing act of humanity. And yet Savin didn't sense any demonic vibes from her. He could pick a demon out from a crowd milling in the Louvre at fifty paces. Even the ones who had cloaked themselves with a sheen.

He stepped forward. The woman cringed. Savin put up his hands in placation. With the sigils on his forearms exposed, he advertised what he was to her. Just in case she was demon. She didn't flee. Nor did she hiss or spew vile threats at him.

Now Savin wondered if she had been hurt. And perhaps it had nothing to do with what had just gone down in the lavender field. Had she been assaulted and fled, or had some asshole abandoned her far from the city?

"It's okay," he said firmly. "I'm not going to hurt you. My name's Savin Thorne. Do you need help?"

"S-Savin?" The woman's mouth quivered. She dropped her hands to her sides. "Is it… Is it really you?"

He narrowed his gaze on her. She…*knew* him?

"Savin?" She began to bawl and dropped to her knees. "Savin, it's me. Jett."

Savin swallowed roughly. His heart plunged to his gut. By all the dark and demonic gods, this was not possible.

Chapter 2

Twenty years earlier

Savin grabbed Jett's hand and together they raced across the field behind their parents' houses. The lavender grew high and wild, sweetening the air. Butterflies dotted the flower tops with spots of orange and blue.

Jett's laughter suddenly abbreviated. She stopped, gripping her gut as she bent over.

"Wait!" she called as Savin ran ahead. "I'm getting a bellyache. Mamma's cherry pie is sitting right here." She slapped a hand to her stomach. "I shouldn't have eaten that third piece!"

Savin laughed and walked backward toward the edge of the field where the forest began. The dark, creepy forest that they always teased each other to venture into alone. Neither had done it. Yet.

Today he'd challenged her to creep up to the edge and touch the foreboding black tree that grew bent like a crippled man and thrust out its branches as if they were wicked fingers. If she did, he'd give her his Asterix comic collection. Fortunately, he knew she wouldn't do it. Jett was a chicken. And he teased her now by chanting just that.

"I am not!" she announced as she approached him, still clutching her gut. Her long black hair hid what he guessed was a barely contained smile.

"You can't use that excuse to get out of it this time." Savin planted his walking stick in the ground near his sneaker. The stick was one he'd found in the spring and had been whittling at for a month. He'd tried to carve a dragon on the top of it, but it looked more like a snake. "Girls are always chicken!"

"Am not." Jett stepped out of the lavender field and stopped beside him to stare into the forest that loomed thirty paces away.

The trees were close and the trunks looked black from this distance. Savin nudged Jett's arm and she jumped away from him and stuck out her tongue.

"I don't need your comic books," she said. "Anyway, I'll get them all when we get married someday."

Jett was the one to always remind him that they'd get married. Someday. When they were grown-up and didn't care about things like comic books and creepy forests. Which was fine with Savin. Except he thought maybe he should kiss her before that happened. And actually love her. Jett was a girl with whom he raced home from school, ran through the fields and played video games. They spent every day with each other. But love? Right now that sounded as creepy as the forest.

"Whatever." He stubbed the toe of his sneaker against the walking stick.

"Why don't you go in there?" she cooed in that cotton-candy voice she always used when she wanted him to do something.

It made Savin's ears burn and his heart feel like bug wings were fluttering inside.

"Maybe I will." He took a step forward and planted the stick again.

Looking over the forest, he thought for a moment he saw the air waver before him. Did something flash silver? Of course, a haunted forest might be like that. He didn't dare say "maybe not." So he took another step, and then another.

And he heard Jett's gasp behind him. "Savin, wait—"

He turned to see Jett's brown eyes widen. She pointed over his shoulder. When he swung around to face the forest, Savin didn't have time to scream.

Sucked forward through the air, arms flailing and legs stretched out behind him, he dropped the walking stick. Cold, icy air entered his lungs, swallowing his scream. Yet beside him he heard Jett's scream like the worst nightmare. The world turned blacker than the cellar without the lights on. And the strange smell of rotting eggs made him gag.

Of a sudden his body dropped, seeming to fall endlessly. Until he landed on his back with a crunch of bones and a cry of pain.

He lay there, silenced by the strangeness of what had happened. Had a tornado swept him off his feet and into the depths of the dark forest? Had the sky opened like a crack in the wall and sucked him inside? What was he lying on? It felt…squishy and thick, and it smelled like the worst garbage.

"Savin?"

Jett was with him. He sat up, looking about. The landscape was brown and gray, and a deep streak of red painted what must be the black sky. His fingers curled into the mud he lay on, and he felt things inside it squirm.

"Jett?"

"Over here. Wh-what happened? What is that!"

An insectile whine preceded the approach of a creature that looked like something out of one of those nasty video games his parents had forbid him to play. Jett scrambled over to Savin. He clutched her hand and they both backed away from the thing that walked on three legs and looked like half a spider…with a human face.

"Run!" Savin yelled.

They ran for days, it seemed. They encountered… things. Monsters. Creatures. Demons. Evil. They were no longer anywhere near home. This was not the outer countryside surrounding Paris. There was no lush lavender field to run through. Or even grass. Savin wasn't sure where they were or how they'd gotten here, but it was not a place in which he wanted to stay.

Jett cried as often as she wandered in silence and with a drawn expression. She was hungry and had taken on many cuts and bruises from the rough, sharp landscape and the strange molten rocks. Every time something moved, she screamed. Which was often.

This had to be hell. But Savin honestly didn't know why they were here. Had they died? They hadn't encountered people. But they did see humanlike beings. Strange creatures with faces and appendages that morphed and twisted, and some even had wings. None had spoken to them in a language they could understand.

"I want to go home," Jett said on a tearful plea.

Savin hugged her close, as much to comfort her as for his own reassurance. He wanted to go home, too. And he wanted to cry. But he was trying to be brave. He'd hand over all his Asterix comics right now if only they could be home in their own beds.

"We'll get out of here," he murmured, and then clutched Jett even tighter. "I promise."

They tried to drink from the stream that flowed with orange water, but it burned their throats. Jett's tears permanently streaked her dirtied face. Her eyes were red and swollen. Her hands were rough and darkened with the gray dust that covered the landscape, and her jeans were tattered.

Savin had torn up his shirt to wrap a bandage about her ankle after she'd cut it on what had looked like barbed wire. But after she'd screamed, that strange wire had unfurled and slunk away.

They sat on a vast plateau of flat gray stone that tended to crack without warning, much like thin ice on a lake. No other creatures seemed to want to walk on it, so they felt safe. For the moment.

Savin had fashioned a weapon out of a branch from a tree that had appeared to be made of wood, until he'd broken off the branch and inspected it. It was metal. That he could break. But the point was sharp. That was all that mattered. He'd already killed something with it. An insect the size of a dog, with snapping mandibles and so many legs he hadn't wanted to count them.

"Do you hear that?" Jett said in a weary whisper.

Savin followed the direction she looked. An inhale drew in the air. For some reason it smelled like summer. Fresh and...almost like water. Curious.

"I miss my mama and papa," Jett whispered. She shivered. She shook constantly. They hadn't eaten for days. And Savin's stomach growled relentlessly. "If I die, promise me you won't let one of those monsters eat me."

"You're not going to die," Savin quickly retorted.

But he wasn't so sure anymore.

Jett stood and wandered across the unsteady surface, wobbling at best. Savin thought to call out to her, but his lips were dry and cracked. He wanted something to drink. He wanted his feet to stop burning because he'd taken off his sneakers after the rubber soles had melted in the steel nettle field. He wanted safety. He'd do anything to escape this place he'd come to think of as the Place of All Demons.

"I see water!" Jett began to run.

Savin couldn't believe she had the energy to move so swiftly. But he managed to pick up his pace and follow. She was fifty yards ahead of him when she reached the edge of what looked like a waterfall. *Actual water?*

"Jett, be careful!"

But she didn't hear him. And when she turned to wave to him, all of a sudden her body was flung upward—as if lifted by a big invisible hand—and then her body dropped.

Savin reached the edge of the falls and plunged to his knees. He couldn't see Jett. Her screams echoed for a long time. And what initially looked like clear, cool water suddenly morphed into a thick, sludgy black flow of lava that bubbled down into an endless pit. He couldn't see the bottom.

"Jett!"

* * *

He lay at the edge of the pit for a long time. Days? There was no night and day in this awful place, so he couldn't know. After he'd decided that Jett had died in the lava, Savin had vacillated between jumping in and ending his life, and crawling away. No one could survive such a fall. Perhaps that was for the best. He hoped she hadn't suffered. He hoped she was in heaven right now, happy and safe.

But as much as he wanted to give up, he also didn't want to die.

Savin finally crawled away from the lava falls. He hadn't the energy to stand. He'd lost his walking stick in the lavender field. The next creature that threatened him? Bring it on. He didn't like the idea of being eaten alive, but maybe the thing would chomp on his heart and kill him fast.

He crawled endlessly. Nothing tried to eat him.

Calluses roughed his fingers, and his T-shirt was shredded. He couldn't feel his feet anymore. And his throat was so dry he couldn't make saliva. So when he heard the voice of a woman, he thought it must be a dream.

Savin lay sprawled on an icy sheet of blackness that smelled like blood and dirt. Again, he heard the voice. Was it saying...*help me*?

It wasn't Jett's voice. Was it? No. Impossible. Though his heart broke anew over her loss, he couldn't produce tears.

"Over here..."

With great effort, he was able to lift his head and saw what looked like lush streams of blackest hair. *Was it Jett?*

He crawled forward. His fingers glanced over something soft and fine, like one of his mother's dresses. It was blue and smelled like flowers. A woman lay on the ground, blue and black hair flowing about her in masses that he thought made up her dress. He couldn't get a good look at her face because he was too weak to sit up or stand.

"Do you want to go home?" the woman whispered.

He sobbed without tears and nodded profusely.

"I can help you out of Daemonia."

That was the first time he'd heard the name of this terrible place.

"Please," he rasped. "I'll do anything."

"Of course you will, boy. I ask but one simple thing of you."

"Anything," he managed.

"Come closer, boy. If you kiss me, I will bring you home."

Kiss her? What strange request was that?

On the other hand…all he had to do was kiss the woman and he could return home to his soft, warm bed?

Savin pushed himself up onto his elbows and looked back the direction from which he'd crawled. He'd promised Jett he'd protect her. He'd failed. He should stay in this awful place as punishment. But he wasn't stupid. And he wanted to see his parents.

"A…kiss?"

"Just one. And then you can go home."

Savin crawled closer to the woman until he hovered inches from her face. She smelled like a field of flowers. Her skin was dark blue and her eyes were red, as were the eyes of all the creatures in this terrible place.

He wavered as he supported himself with a hand and leaned closer.

And then he saw her lips.

Savin cried out. He tumbled to the side and rolled to his back. Her lips were covered with worms!

"Just one kiss, boy. Your parents are worried about you."

Now a teardrop did fall. Savin gasped and choked as he could only wish for the safety of his parents' embrace. And then…he forced himself to lean over the woman and kiss her awful mouth.

Chapter 3

He was called a reckoner now.

Savin Thorne sent demons who had come from Daemonia back where they belonged. He was hired to do so and rarely hunted them himself. He left the hunting for others. Once the demon was subdued or contained—usually in some style of hex circle—then he stepped in and worked his magic. A demonic magic afforded him, he believed, because of the demon within him. She had hitched a ride to the mortal realm when she sent him home following that foul kiss. He knew it was a female. And he could not get her out of him. He didn't know her name, so had come to refer to her as the Other. He'd love to expel her from his very soul, but he'd tried every possible spell, hex and banishment without success.

He'd accepted that life from here on would be spent sharing his bones and flesh with the demon he'd once kissed out of a vile desperation.

Rain spattered Savin's face and streaked through the headlight beams. The woman kneeling on the ground before him waited for his reaction. She'd called him by name. And her name was…

Mon Dieu, he'd thought her dead.

"Jett?"

She nodded, blinking at the falling rain. "I…I finally got out."

"Finally…" Words felt impossible.

It was incredible to fathom. This frail, dirtied woman was Jett? All grown up? Had she been in Daemonia all this time? Twenty years? If he had known she'd survived the fall, he would have found a way to get to her, to rescue her from the unspeakable evils. Somehow.

Savin's heart thundered. His fingers flexed at his sides. He didn't know what to do. How to react. He should have been there for her when they were nine and ten and lost in the Place of All Demons. He'd promised her he would protect her. And he had failed.

Yet somehow Jett had survived. Had she escaped through the rift that had opened earlier? She must have.

She must be so… Twenty years! She had no home. No life. She had literally been dropped into this world.

"Jett." Savin dropped to the ground before her, his knees crunching the wet gravel. Without reluctance, he hugged her to him. She was frail and shaking and they were both soaked from the rain. "I thought you were dead. Oh, Jett, I'm so sorry. It's really you?"

He leaned back and studied her face. He remembered the sweet round face of the girl with the long black hair and the giggles that never ceased. Her eyes had been— Yes, they were brown. It could be her.

It had to be her.

"You've gotten so big," she said, and then managed a

weak laugh. "Yes, it's me. Jett Montfort. I'm out. I'm...
Oh, Savin." She searched his eyes. Rain lashed at her
pale skin and lips. "I want to be safe."

"Of course. Safe. You are now. With me. I'll..."

What would he do? He couldn't leave her alone on
the side of the road. She needed a place to stay. Clothes.
Warmth. Food? How in the world had she survived in
such a place for so long? It didn't matter right now. She
was frightened and alone.

"Will you come with me?" he asked.

"Where to?"

"My place. I live in Paris. I'll help you, Jett. Whatever you need, I'll help you to get." And before he could
regret another vow, he said, "Promise."

She nodded, her smile wobbling and tears spilling
freely. "Please."

And when he thought to stand and help her up, instead Savin scooped her into his arms and carried her
to the passenger side of the truck and set her inside. He
tucked in her thin dress, which was nothing more than
jagged-cut fabric clinging to her torso. She was covered
with dirt and scratches, but the rain must have washed
away any blood. She'd been hurt. Traumatized, surely.

She was a strange survivor.

And he owed her his life.

"You're safe now." He squeezed her hand, then closed
the door and ran around to hop behind the wheel.

Legs pulled up to her chest and arms wrapped about
her shins, she bowed her head to her knees and closed
her eyes as Savin drove into the city.

What strange luck that her escape into the mortal
realm should be met by the one person she knew and had
thought of many times over the years. It couldn't be a co-

incidence. And yet Savin was a part of the demonic world in a way that disturbed Jett. She'd watched as he stood before the tear between the realms and reckoned demons back to Daemonia. He was powerful. And dangerous.

To her, he could prove most threatening.

Yet in her moment of need, Jett had accepted his offer of safety. Because she was exhausted, tattered and worn. And yet triumphant. She'd done it! She had escaped to the mortal realm. And whatever happened next would challenge her in ways she couldn't imagine. She had prepared mentally, but the physical challenges would be unknown. She owned a specific power. She could survive this new adventure.

As the truck entered the city, she watched headlights flash past in swift beams of red and white. It had been a long time since Jett had been in a cosmopolitan city with vehicles and buildings of human manufacture. She remembered Paris. The historical monuments and buildings, the gardens and sculptures. The elite shops and the River Seine. It hadn't seemed to change.

She had changed. Everything she knew about every single thing had changed.

And Savin remained the one pillar she needed more than she could fathom. He'd grown older, as had she. He'd gotten big and tall. The man was a behemoth wrapped in muscle and might. His dark brown hair was still shoulder length and tousled, as it had been when they were children. But now he wore a mustache and beard and a brute glint lived in his eyes. He had become a man. A very attractive man.

Jett couldn't prevent the frequent glances out the corner of her eye to the man driving the truck. She had not seen such a handsome being in…a long time. And he occupied every air molecule with his presence. He overwhelmed the space in the truck. Being near him made her heart flutter, in a good way. That was something it had not done since she was a kid.

But was this man now her enemy?

No. She wouldn't think like that. She needed help from Savin. And possibly protection. Even though he was the one person she'd best run from, he was all she had right now.

When finally he parked the truck and jumped out to run around the front of the hood and open her door, Jett stared out at the dark building front where he said he lived. This was the fourteenth arrondissement. Not far from where she recalled a massive cemetery sat in Gothic silence amidst the bustling city. While she and Savin had lived in the country when they were children, their parents had alternated taking them into the city on the weekends to visit the parks and museums. Memory of those times made her heart again flutter.

Could she have back that innocence? Did she want it back? What *was* innocence but a foul waste of power? The darkness within her would not allow her to ruminate on the past for long. Just as well. Time to move forward.

Now Jett had ventured into the city again. With Savin. And he didn't suspect a thing about her, nor had he asked how she had survived for so long in Daemonia. Which was how it must remain.

She slid her fingers against the wide hand he offered, and stepped down onto the sidewalk. Her bare feet were scraped and bruised from running across the vast smoke-ice planes where cracks in the landscape were edged like razors. Pain had become but a bother to her. Healing would come quickly. Perhaps. She must be cautious about utilizing the skills she had been taught.

"Your feet hurt?" Savin asked when she wincingly stepped forward.

Pain in this mortal realm felt different than when she'd been in the Place of All Demons. It was acute. And the cool air brushed her skin roughly. A shiver ensured that she had grasp of the sheen she wore. She must be cautious.

Without another word, Savin whisked her into his arms and carried her inside the building and up four flights of stairs without a catch to his breathing. Jett clung to the front of his shirt, noticing beneath her fingers the hard, sculpted muscles. And he smelled like nothing she had smelled before. Freshly exhilarating, yet rough. It appealed so strongly she nudged her nose against his shirt and inhaled. Was this what the princess felt like when rescued by the knight? How many times had they played such a game when they were children, always alternating who got to be the rescuer and who had to lie in dismay in wait of saving?

Now that game had become reality.

Why she had such a silly thought startled her. She had tried not to think about the simple human life she'd lost while in Daemonia. Too dangerous.

He set her down, yet supported her by the elbow, before a door. A door inscribed with demonic repulsion sigils. Jett knew them well. One did not live in Daemonia for so long without gaining such knowledge.

She tentatively reached to touch one of the symbols— and flinched.

"Keeps the nasties out," Savin commented. "Necessary. But, uh… Hmm… You've just come from there.

Must have some residual gunk on you that will alert the wards. Let me take them down for you." He swept a hand over the sigils and muttered a word she recognized as a demonic language. He knew so much? "There. Now it shouldn't tug when you cross the threshold."

He pushed the door open. Cool shadows invited Jett to step inside the narrow loft as easily as if she were crossing the threshold of her childhood home after returning from a day at school. No tug from the sigils, either. Whew.

Behind her, Savin muttered a reversal to seal the wards and closed the door. That action did pull at her system, but she disguised the sudden assault with an inhale and a sigh.

When she saw him reach for the light switch, she said, "No. Uh… I can see well in the darkness. I, uh…think it will take a while to adjust to the bright."

He lowered his hand. "Yeah, okay. There's moonlight anyway." He gestured to a line of windows that ran across the ceiling, skylights catching the moonlight. Pale illumination sifted down over furniture and the cluttered walls of a living area. "This top-floor apartment is small, but it has its perks. You thirsty?"

She was. And suddenly so cold, even though it had been warm outside. Jett rubbed her hands up and down her arms and glanced at the front door. No sigils on this side. Yet she was literally trapped now.

What had he asked? Right. She nodded. "Yes, water. Please."

He retrieved a glass from a cupboard and Jett marveled at the clear, clean water running from the tap. She'd forgotten how pure things could be. Unadulterated by the darkness she had learned to caress and rely on for comfort. When he handed it to her, she held the glass for a moment, taking it in. So normal. She remembered when her mother would hand her a glass of water. Drink it down. On to the next adventure, like chasing rabbits through the cabbage patch with Savin.

"I'm not going to ask if you are all right," Savin said. Deep and calm, his voice chased away her shivers. "You can't be. You just came out of Daemonia. Maybe I should let you settle in and feel your way around the place for tonight?"

She nodded. "Please."

"I bet a shower will feel great. Come this way."

She followed him through the living room stuffed with dark, wood-trimmed furniture and saw many guitars hung on the walls. Amongst them she noticed more demon sigils scrawled on the bare-brick walls. Some glinted at her, but none seemed to notice her presence.

"I've only got one bedroom," Savin said, "but it's a king-size bed. Comfy. You can sleep in that tonight and I'll take the couch."

She didn't want to put him out, but—at sight of the bed, lush with a thick gray coverlet and pillows—pillows! She'd not laid her head on a pillow for so long. Jett decided to quietly accept the generous offer.

Ahead, he flipped on the light in the bathroom and she blinked and stepped back. It was so bright.

"Oh." He noticed her discomfort. "It's on a dimmer." He turned a dial and the light softened. "You can shower and there are towels in the cabinet. I probably have a shirt you can wear to sleep in. Does that sound good?"

She nodded again and realized she clutched the water glass to her chest. So precious, the clean water.

Savin rubbed his bearded jaw. His deep blue eyes

beckoned her to wonder if they were real. Never had she seen such blue irises. Lapis lazuli, she remembered, was one of the stones she'd collected as a child. Though to consider his eyes now, they looked sad. Concerned.

"Tell me what you need, Jett."

She didn't know what she needed, beyond the temporary safety she felt standing before Savin's powerful build. In his home. Behind the sigils that would keep out demons. Of utmost concern was keeping any and all of those sorts away from her.

"This is good. I will shower and sleep. I feel like I can sleep." She rarely slept. To imagine lying for hours without nightmares? It seemed an impossibility. "You are too kind."

"It's not a problem. I'll be out on the couch if you need anything. You're welcome to wander about, help yourself to whatever appeals in the fridge. Just…uh, do what you need to do. Make my place your own. We'll talk in the morning."

Another nod was all she could offer. She didn't want to talk about that place. Not right away. In order to move forward, she needed to put that experience behind her. To truly be free. But she was curious how Savin had escaped and how he'd come to be a man who reckoned demons out of this realm.

"Good night," he offered. When he brushed past her, the heat of his skin shivered over hers.

Jett lifted her head and sucked in a breath. As she followed his exit from the room, the flutters returned to her heart and her skin flushed warmly. Was this what desire felt like?

Chapter 4

Savin did not sleep much that night. He lay there in the cool darkness, bare feet jutting over the end of the couch, thinking about the woman who slept in his bed not thirty feet away in the other room.

After watching Jett being literally sucked over the wicked lava falls in Daemonia, had he given up on her too quickly? Should he have lain there at the edge longer, waiting for her to emerge? He'd thought he had sprawled there for days. But he'd learned it was impossible to gauge time in such a place. He'd never cried so much as he had after losing his best friend. The remembrance zinged in his muscles with stinging aches and he almost thought to feel his skin burn now as it had then.

That harrowing experience had been seared into his very bones. It had become a part of him. It was him. It was the reason why he reckoned demons. Such creatures did not belong in this realm. No human should have to experience what he had lived through.

And now Jett was back. Alive, and seemingly sane. But how damaged must she be after living in that place for twenty years? He couldn't imagine. The demons he reckoned to Daemonia were often vicious, wild, physically disgusting and, many times, homicidal. For a human to exist in such a place, and with those creatures, for any longer than he had survived there seemed incomprehensible.

Yet there existed demons of all sorts, natures and aptitudes, and some were even—surprisingly—benevolent. Edamite Thrash being one such example. Savin could only pray Jett had been guided and sheltered by one possessing a modicum of kindness.

He had so many questions to ask. Why had they gotten sucked into Daemonia? It was something he'd asked himself thousands of times over the years. Never had he gotten an answer. Might Jett have brought back that answer with her? He wanted to know, if she could tell him. But he must be careful with her, allow her time to heal and to adjust to the mortal realm.

Hell, he was thankful she was alive.

Hours later, the sun prodded Savin out of a snore. He rubbed a hand over his head and then his shaggy beard. He needed a shave. He tended to avoid the manscaping bullshit and suffice with a shower and comb. He wasn't trying to impress anyone.

Except now a pretty woman lay in the other room. He didn't want to scare her. Might be time to dig out the razor.

Rising, he tugged off the long-sleeved shirt he'd slept in and unbuttoned his jeans as he walked toward the back of the flat. There were no doors between the living room and bedroom, so he peeked inside before entering. Jett lay still and was covered by the sheet, so he quickly snuck through the room and into the bathroom, closing that door quietly behind him.

Turning to meet his reflection in the mirror above the freestanding porcelain sink, he sneered at the gruff man who rarely smiled back. How long had his eyes been so dark and sullen? Was that the appearance of a wild man or a scruffy hermit? He really had developed a lack of concern. Kept the demons back, he figured. They feared his appearance. Heh. Not really. That was what the sigils were for. Protection and repulsion.

He traced one of the finely tattooed sigils on the underside of his forearm. Composed of circles within circles and some directional arrows along with demonic repulsion sigils. Sayne, the ink witch who'd put the bespelled ink down, had promised him they would be effective against most demons. Of course, he could never be impervious to all because there were so many breeds of demons in existence.

There had been one occasion when Savin met a demon who had not been repulsed by any of his sigils. That demon had initially been locked in a cage in the bowels of the Acquisitions' headquarters. Later, Savin had ended up working with Gazariel, The Beautiful One, to help track down a vicious vampiress intent on invoking a spell that could end the world by smothering all mankind with the wings of fallen angels. That was a long story.

Savin found his way into some serious shit at times. Like it or not.

Hell, he liked it more than not. Kept life interesting. And, well, it was what he knew how to do.

Flipping on the shower, he stripped down and grabbed

the razor from the medicine cabinet. Time to make himself more presentable for his guest.

Jett sat up on the big, wide bed. She'd slept? Grabbing a pillow, she hugged it to her chest, burying her face in the rugged scent of Savin Thorne. She hadn't smelled anything so good. Ever. The man entered her pores on a brute whisper of masculinity and crisp fall leaves, and stirred up thoughts that didn't so much surprise her with their eroticism as rise to embolden her.

Was she still asleep and in a dream?

While she was in Daemonia, dreams had been elusive. Actually, nightmares might have been the only reverie possible there. When attempting to recline and rest, she'd learned to shut down her thoughts. To sleep? Surely, she had. According to Savin, it had been twenty years that she had been absent. A person couldn't survive so long without sleeping.

"Twenty years," she whispered.

Twenty years according to the mortal realm's time-keeping.

It was impossible to track time in Daemonia. Night and day did not exist. The seasons of gray and white and rust did. Gray crept in on mist and eeriness. White had shocked with ice and the crackly lava flowers she'd grown to enjoy despite their charcoal scent. And rust? Fire and screams.

It was late summer here in Paris. Perhaps. She hadn't taken careful note of the field and surroundings last night before Savin pulled up on the road beside her. But it was warm. Such comforting warmth teased at her skin. In all her time in that place, she'd not known such a gentle and undemanding temperature.

Now she was determined to open her arms wide and

embrace it all. Take it back in and flood her system with the muscle memory of a normal life. She must once again become a part of the human race.

Was it possible? She didn't have a clue. But she would not relent until she was proved either right or wrong.

A clatter from inside the bathroom clued her she was not, indeed, dreaming. Savin must have finished in the shower. And before she could decide if she should leave the bedroom to give him some privacy, the door opened. Steam wafted out on a sage-scented cloud. And a god wearing but a towel emerged.

"Oh, you're up." Savin hooked his hand on the towel where it was tucked at his hip.

Jett dragged her gaze from his face—he had trimmed what had been a wild beard to something a bit more ruly—down over his wide and solid chest. That was a lot of muscle, and all of it was tight and undulated in curves and hard planes and… She had seen demons who looked like they pumped iron in a gym. They'd had muscles of blackest flesh or coldest steel. Some breeds' physical makeup had been so terrible as to reveal bone and organs. But this man? Those muscles did not wrap about a rib cage that lacked within it a beating heart. Savin Thorne was a hot drink of the clearest, cleanest water she'd ever desired.

"Did you sleep?" he asked.

"Sleep?" Adjusting her gaze from the tantalizing ridges of muscle on his abdomen, Jett hugged the pillow tighter to her chest, sensing a weird increase in her breaths. Which, when checked, she realized was want. Need. Hunger for the man's muscles pressed up against her body. "Uh, yes. Surprisingly. I think that's the best sleep I've had in ages."

"That bed is comfortable. I, uh…"

He glanced to the cabinet on the other side of the bed that stood up against the wall.

"Oh, you need to get dressed. I should let you have some privacy." She dropped the pillow and walked to the edge of the bed on her knees, but Savin beat her to the cabinet, and if she climbed off the bed, she'd step right up against him.

"It's cool," he said. "I'll just grab some things and change out in the living room. I'm sure you want to use the bathroom. You can use whatever you like. I might even have an extra toothbrush in one of the drawers. Toothpaste is in the cabinet."

Toothpaste. That sounded so decadent.

"How about we take a walk down the street and find something to eat?" he offered as he claimed some clothes. "Then we can talk."

"Talk?" Not about Daemonia. She wasn't ready for that. And she wasn't sure she would ever be. "Sure. It'll be great to get out in the fresh air. It's not something I've had…" Uh… No. She wasn't going to detail what was now her past. "Thank you, Savin. It was weird luck that you were out there in the country to help me."

"It was. But also not a coincidence." He took her in with a shadowed glance. His eyes were deep blue and his thick brows were low above them, granting him a dangerous mien. A force to, literally, be reckoned with. "That place where the rift to Daemonia opened last night is exactly where *it* happened."

Jett nodded. It. Yes, it had been. That day long ago when her life had been irrevocably altered.

"Sorry." He winced. "You probably don't want to talk much about all that. We'll take it slow. I'm hungry.

Soon as you're ready, we'll head out. Feel free to raid my clothes. You might make a dress out of one of my shirts, you're so tiny."

He strode around the corner and Jett slid off the bed to look through the clothes cabinet. She'd found a T-shirt to sleep in last night and it hung to her thighs. Her hand glided over a pair of gray sweatpants with a string tie at the waist. It should serve until she could buy clothes that fit her.

Might Savin lend her some money to get her life established? She would need it because she had no means to a job or even knowledge of how to acquire the basics such as food, clothing and shelter.

Had she done the right thing?

The innate part of her that had seen to her survival in the Place of All Demons rose within her, reminding her she was not the same girl who had been taken out of this realm so long ago. She was stronger, and more vital. And she would have whatever she wanted, using her wiles if necessary. Let no man, or demon, stop her.

"I will," Jett whispered decisively. "And he will help me."

In the bathroom, she found a new toothbrush and Savin's comb. Her hair was a tangle and hung to her waist. Also, it was no longer the color it had been while she was in Daemonia. She wasn't sure if she missed that or not. She'd often worn it braided and back, but she no longer had consorts to aid or help her dress. Such a loss.

A moment to focus inward and ensure that all would be well—and secure—served her temporary solace. Maybe? She was trapped within something she was not in this realm, just as she had been in the other realm.

And she was already questioning her decision to escape. She'd left behind things. Privileges. A certain status.

Jett shook her head. She had to stay on focus. She had wanted this. Had striven for escape. And the best person to help her achieve normality had been right there, waiting for her. Surely, that was a positive sign. For now, she was safe around Savin. Yet she could not overlook that the wards protecting his home pulled at her when she got too near the front door. She needed to be outside, free from any repulsive magic.

Pulling up the sweatpants, she tugged the ties and bunched up the excess. It still didn't fit smartly, so she'd be forced to hold them up while she walked. But the invite to get outside could not be refused. She craved fresh air and would swallow it in gulps.

Out in the living room and sitting on the couch, Savin strummed an acoustic guitar. When Jett entered, he stopped and stood, setting the instrument aside. "You found clothes. That's good."

She clutched the front of the pants.

"Or not." He winced. "There's a women's shop two buildings down from here. You want to stop in before we eat?"

"I'd appreciate that, but I have no means to pay."

"Jett, don't worry about it. You have nothing. I've got your back."

She nodded, again finding it hard to speak when he had already been so generous. At the same time, a part of her, the part that had shone and assimilated while in Daemonia, smiled and straightened her spine. Of course he should serve her and make her comfortable. She deserved it.

"Let's go out, then," she said. "I'm eager to breathe in Paris."

Chapter 5

In the women's clothing shop, Jett found some black jeans with sequins dashing down the sides of each leg seam, and a blousy red top. Black boots with high heels had given her a giddy thrill. Savin had suggested she grab a few more things, and while she had been initially reluctant, she quickly warmed to the shopping gene that Savin knew all women possessed. He didn't mind bulking up his credit card bill. Seeing Jett's satisfied smile had been well worth it.

Of course, the smile had been too brief. It was almost as if she'd caught herself in a moment of joy, then quickly slammed the door shut on the freedom. It would require time for her to rise above her experience, surely.

Now she sat across a metal table from him on the sidewalk before his favorite sixth-arrondissement café. Four bags were corralled around her. She looked over the menu while he had ordered black coffee and three *pains au chocolat*. That was the first course for him. He would go in for the potatoes next.

"I'm not sure what I want," she said, setting down the menu. "I feel hungry. Or do I?"

"You can have one of my pastries and then order something later if you're still hungry." He noticed her scowl. "It's not a test, Jett. You can try as many things as you like."

She managed a roundabout shrug-nod. He assumed it was overwhelming for her to be someplace so simple as a sidewalk café after coming from— Well, he wasn't going to ask about it. He'd wait until she brought it up. It seemed the kindest thing to do.

"Paris smells like I remember. Old, yet hopeful," she said after the waitress dropped off Savin's order. She accepted a plate with one of his pastries on it and picked up a fork. "And the fountain down the street sounds so happy."

He'd forgotten about that fountain. A guy could hear it if he really listened. He'd lived here so long it had faded into the background. Just another city sound. What his senses were most focused to? Demons. They brandished a distinctive hum to their aura. If one walked close enough to him, it registered as a twinge in his veins. Some, he even smelled the sulfur. And while they could cast a sheen over that hum, the scent and their innate red pupils, if Savin caught sight of them at the right angle, the red glinted.

Jett paused with her fork poised over the pastry. "Can I ask you a few things?"

"Of course. Ask away."

"You were sending demons back into Daemonia last night, yes?"

"You bet. I'm a reckoner, Jett."

"That is what I guessed. How did you ever come to do such a thing? And, uh…just how long have you been…back?"

He set down the pastry and brushed the crumbs from his beard. She wouldn't like hearing this, but he wasn't going to lie to her. Savin had a thing about loyalty to friends. He didn't know any other way to exist.

"I've been back," he said, "since I was ten."

Her jaw dropped open and the fork hit the plate with a clink. "But you were ten then. When we…" She pressed her fingers to her mouth, and her eyes averted to study the sidewalk.

"I was in Daemonia for what felt like weeks," he offered. "Maybe a month?"

"Time doesn't exist there," she said softly. The fragile pain in her tone cut Savin to the core. Should he have been so forthright?

"Right. No way to measure time there," he said. "But I did find a way out."

"That's so good for you." Her smile was again brief. Not easy. "And…your parents were there for you?"

"As soon as my feet hit mortal ground outside the wicked forest, I ran back home through the lavender field and straight into my house. My parents were over the moon. I didn't think my mom would ever stop hugging me."

Jett's eyes still did not meet his, and he could imagine what she was thinking. How she had lost that opportunity for a cheery family reunion. Hell, he shouldn't have mentioned that part.

"I tried to explain what happened, but they thought me…" He twirled a forefinger near his temple. "And when your parents asked me where you were, I didn't know what to say. Would they believe a kid who said some strange force sucked us into a different realm? Kids always get accused of having wild imaginations. And I remember your mom, in particular, was Catholic."

Jett nodded. Smirked at the memory. "To the extreme. So much guilt."

"Right. Religion is…not for me. Anyway, after giving it some thought, I decided that being lured into the woods by a stranger and the two of us being separated was the only story they'd believe. That's when the police arrived. They questioned me for hours. I cried a lot."

"I imagine so."

Savin lifted his chin and swallowed. Ignoring the stir of the Other within, he reached across the table and touched her fingers. "Those tears were for you, Jett. I just wanted you back."

She nodded and yet pulled her fingers from under his touch. Wrapping her arms tightly across her chest, she leaned forward, protecting herself as best she could. "Were my parents upset?"

"Inconsolable." He waited until she finally gave him her gaze. That soft brown stare that had once teased, cajoled and challenged him. "They loved you, Jett. But I know it was difficult for them to accept that I returned and you did not. Nothing was the same after that."

"What do you mean?"

"Well." How to say it kindly? Surely, she might seek her parents now. And while he'd been but a kid, Savin had understood exactly what had occurred in the neighbors' house down the street in those months following his return. The truth needed to be told. "Your parents split up about a year after it happened. I was still young and only heard the whispers from my parents, but I understood that your father moved out of the country."

"He did? That's… Wow." She sat back on the metal chair and pulled up a knee to hug against her chest.

"And your mother…"

"My mother?"

"What was her name again?"

"Josette. Josette and Charles Montfort."

"Right." Savin raked his fingers through his hair. "I'm not sure what happened to Josette. After your dad left, my parents told me never to speak to Madame Montfort because I'd upset her. So I walked the long way around the neighborhood to get to school. Not that I stayed in school much longer than a few years."

"But you were ready to enter middle school?"

"I managed middle school. Barely. My mom called it ADD. I knew differently. I dropped out in the first year of high school. The whole world, and the way I saw it, was never the same after— Well, I'm sure you understand. Anyway, I moved to the city when I was seventeen and lost touch completely with the Montforts."

"I see." Jett toyed with the pastry flakes on the plate, then rubbed her hand along her thigh. "I guess I can understand the divorce. My parents must have been shattered about my disappearance. They…fought a lot."

"I remember you telling me about hearing their arguments. It happens. People change and seek new directions."

"But another country? You don't know where my father went?" she asked.

He shook his head. And one final terrible detail. "He got remarried, Jett. That's all I know."

She nodded, taking it in. Her fingers clasped tightly on her lap. Everything about her closed. "I wonder if my mother is still in the same house."

"Impossible. That area we were in last night is where the lavender field once was. The houses were torn down years ago, Jett. There's only a thin line of trees left from the original forest. They're putting up new buildings and a golf course. I'm not sure where your mother went."

"Would your parents know? I mean…" She exhaled heavily, and when she met his gaze, Savin expected to see tears, but instead a steely determination glinted in her dark irises. "I have no one now. I need to start anew. But I can't do that without support. And survival aside, I'd like to find my parents. Because…"

"Of course. I can ask my maman for you. My dad died ten years ago."

"Oh." She dropped her gaze from his. "Death is— You resemble him, from what I remember."

Savin winced at her tone. It had been so…dead. Like she had forced herself to say something kind. Like she didn't really feel for him. It was a weird thing to notice. But again, he reminded himself, she had been through a lot.

"So you got out fast," she stated. "And did you always want to be a reckoner after that?"

He snorted. "Hell no. I had no idea what a reckoner even was until seven or eight years ago when John Malcolm—he's an exorcist—found me and told me I needed to be trained to do what I could do naturally. It's the weirdest thing I've never asked for, but have accepted because it seems that's what I'm meant to do.

It's a strange and repulsive calling. I just want to keep humans safe from demons."

She nodded.

"You need to know something, Jett. When I came back to this realm, a demon hitched a ride in me. I call her the Other."

"The Other?" she said with a gasp.

Yes, she remembered. They'd played a board game when they were kids that had been a bit like Dungeons and Dragons, and the creature who had lived in a dark cave had been called the Other. That was the name for the villain they had always adopted when playacting any sort of fantasy quest, adventure, or even when taking a tromp through the basement without the lights on.

Savin shrugged. "I was a kid. At the time, it was a name that fit. She's the one who helped me get home. The bitch is still in me. She's incorporeal. Can't get her out. I'm not sure how to. I've tried, believe me. But we've developed a mutual respect for each other's boundaries and I put up with her occasional fits."

"Fits?"

"When angered, she can toss me across the room. Freaks the hell out of me. She's been a bit prickly today. Weird. I'm chalking it up to our experience last night. But there are…measures I take to keep her calm."

"Measures?"

He reached into his back pocket and laid on the table a tin box that he never left home without. He had a few more tucked in all the other places he might need a quick fix, such as at home and in his truck. "Morphine. It seems to keep the bitch chilled without affecting me too much."

"Oh. Yes, morphine. It is a commodity in Daemonia. Smuggled in illegally from the mortal realm."

He shrugged. "Yeah, I knew that. That's how I figured it might be something I could use to control her." He tucked away the tin box. "Since my return, I've been able to see and feel a demon's presence. In my very bones, you know?"

She swallowed and nodded again, strangely telling in her silence.

"And for some reason," Savin continued, "I can invoke demonic rituals and languages to send them back to where they came from. It's been an innate skill after my return. So after Malcolm trained me, I figured I hadn't much choice but to become a reckoner. Wasn't as if I had a vibrant social life or dreams and goals of becoming a corporate raider or even a chef or fireman. I'm just weird Savin Thorne who sees demons and feels them all around. I've learned to work with it."

"You don't seem so weird to me. Rather handsome, too." She lowered her gaze, but her voice took on a confident tone. "You've grown up since I last saw you."

"So have you." He felt something close to a blush heat his neck. Savin quickly rubbed at his beard to hide his sudden nerves. Not that he didn't enjoy flirting with a beautiful woman. He just…was surprised by his sudden and easy interest in Jett's sensual appeal.

"So you can see demons in the mortal realm? All of them?"

"Not all. Most. And it's not so much that I can see them—some I can—as that they give off a vibration that I can sense when they are close. But some are clever and wear a sheen expertly. You know about that stuff, yes?"

Another silent nod.

"Right. Probably hard not to get educated on the demonic realm when stuck in that place. Listen, Jett, I know you probably want to avoid questions about Daemonia, but can I ask one thing?"

"Of course you can."

"Were you treated well?"

She straightened her neck and slid her palms along each chair arm. It was almost as if she had realized she was safe now and could be the woman she was. A regal confidence bloomed in her eyes. "Well enough. I survived. And I am in one piece. And now I'm here. That is what matters, isn't it?"

"It is."

Yet her confident front did not hide the fact that she was frightened. Savin could feel the fear coming off her.

The waitress stopped by and set the roasted potatoes, sprinkled with rosemary, before him. Jett decided on tea and he didn't push her to order more.

His cell phone rang and, seeing it was Ed, he told Jett he needed to take the call. "Yeah, Ed, what's up?"

"We managed to wrangle a dozen demons after leaving the site last night. I've got them contained here at the office in the basement holding cell. Would you be able to swing by and reckon them?"

He glanced across the table. Jett was poking about in one of her shopping bags, the tissue paper crinkling. "Sure. Give me a couple hours and I'll head over."

"Great. I'll give you more details then."

"The cellular phone has advanced measurably in my absence," Jett commented as he tucked away his phone. "I remember them being large and—what were they— flip phones?"

"They get smaller and sleeker every year. And the

cameras on them are amazing. I've even got a demon tracking app."

"What's an app?"

"It's a…" Savin chuckled. "A program designed to do something specific and usually make life easier. Though I'm not much for selfies."

"What's a selfie?"

"Something I think you would be excellent at." He winked, and her lift of chin preceded a slight curve of her mouth. Yes, she would put all the selfie queens to shame with her natural beauty. "I'll give you the tech talk later," he said. "You won't need to learn much to get up to speed. Except that swiping right can get you in more trouble than you are prepared to confront."

And that was all he was willing to divulge regarding his failed Tinder experiment.

"I have no idea what you just said, but I think I'll be fine without a phone for now. Getting up to speed on existing in this realm is going to take some time. You have somewhere you need to be?"

"Yes, that was Edamite Thrash. He's a corax demon. Good guy. I'd never reckon him. He keeps an eye on the demons in Paris and isn't afraid to move in when one steps out of line. Sort of the demon police patrol over Paris."

"Edamite Thrash." She seemed to make note of the name.

"I have some business across the river with Ed."

"Reckoning?"

Savin nodded. "I won't invite you along. I suspect you'll want to keep yourself as far from anything having to do with demons as you can."

"Sounds like a dream. But is it possible in this city?"

He felt awful that her dream was so dismal. "It is. Demons are populous in Paris, but the smart ones tend to mind their manners. I'll walk you back to the flat and then make it a quick job."

"I can find my way back on my own."

"I do need to get my truck." He wolfed down some potatoes and finished his coffee. Seeing Jett's longing look at some passing tourists, he offered, "Unless you want to walk by yourself for a while? I don't want to be too forward."

She gave him that silent nod again. Somehow submissive, which bothered him.

He tugged out his wallet and laid a couple twenty-euro notes before her. "You take that and go off walking by yourself. Buy what you want. If your appetite comes back, you'll be covered. Yes?"

"Thank you."

"I'll leave the door to my place unlocked. Don't let the demon wards freak you out. Sometimes they tug when you enter."

"Didn't even notice them last night," she offered airily.

"They're not all-purpose, but they've served me well. I'll loosen them up for you anyway." Because she probably still had residue from Daemonia on her. "And feel free to tuck your new purchases into a drawer. Make yourself at home, Jett. My place is your place until you feel like you need to get the hell out. Deal?"

"Deal."

He signed the check, then stood, and thinking he should shake her hand or something, he decided that was stupid. And would she get the friendly double-cheek-kiss thing? It wasn't something he ever did—why was he fretting about this?

Abandoning his ridiculous thoughts, he tossed out a "See you later?"

"I look forward to it."

So did he. Because those beautiful, sad brown eyes made him hungry for things other than food. A man shouldn't have such thoughts for a woman he hardly knew. And yet he did know her. The nine-year-old Jett. The intrepid, laughing best friend he'd promised to someday marry. Seemed like a long shot now. She was different. Could she get back to the usual? Did she want to? What had she been through?

He wanted to help her. He really did. And he needed to protect her. Things that came out of Daemonia might be required to return, no matter their species. Might someone—or something—come looking for Jett?

Jett wandered the cobblestoned streets and sidewalks through Paris, inhaling the smells of gasoline, cooked food and ancient limestone. The sounds of rushing cars, chattering tourists, Notre Dame's bells and the laughter of children lightened her mood.

The sights were both historical and contemporary. The old buildings that had been around for centuries, and that she could recognize, gave her comfort. The city had not changed in her absence. And the people had only marginally changed, fashionwise. But there were so many cell phones now. Did everyone carry them always? Including the children? How bizarre to want to walk down the street having a conversation with a person on the phone while your family or friend walked next to you, doing the very same.

The city was as she'd remembered, and yet those
memories were so old everything had become new
again. She found herself smiling despite not having used
those muscles around her mouth for a long time. A satisfied sigh followed.

She could make this her home once again.

As she was weaving through tourists who crowded
the sidewalks, the scent of roasted meat lured her to draw
in the savory aroma. But she didn't feel hungry. After
one bite of Savin's pastry, she had realized it tasted like
stale paper. It was not what she'd eaten in Daemonia. All
senses had been engaged during meals, lush scents and
flavors combining to satisfy in the most bizarre manner. The humans would not know what to call the demonic foods, and some dishes might even repulse them.

She could grow accustomed to roast chicken and potatoes again. She must.

Savin had taken her bags back to his place, so Jett
swung her arms as she crossed a busy intersection.
The river was close. The water smelled dark, yet much
cleaner than anything she had known in a while.

A passerby rudely brushed her shoulder and kept on
walking, his attention on the cell phone at his ear. But the
sensations Jett got from that quick contact shocked up
her arm. *Demon.* It was an innate knowledge. He didn't
turn to regard her. He couldn't know acknowledgment
was required. Rather, submission.

That was a good thing. Maybe?

Part of her decided it was. The darkest part of her
crossed her arms and gave a huffy pout. Really. Where
was the subservience? Should not all demons know and
fear her? It was going to take time to adjust to being just
another face in the crowd.

Shaking off the surprise of having been so close to a demon—and not feeling compelled to follow—Jett wandered to the river's edge and leaned over the wide concrete balustrade. If demons walked the streets without notice, that meant surely the city must be populated with all species of paranormals. Something of which she'd not been aware when she was an innocent child.

And now knowing so much served her both bane and boon. All grown up and in the know, she could be smart and protect herself from anything that wished to harm her. If that *anything* knew who she was. Something she intended to conceal as long as physically possible.

Holding a hand out over the water, Jett closed her eyes and drew in the power of nature. Flowing water had always strengthened her. She harkened it to that fateful plunge over the falls. Rather, that *push*. She'd initially thought Savin had caught up to her and shoved her screaming and flailing over the edge. But she'd corrected that after the long fall. He hadn't been close enough. He could never have known what had occurred during that fall.

Similar to the fall an angel makes from Above? It was a tale she'd made up, a secret belief that had helped her through hard times. Innocence falling to destruction and ruin, and all that fantastical stuff.

But that truth wasn't something she could share with Savin. Maybe? No, she wasn't nearly so ready to completely trust the man. It had been twenty years. So much had happened. Both had changed and been altered by their stays in that nightmare place. Jett would be wise to tread carefully around the man who could reckon demons out of this realm.

Hearing the loud chatter of a woman next to her, Jett

turned, expecting to find her conversing with another, and only saw the one woman.

"Technology," she muttered Savin's explanation. "What else has changed?"

For one thing, the movie screens. Or were they television screens? Whatever they were, there was one set up in the parvis before Notre Dame just across the river; it played a film on the cathedral's history. The screen was so large, and the images remarkably clear, even from where she stood.

The cars that zoomed past on the bridge were the same as she remembered, save newer and probably faster. The people all looked the same. Fashion in this touristy district still left much to be desired. Jett could spot a true Parisian by her smart, elegant style. Or there, the woman riding the bicycle in a skirt, with her high heels tucked in a side bag. Definitely a city native.

The food all seemed familiar. The Notre Dame Cathedral was still an awesome monument. The whine of tired children tugging on their parents' legs was familiar, as well. So much remained familiar to her, and that was heartening.

Yet where were the bowing sycophants?

Jett's eyes sought someone, anyone who might recognize her importance. And she realized her sheen was beginning to wane, allowing her darkness to rise, so she tightened her hold on it and spread her focus over her skin once again. Mustn't drop her mask. No matter how good it felt, or how much she desired recognition.

After walking awhile, Jett shrugged her achy shoulders and yawned. The crowd and the bright sunlight taxed her energy. She was beginning to require more focus than usual to stay in this form. So she headed back toward Savin's place, wandering quickly past the Montparnasse Cemetery and then the Luxembourg Gardens, taking in all things, but also looking forward to rest. She'd breathed enough fresh air for today.

Most of all, she looked forward to seeing Savin again.

The only friend she had ever known had reentered her life. And that was remarkable.

But what he'd told her about her parents. They'd divorced. And he had no clue where either was right now? Besides the memory of her best friend, her parents had been her only connection to this realm. For the longest time she had whispered the Catholic prayers her mother had taught her, until the words had begun to literally burn on her tongue. And long after she'd learned not to invoke the Christian God in that place, the simple image of her mother or father had worked to keep up her spirits.

She needed to find them to truly return to this realm she wanted to once again call home.

Arriving at Savin's building, she took in the vibrations cloaking the immediate area. Like Savin, she could read the air and sense demons when nearby. As well, she could vibrationally map out the living beings in the area. Sort of like sonar, she supposed. Savin was above in his home, already returned from his task. She knew it because his scent carried to her. That delicious essence of man that she'd slept wrapped in all night.

There were wards outside the limestone-faced building. Invisible, yet she could feel Savin's signature sealing them. Wards against demons and a few other species, perhaps vampires and werewolves. They tugged at her musculature, as they had last night, when she mounted the inner stairs and climbed up four stories, but it wasn't anything that would rip her apart or send her screaming.

Facing the wards drawn on Savin's front door, Jett rechecked the sheen she wore, a masterful disguise. She'd need to relax and let go soon. Just an hour or so. A means to recharge.

Yet the last place she could do that was inside a fully warded reckoner's home.

Or maybe, it might serve as the safest place possible.

She knocked on the front door, then tried the knob. It was open, and as she popped her head inside the flat, Savin called for her to enter. A fierce tug at her skin pulled and prickled as she crossed the threshold, but she made it inside and closed the door behind her, thus squelching the ward's seeking force. It sought to repeal a demon. She was still strong enough to thwart the weakened repulsion.

Now she dropped her shoulders and exhaled wearily. "You beat me back," she commented.

Savin sat on the couch, a glass of what smelled like alcohol in hand, which he tilted to her. "It was a quick call. Four more demons sent back to where they belong. And you have been out the whole afternoon. You walk around the city?"

She sat on the wooden-armed chair across from the couch and pulled up her legs to hook her feet on the leather cushion. It was cool and not so bright in his place, and she appreciated that. "Paris is beautiful. I never appreciated the architecture when we were kids. So many people, though. I'm tired out!"

"Yeah, it's August and the tourist crush is ridiculous. No wonder all the locals head out of town this time of year. I left your new things in the bedroom for you. You want a drink?"

"I recognize the smell of whiskey from when my father used to have a 'sip' after an evening meal. But I've never tried alcohol. At least, not anything made in this realm."

"Really? I suppose." He swiped a hand across his jaw.

She sensed he tried to be tactful and not ask about her experience, which she appreciated.

"Want to try some?"

"I'd never refuse a challenge from you."

And while that statement was something that she would have said as a kid to Savin's challenging glint in the eye, now it felt bold and powerful. Adult. And in response, Savin's gaze seemed to slip across her skin in a welcome manner. Jett wriggled on the chair, lifting her chin. She liked to be admired by him.

He stood and collected another glass in the kitchen, then returned to pour her a portion from the bottle.

"Do you play all those guitars?" she asked as he handed her the glass. She sniffed it. Very strong, and not too appealing.

"Most are collectibles," he said. "A few are prized possessions. That one is signed by Chuck Berry. Saw him at a concert a decade ago and met him when he was exiting out the backstage door. I like to play my own compositions. A little blues à la Chuck Berry, a little Southern rock. Some headbanging riffs mixed with a touch of classical. I'm also teaching myself musicomancy."

Jett sat up a little straighter. "Is that some kind of magic?"

"Using music. But it's slow going. Hell, I tend to sit and drink far too much whiskey, and then my playing gets looser and more random. I suspect that's a good reason why I have yet to accomplish musicomancy." He winked and tilted back the remainder of his drink, then poured some more. "I use the diddley bow for the magic stuff." He gestured over his shoulder, and Jett noted a strange guitar-like instrument with a turtle-shell-sized body and a long, thin neck and only one string. "Made that one myself. That's another hobby of mine. Fiddling around with making things. Made a bunch of navigational devices that I use for my work, as well. Guess I got the creative gene from my dad. You remember when I took apart your Nintendo controller?"

"I don't think I forgave you for that. And I wouldn't necessarily call destroying things being creative," she teased. "You tended to take apart anything you could get your hands on."

"Yeah." He chuckled. "Now I put things back together. I figured out how it all works. Now I'm all about restoration and creation. No destruction."

Destruction. The word felt comfortable to Jett's senses. It had been so easy to destroy that which annoyed her. But just as she noticed herself smiling about such memories, she chased away the thought. She would not slip around Savin. She must not.

She sniffed her glass, then took a sip. It burned down her throat, but it was actually tasty. As she drank more, the burn lessened. Another sip and the dark liquid smoothened on her tongue. "I like this."

"Much as I hate to be the one to corrupt you, I can't argue an appreciation for a good aged whiskey."

"I am beyond corruption, Savin. So don't worry about that."

"Everyone is corruptible."

"Yes, well, there's nothing about me that can get any more corrupted. So trust, you won't harm me. No matter what vices or sinful challenges with which you should tempt me." She held out her glass toward him. Her voice thickened into a husky tone. "More."

Glass clinked as he poured her another portion. Then he topped off his drink. The lingering look he gave her was in reaction to her sensual tease. Good boy. He understood her. She could work with that.

"Can I ask you one thing? It's personal."

"I don't have any boyfriends, if that's what you're wondering." Jett chuckled softly and pressed the cool glass against her lower lip. The man was so sexy. And she understood the meaning of that word now. How quickly she relaxed around him. And desired. She was feeling…sensual. Must be the whiskey. Yes, she did like this drink.

"No, that's—" Savin looked over the rim of his glass. "Could you have boyfriends…you know…there?"

He wanted to know about her love life in Daemonia? Ugh. "Is that the question you wanted to ask?"

"Do I only get the one?"

Jett sighed and allowed her shoulders to relax against the comfy cushions. She crossed her legs, and with a slip off of the heel, she dangled her shoe on her toes. "Fine. Ask me anything. But I'm allowed to refuse any answer."

"I don't want to grill you, Jett. But I am curious. In turn, you can ask me anything."

"You've been open with me so far. I owe you that much."

He leaned forward, resting his elbows on his knees, the whiskey glass dangling from one hand before a leg. "How did you survive in that place? Was there shelter? Buildings? Towns? A place of safety?"

"There's never safety in Daemonia," she said curtly. The whiskey slid quickly down her throat and she slammed the glass on the chair arm. "But there are dwellings. And cities and citadels. Castles, hovels and all means of residence. I…had a place to live." She couldn't tell him everything. She'd never get out of this flat in one piece if she did that. "And I was generally free from the treacherous elements that I'm sure you remember."

"So someone took you in? That's good. I couldn't imagine you wandering that horrible place for so long and on your own."

"There is no alone there." Jett cast her glance up toward the windows fitted in the ceiling. The sky was darkening. Thankfully. "Nor was there a sun. But you know, the many moons were pretty. Save for the fire moon. That one hurt if I forgot myself and walked out beneath it."

"Like a sunburn?"

He might never understand that in Daemonia everything was multiplied, magnified, extremely enlarged, enhanced and so, so dangerous. He'd had but a taste as a child.

"A bit," she offered quickly. Now she stood and grabbed the half-empty whiskey bottle and refilled her glass. Growing more confident, she sat on the couch, snuggling up about two feet from where Savin sat and facing him. The whiskey warmed her, and the exhaustion she'd been feeling earlier cooled to a comfortable relaxation. "Any more questions?"

"So many. But I won't inundate you. I genuinely thought you were dead after that fall, Jett. Were you angry with me? For not coming after you?"

He lifted his chin just as their eyes met. Alpha in his command, and unwilling to show any weakness. She'd dealt with men like him. And yet she could feel his heart beating rapidly. He was frightened at his own emotions.

And she, well, she had long ago abandoned the sillier emotions such as fear, shame and empathy.

"I was never angry with you," she said truthfully. "And I hoped for so long that you had made it back home. My wish came true. I'm glad for that."

"I should have leaped over that cliff and tried to save you."

"It would have been a suicide leap, Savin. You were wise to stay put. Trust me on that one."

How she had survived the lava falls was a question she'd never gotten an answer to. And really, she'd decided long ago she didn't want that answer. There had been a reason she was whisked into Daemonia. A wicked, selfish reason for which she could never forgive the perpetrator.

Savin considered her words. Surely his next question would be, how had she survived? So she would redirect his thoughts. "What about you? Do you have any girlfriends?"

His brow quirked; then his lips dallied with a smile before he shook his head. "I'm not so talented with the suave and smooth. All that dating stuff feels awkward."

"A man so handsome and kind as you has trouble with women? Surely, you've dated."

"I have. I do. Eh. It never lasts. I'm human, Jett, but this demon inside me makes it difficult to relate to human women. I'm different than most. I know things I shouldn't know about things that shouldn't exist. And I have to protect that side of me from discovery. You know? I did date a vampiress once. I don't like the idea of getting bitten, though, and that did seem to be a requirement to a happy relationship."

"Did she bite you?"

"I wouldn't let her. It was tempting. I understand the bite is orgasmic. Oh, uh, sorry. I shouldn't talk like that around you."

"Why not? We're both adults. I am a grown woman." And she was feeling more of herself with every moment she sat near Savin. He'd toyed with getting bitten by a vampire? Jett traced the bottom tip of her canine tooth. It was sharp, but not as pointed as usual without her sheen. "I know things," she said. "Trust me, I'm not an innocent."

"All right, then." He considered his glass, and Jett sensed his sudden discomfort.

"Vampires! So many creatures walking this realm," she tossed out to break the tension. "All the things we once thought were only make-believe. All of them predators and prey."

"I've never been prey and don't intend to start. Trust me on that one." He chuckled and shook his head. "Hand me the bottle. Let's finish it off."

She grabbed the bottle and went up on her knees to slide closer to Savin, setting the bottle on his thigh. When he gripped it, she placed her hand over his. He turned his head, and the scent of him invaded her pores on a tease. As a woman, she had needs. And those needs screamed for satisfaction right now. A new turn at satisfaction, actually. One that she might not regret, or that would leave her shivering in revulsion.

"My turn to ask the questions," she said. "Or rather, I've a request."

He studied her hand still resting over his, and she released him so he could pour the last inch into his glass. He tucked the bottle on the other side of his thigh, then said, "Shoot."

Boldness had been bred into her over the long and unending years of her exile. And she was feeling her mettle now that she'd begun to acclimate to this realm. Jett touched the ends of Savin's dark hair and swept them over his shoulder. With the back of her forefinger, she traced along his neck up to the bristly beard hairs. He was warm, much more so than she'd expected. Fiery, even. But never dangerous, at least, not to her darkness.

"Do you think I'm pretty, Savin?"

Now his gaze locked on to hers, and she felt the heat of him scurry over her skin. It danced about her arms and torso and tightened her nipples. Mmm…he was not a man to be ignored.

"I do."

"Do you remember when we were kids and I asked you to kiss me and you said you couldn't until we were older because we'd have to be married and you'd probably have to like girls to do so?"

He nodded and, with a tilt of his head, chuckled softly. "You remember that? I've always respected women. My mother taught me that."

"Yes, you are a kind man. But. Are we old enough to kiss now?"

Her finger wandered over his chin and followed the line of hairs below the center of his bottom lip. She traced lightly over his mouth. All the while his gaze was intent on hers. Desire smoldered in his deep dark eyes. And she could smell it on him, even though it was a scent that had usually offended her. Not so from Savin. He was a real man. Not a demon.

"Kiss me," she whispered. She moved nearer until their noses were close enough to brush. He smelled like the brisk Paris air and fiery whiskey, with a rich earthy tang of man.

"Jett, I—"

"Yes?"

A hush of his breath played over her lips. "Are you sure?"

"I never ask for things I don't want. That's a waste of words."

She ran her fingers along his cheek and back through his hair.

She would not kiss him. He must come to her. Otherwise, she would not know if he was merely doing as she asked or if he genuinely wanted to. But the heat of his body so close to hers was incredible. Tempting. And she felt dizzied, yet also emboldened by the alcohol. If he refused her request, it would crush her.

When his mouth met hers, the connection felt tentative for but a moment. Savin's hand slipped along her neck, gentle but guiding, as he tilted her head to better receive the taste of his desire. He invaded her with his presence in a way she had never known. And she wanted to keep it. To know him as only adults could know each other.

His mustache brushed her upper lip, and their noses nudged. Eyes closed, she gripped at his wavy hair. Their intense connection rocketed up the delicious tingle that began at her mouth and coiled rapidly throughout her body. Jett slid a leg over his lap, her knee hitting the whiskey bottle, and straddled him. He slipped a hand along her back, not breaking the kiss, instead keeping her firmly in place upon him.

She wanted to taste him, to drink the whiskey from his tongue. That wish was granted as he dashed his tongue along the seam of her mouth. Such a spectacular sensation giddied up her spine. The man's throaty groan clued her he enjoyed kissing her as much as she did him.

His tongue was hot and slick as he tasted her teeth, tongue and her lips. She copied his movements, daring him into a deep dance that ignited the coil of want in her belly, and lower. It was not a sensation she had known—too easy, too comfortable—and it alerted her for a few moments, but she would not let him know her caution rose. The width of his hand spanned her back as he gentled that sudden anxiety with the realization that he might only protect her and—if she was lucky—give her pleasure.

He must. She deserved it.

Bracketing his face with both palms, Jett tilted her head, seeking to devour his whiskey sweetness. When she brushed her hard nipples against his chest, again the man moaned. Yes, she liked his reaction. He was under her command now. And that empowered her.

Yet when he slipped out his tongue and kissed her mouth, then bowed his forehead to hers to end the kiss, she wanted to greedily pull him back for another. So she did. This time the clutch of his hand against her hip was more urgent. And his other hand slid over her derriere and squeezed.

She wanted to feel his body against hers, skin to skin, to know what his muscles felt like flexing with movement, melding against her body, and to own him.

But she was getting carried away.

Jett lashed her tongue along Savin's lower lip, then met his gaze.

"Whew!" he said.

Exactly. And kneeling over him, firmly in his embrace, she could sense…something similar within him. The demoness he claimed had hitched a ride to this realm with his escape? The Other. Her presence was faint, barely a shimmer that traced the man's veins. And yet she wanted Jett to know of her presence.

Oh, she was aware.

Jett thumbed Savin's mouth. "I've never been kissed like that."

His eyebrow quirked.

"Actually, I've never been kissed until now."

"You're— Really?"

She nodded. "Finally, that kiss you promised me when we were kids has been granted. And don't think you have to stop giving them to me."

"That was an intense kiss. A guy would never know you'd not done such before." He looked aside. Were his thoughts going to places she didn't want them to go?

Jett kissed him again. She would claim this man, body and soul. Because that was what she did to survive.

Chapter 6

There was only one way to be safe, and that would mean relinquishing the power Jett had gained since living in Daemonia. She felt sure she could accomplish the task. She would never return there. Not even if a sexy reckoner decided her time was up.

However, to let go of what she had gained would be a supreme sacrifice. She'd not yet dared to test those powers here in the mortal realm. Perhaps they were already diminished?

But first, she needed an answer to a question that had haunted her all through her absence. And the only way to do that was to locate her parents; one or both. Though she suspected her mother might be the best bet, according to what Savin had told her about her father moving on after her disappearance.

Her father. He could be the missing key. What did she really know about her father?

She'd asked Savin if he could ask his mother about her parents. Since they'd lived so close when they were children, and she remembered their mothers being friends, perhaps Madame Thorne could aid in her search. With luck, she would have an answer to her oft-wondered-about question soon.

Teasing her finger along the granite countertop in Savin's kitchen, Jett marveled over the simple stone. Nothing like this in Daemonia. There the minerals and earth had been volatile and ever changing. One could never take a step without being certain one's foot would land on a solid or moving surface. It was good to be home. Almost home. Would she ever call a place home again?

Savin wandered in from the bedroom. The man wore loose-fitted jeans and a long-sleeved shirt that struggled to contain his biceps. "I'm heading out for some groceries, and I just got a text from Ed, the corax demon I reckoned for yesterday. He was the one who sensed the gates to Daemonia were opening, and was there the night you came through. He isn't sure Certainly's spell to close the rift is holding."

"And who or what is Certainly?"

"Certainly Jones is a man. A dark witch."

Yet another person of whom she should remain wary. Witches never survived Daemonia. The dark ones did like to conjure from that source, and such invocations never seemed to go well. At least, not for the demon.

"I thought you were the reckoner," Jett said. "How are you involved with wrangling demons? Do you hunt, as well?"

"Nope. Don't like to hunt. Dead giveaway, too, because demons sense me as easily as I sense them. But

I'm in on this whole keeping-the-rift-closed adventure, so I'll help Ed and CJ any way I can. You going to be okay here by yourself for a while?"

"Of course. I'm a big girl."

"That you are." His eyes twinkled, and Jett remembered their kiss last night. She would take another from him soon, if she had her way. And she generally did. "Any requests for food?"

"No, but if you could call your mother, I'd be appreciative."

"Right. I haven't forgotten. I might stop by her place today. She lives in the sixteenth near the park now. Has a nice little apartment. She's going to flip to hear you're back."

"Is that a good flip or a bad flip?"

"My mother knows about me and the demon stuff. She says she believes me, but I also know she can't bring herself to label her son crazy, even though she suspects that could be a possibility." He shrugged. "Such is life. I'm going to pick you up a phone while I'm out, too. Not that you need to start texting and taking selfies, but it'll be a good way for us to keep in touch when I'm gone."

"You are too generous, Savin. I feel as if I owe you so much already."

"Don't think like that. I'm glad I can offer you a place to stay. It's nice having someone around to talk to."

"And kiss," she offered, following him to the front door.

"And kiss." He turned and looked down at her. He was too tall and wouldn't be able to get close enough for a kiss without bending his knees. But Jett waited anyway. For a few seconds they held gazes. He seemed… nervous. "Uh, I should go, then."

"Kiss me first. I want to make up for lost time."

He leaned down and his breath hushed against her ear as he spoke. "It's impossible to get back time."

"Time grows longer when you kiss me."

His eyebrow quirked, followed by a slow smile that punctuated his cheeks with subtle dimples. Now, that was impossible to resist.

Jett initiated the kiss that lured her to her tiptoes and into the burly man's embrace. His arms wrapped about her back, and her body tilted against his. Their connection grew lush and deep. She moaned against his mouth. Pleasurable vibrations sparkled in her chest and shimmered lower. Standing in Savin's arms stirred her wanton instincts. This was a new feeling. Yet it teased at her darkness. How she wanted to push him against the wall and tear off his shirt—

"You sure do like my kisses," Savin said as he pulled away. "Or else you've had a lot of practice."

"I told you last night you are the first man I've kissed. I'm glad for that. And you tempt me to want to kiss you all day. Hurry back. I want to start up where we're leaving off."

"I like the way you think." He winked, then opened the door. "See you in a bit."

The door closed behind him and Jett felt the wards zap at her. Stepping back with a skip, she hissed at the intrusive repulsion. It was more an annoyance than anything. But now as she glanced about the kitchen and living room, she realized she was once again imprisoned. Even if she didn't mind the prison so much this time around, she could not breach those wards without pain.

She had to find her own place. Her own identity. And

yet she wanted to do that *and* keep Savin in her life. He fit her. It was as if they had never been separated.

This time her smile came easily as she spun into the kitchen.

Jett opened the fridge door and inspected the contents. Lots of sandwich meats, cheese wedges and bottled energy drinks in wild colors. She was a little hungry but had yet to figure out her appetite. She grabbed a bottle that boasted a protein-packed chocolate elixir and tested it.

"Not terrible."

Drink in hand, she wandered about the place. It was cool and quiet. The skylights beamed in subtle sunlight. Nothing too bright. She suspected it would take a while to fully adjust to the daylight. But the part of her that took comfort from the darkness prodded at her. *Stay in the dark*, it nudged. *Dark is safe. Dark is home.*

Rubbing a palm over her upper arm, Jett winced. Yes, the darkness was a safe and tempting place. There was so much light here in the mortal realm. Had her decision to escape here been wise?

Standing in the center of the living area, she suddenly felt lost, abandoned. Like a nine-year-old child who had been thrust into the unknown. Her cries would never be heard or comforted. She needed safety. So she began to allow the sheen to dissolve—

"No!" Jett lifted her head and fisted a hand at her side. The fall of her sheen stopped. "I can do this. I will do this. I am human."

And her dark half, defeated for the moment, slunk away into the shadows. But she would continue to lurch up closer and closer until Jett could no longer keep her back. How could she? That darkness was her reality.

She smirked. Savin had an incorporeal demon inside him? In a way, they were two alike. Jett had no idea how to ask him for help with her problem. And best she not. No reckoner was going to calmly take her by the hand and treat her kindly should he learn her truth.

Tilting back half the bottle of protein drink, she set it on the wooden chair arm and forced herself to think of anything but her past. Because that was where it now belonged—forgotten in the past.

Her eyes moved about the vast brick wall behind the couch. So many guitars. And the odd one with a single string he'd made himself. Fascinating. Savin practiced musicomancy? She wasn't sure how that magic was utilized, but it didn't sound like something she wanted to experience. Especially when wielded by a reckoner.

On the other hand, she needed to be smart and remain aware. Never look away and always glance over her shoulder. It was a motto that had helped her to survive. Best she learn everything she could about the use of music to invoke magic.

Jett strummed her fingers over the six nylon strings on one guitar. It sounded soft and simple. She imagined Savin could make the instrument sing. As he'd made her insides sing when kissing her. She was not a woman who could be satisfied with mere kisses for long. The man was an inferno, and she wanted to plunge into him. Flames were her sanctuary. It was where she felt most powerful.

Wandering into the bedroom, she approached the freestanding cabinet that stretched as high as her head. Half a dozen metal objects sat on top of it. Crawling onto the high bed, she stood on the mattress and leaned over to catch her forearms against the cabinet top. There were six different metal cases and objects. Brass housings edged them all and intricate carvings decorated the brushed metal surfaces. Wooden pieces were fit in here and there, and some gears and even a combination dial were attached to one of them. They resembled intricate navigational devices from a time long ago. Some had symbols embossed on the metal or burned into the wooden surfaces.

"Sigils," she said with knowing.

A few she recognized as demonic. She knew the words for them but would not speak them, for she could not know what such a recitation would conjure in this realm. Obviously, Savin also had that knowledge.

"His means to track demons?" she wondered as she tapped the cover of one case. But no, he'd said he did not hunt them. Which could only mean... "A device to reckon them back to Daemonia."

It was shaped like a book with an elaborate multitier brass wheel on the front and a dial in the center that did not turn to numbers but rather alchemical symbols. More sigils circled the wheel on four levels. Jett turned the center dial and heard a click. She tested the cover to see if she could open it; it did not. She supposed there was a code or series of turns to open it, much like a combination lock. The vibrations that hummed from the device were weak, yet she sensed it was perhaps honed to work only for a specific user.

Jett did not like being kept out of a secret whether it be delicious or dangerous.

With a sneer, she set that one aside and traced a fingernail over a circular device that featured metal bars jutting out from the center, and at the end of each bar was a small black crystal. Savin had mentioned he made these things. The craftsmanship was stunning. He was talented. As she moved a fingertip over each crystal, the device shook. It *felt* her.

A creak from the other room alerted Jett. She turned to check over her shoulder. Had Savin returned so soon? She listened for a few breathless seconds, then decided she was spooking herself. The thought was ridiculous. Someone such as she, spooked?

Never.

She would not understand these devices, and that was frustrating. With a snap of her finger she should be able to summon an answer.

Jett studied her thumb pressed against her middle finger, ready to snap.

"No longer," she said.

She must learn to exist in a new manner now. With new rules, or, rather, the old rules of the mortal realm she'd once known.

Replacing the device where she'd found it, she perused the rest of the items. At the corner of the cabinet sat a metal tin much like the one Savin had shown her at the café. Morphine? She opened it to find inside a syringe, and rather an old-fashioned one at that. It wasn't disposable or plastic like the sort she'd once seen her father's brother use because he had diabetes. This device was metal and wasn't rusted, but the glass tube did reveal discoloration. And nestled in the red velvet beside the syringe was a white vial with the fading word *Morphia* on it. An elaborate brass cap screwed on the top.

"Like something out of the nineteenth century," she whispered. It couldn't be sanitary or even safe for Savin's health.

He'd said he needed it to keep the demon inside him

subdued. Addicts in Daemonia drank morphine like some kind of sweet beverage and then lapsed into an eyelid-twitching reverie. If they had eyelids, that was.

What demon had hitched a ride in Savin Thorne to come to this realm? And why? If she was incorporeal, she had to have known before leaving Daemonia that she could never leave her host. Or rather, she might switch bodies, but only at great risk. Hmm… On the other hand, sometimes corporeal demons could only maintain that form in Daemonia, and a trip to the mortal realm reduced them to seeking a human host as an incorporeal passenger.

Should Jett have known about that apparent escape from Daemonia? It sounded as though Savin might have been there only a short while, so at the time, Jett wouldn't have had reason or the capability to tap in to what had occurred with his exit.

Now she was curious to learn more about his demonic passenger he called the Other. But she had to be careful because her sheen could crack at any moment. The last thing she wanted was for Savin to see her true nature exposed.

"I will learn what drives you, Savin. And I will have more than kisses from you. I need intimacy," she decided. "To finally feel like a real, human woman."

Ed had been heading out to meet with one of his troop leaders, so he directed Savin to speak to Certainly Jones, who worked in the Archives. The Archives kept a vast storehouse of all documents, texts and artifacts related to every known paranormal species. As well as the most rare and volatile magical objects, devices and even creatures. It was rumored that to obtain some of those things, by trick or by sword, they utilized retrievers in the branch called Acquisitions to do so.

Savin knew their methods were peccable, and that was fine with him. He wasn't big on following the law to a tee. And here in this realm, there was no paranormal code of ethics beyond "Don't make yourself known to humans."

But he was human, and he did know. And he was glad he knew about all the things that should only be myth or legend. Then some days he wasn't so glad. The things he had seen in his short lifetime would turn a man's hair gray and force him to drink. His hair was still brown, but the drinking part...

Upon entering the Archives, he'd let CJ test the wards tattooed on his skin for efficacy and deflection. With Savin's approval, the dark witch had whispered a spell to place a sort of "plastic wrap protector" over those tattooed sigils that could interact negatively with the wards in the building. Still, they retained their power to protect him should some*thing* wish to invade or harm him while he was here.

Feeling the wrapper tingle over his skin, Savin shook out his muscles with a good doggy shake. He then nodded thanks to the witch. "Ed says you're nervous about the wards on the rift."

"I am. And I appreciate you remaining involved in this, Thorne. It's good to have a reckoner handy when all Beneath breaks lose."

Beneath was the paranormal version of the humans' hell.

"I think Daemonia ranks worse than Beneath."

"Fair enough. I've been to Daemonia for a visit myself. Been there, done that, wasn't about to get the T-shirt."

Savin knew that, because CJ was the one he'd gone to in an attempt to get rid of his passenger demon. After his return from Daemonia so many years ago, CJ had been successful in banishing all the unwanted demons from his soul. Yet they both remained baffled on how to oust Savin's guest.

"Right, you know about that adventure," CJ amended. "I wish I had known you when I was full of demons. Would have been much easier to reckon them than the hell I went through getting rid of those bastards."

"It doesn't work that way, I'm afraid." Savin turned a shoulder against the office wall and leaned against it. CJ offered him a clove cigarette, which he took. "I can't reckon a demon within a human host. Tried it on myself."

"That's right. I forgot about that. Sorry, man. You've still got that bitch inside you?" He handed Savin a lighter, then blew fragrant smoke to the side.

"Yes, but let's not call her a bitch today. She's quiet, and I like to keep it that way."

"Got it." CJ leaned against the limestone wall beside Savin and the twosome shared the quiet as they inhaled the sweet smoke.

Despite him being a practitioner of dark magic, Savin liked Certainly Jones. The man had been around for longer than a century and was the ultimate laid-back, bohemian witch. And his woman was gorgeous. Savin had met her one time. Viktoria St. Charles was a cleaner, which meant she and her sister (Libertie, also a witch) cleaned up dead paranormal bodies before they were dis-covered by humans. She also had a sticky soul, which attracted wayward and lost souls. Interesting.

With the Other inside him, Savin wasn't sure what nature his soul was. *Did* she inhabit his very soul? Or merely this chunk of meat he called a body and used while in this mortal realm? He didn't look forward to dying and bringing her along with him. At the very least, he prayed death would release her. Because he'd felt her pull him away when he wanted to kiss Jett longer and more deeply earlier. Bitch.

Yeah, she could hear his thoughts. Screw it.

"Can I ask you something?" he said to CJ.

"Shoot."

Savin held the cigarette before him and blew on the end, brightening the embers. "When you were there, in Daemonia, how was it for you?"

CJ's heavy sigh said so much. No one in their right mind ever wanted to visit that place. But, apparently, CJ had gone there on purpose, for some magical quest. He'd gone into Daemonia of his own accord, and...well, as is usually the case, he'd gotten trapped there. His twin brother, Thoroughly, had to rescue him and bring him home. And with that return, Certainly had been accompanied by at least a dozen nasty incorporeal demons.

"You must understand," CJ started, "that a child's perception—your memory of the place—is going to be vastly different from a grown man's. And I am a man who went there on purpose."

"I know. I was scared beyond shitless. It was all I could do to survive and not go insane. And believe me, part of me thinks you're one hell of an idiot for walking into Daemonia like you did."

"Most of me thinks that, as well. But you know, sometimes a guy has to make the leap and go for the adventure."

"I'm all for adventure. And that part of me admires

your ballsy trip to the Place of All Demons. But is the place...hospitable? How can a person survive there?"

"I'm not sure it's possible for a human to exist in Daemonia for more than a short time. Time is weird there, you know?"

"I know." What he'd thought was weeks in that place had been a little over thirty-two hours by the time he returned to his parents' loving and worried arms. "Do you think a human could survive there for decades?"

Certainly shook his head and flicked ash to the side. "Not without becoming one of them."

"What does that mean? Like a demon?"

"Anything that isn't demon, and which stays there overlong, will ultimately assume, at the very least, some demonic qualities."

Savin hadn't known that. Could Jett...? No. He would have sensed if she had any demon in her. "But they change back to human when they return to this mortal realm?"

"If they don't have passengers. You know as well as I how difficult it is to come out of that place clean."

Savin blew out a breath and lifted his foot to stub out the cigarette on the bottom of his boot. He looked around for a garbage bin and, spying one by a desk, flicked it into the steel container.

"Why do you ask? You ever accidentally reckon a human?"

"No. Never." He hooked his thumbs at his belt loops. Should he tell Certainly about Jett? It didn't feel right. The witch had no need to learn about his houseguest who might have returned to this realm not as human as she seemed. Savin hadn't considered that she could have developed some demonic qualities. Hmm… She was sensitive to sunlight, and still the wards bothered her.

"Need more morphine yet?" Certainly asked.

CJ was also his supplier. The witch provided him with a clean yet powerful drug that appeased the Other. "Soon. Might have about a month's worth remaining."

"That old mixture is hard to come by. Requires worm-wood and dragon's bane. Nasty stuff."

"It's the only thing that works."

CJ nodded. "I'll mix up a larger batch in a week or two. Should keep you in supply for a while."

"Thanks, man. So." Savin rubbed his hands together expectantly. "What's the plan?"

"Ed has two sentries posted out at the site. I visited this morning. I can feel the wards shaking. I think we've got a few days, at the most, before it opens up again."

"How to close it securely?"

CJ leaned against his desk, crossing his legs at the ankle. The guy was barefoot. Savin had never actually seen him wearing shoes. Witches were strange.

"The wards should have held securely," CJ said. "However, there is a reason this suddenly feels loosey-goosey to me."

Savin lifted a brow. "Yeah?"

"I feel as though something got out that wasn't sup-posed to," CJ offered.

"Like every single demon that made its way into this realm?"

"Not exactly. Some demons come here without mak-ing an indelible mark on the realm. They blend in and learn our mortal-realm ways. You know that."

Much as he wished otherwise, Savin knew he'd al-ways have to coexist alongside demons.

"What I'm thinking is that something immense—not necessarily in size, but importance—needs to be returned to Daemonia in order to seal the rift and hex a good lock on it. If something that shouldn't have been allowed comes to this realm?" The witch shuddered. "Realm rules are big on stuff like that. Keeping the balance and all."

"Realm rules?" Savin whistled lowly. "Don't even tell me. I've got enough in this brain that I'd rather not know about, as it is. Something important? Isn't Ed finding most of the demons who got out? I reckoned a handful yesterday."

"He is, but you know demons can cloak themselves. They call it a sheen. Some are so talented they can walk right by you, rub against your skin, and you'd never think they were anything but human."

"I'm better than your average bear at sensing demons. I do have my demon radar sitting inside me."

"Maybe. But you don't sense them all, I'm sure."

"Probably not," Savin conceded. But how to know about the ones he couldn't sense? And did he really want to know? Besides, if it was important or immense, as CJ had described it, surely he would be aware of that disturbance to this realm.

"It's a hunch," CJ offered. "I'm going to spend the afternoon in the demon room, reading up in the Bibliodaemon."

"The Book of All Demons. Doesn't sound like light reading. How can I help?"

"Just stay alert to beyond the usual. Which I'm sure is pretty fucked for you."

"You got that one right."

"I'm going to defer to you as the expert on demons

in this case. Did you encounter anything odd following the spell to close the rift?"

Savin shrugged. Jett was human and finally free. She couldn't possibly have an impact on the continuing issues. And if he did let CJ know about her, the witch might have questions. He didn't want to subject Jett to that. Not yet. Not until she was comfortable being back in this realm.

If he could help locate her mother, that might be a start to returning some normality to her routine.

"Savin?"

"Huh? Oh. No. All's the same. As usual. I'm going to head out. You've got my number if you need me. Do I turn left or right at the end of the hallway?"

"Right," CJ said. "Left always tends to lead one into the sinister, don't you know?"

Savin smirked at the joke. But not really a joke, since he did know his witchery and demon lore. "Talk to you later, man."

He strode down the hall, which was entirely of limestone, carved directly from the earth beneath Paris. So the dark witch didn't believe a human could survive Daemonia without becoming part demon? The notion disturbed Savin. If that was the case, would Jett know if she wasn't completely human?

And if so, would she tell him?

Chapter 7

Savin's mother, Gloriana, was wire-wrapping the new growth on her boxwood bonsai when he arrived at her cozy sixteenth-arrondissement apartment. He kissed her on the head—she was five foot two on a good day; he'd gotten his height from his dad—and she rubbed her hands together as she led him toward the kitchen, where it smelled divine.

"Just took some chocolate madeleines out of the oven," she cooed. "I knew I'd see you soon."

She had a weird sense for things like that. She always knew who was on the phone before picking it up (she still had a landline; cell phones weren't her thing), knew who was at the front door before answering and generally knew within a day or two when Savin would call or stop by. And yet the one time he'd mentioned such precognition to her, she dismissed it as woo-woo stuff. Good ol' Maman. She strived to walk a wide circle around her son's reality.

"I love the chocolate ones," he said as she set the plate before him.

Savin downed three cakes, which were still warm, then got up and checked the fridge for milk. "Your madeleines are the best, Maman. I still think you should go into business and start a food truck."

"I'm considering it."

"You are?" He took the milk carton to the table with a glass and poured. "That's awesome. You and Roxane?" Her best friend, who tended to convince his mother to check out the latest clubs and to wear the highest heels to prove that women in their fifties were only as old as they acted.

"Yes. She's got the marketing skills. I've got the recipes. It could happen."

"I'm impressed. Be sure you cruise around the fourteenth, will you?"

"Oh, *mon cher*, I will deliver yours special every day. I'm working on a cheesecake version. Would you like that?"

"I like them all, Maman, you know that." He downed two more moist and dense cakes in but four bites.

"Now, what's up?" Gloriana asked. "I just spoke to you last week and you generally go a few weeks without getting in touch. New girlfriend?"

Savin set down the half-eaten cake. "What makes you think that?"

She wiggled on the chair and smiled a toothy grin. "You've shaved that unruly beard, and your hair is combed."

"Am I really such a slob otherwise?"

"You do tend to avoid the mirror. So tell me what she's like."

"She's..." Savin pushed the plate of madeleines aside and stretched out his legs, preparing for this strange announcement. He and his mother had always shot straight with each other, even when it came to the weird stuff. "She's not my girlfriend, but she is an old friend."

"Oh? Like from school?"

"Jett Montfort is back, Maman."

"What? Did you say *Jett*? But she..." His mother's lower lip wobbled.

A few years after the event had happened, Savin had told her the entire story about being kidnapped to the demonic realm. After the media's interest had died down and his father had died. He'd had to. The truth had burned like a fire in him every time he tried to act as if it had been a kidnapping. He knew his mother had suspected he wasn't being completely truthful with her.

But as well, he knew the truth wasn't going to land on her believability radar. But she could get close. He trusted telling her things now. Weird things. She could believe him or not. Either way? She still loved him.

"Jett." She pressed her fingers to her mouth. "I can't— But how? Where has she been?"

"If I tell you, you'd never believe me. Well, you know, I told you the truth of it all. It was a wild tale, but every bit of it was true, Maman. I swear it to you."

She nodded. Tears glistened at the corners of her eyes.

"Jett was there, in that place, all this time."

Gloriana gaped.

"Suffice, she's safe now and looks well. I'm letting her stay with me until— I haven't thought beyond offering her a place to stay. I'm sure she'll want to find her own place. But she'll need a job first. Hell, she needs to assimilate and become a part of the human race again."

"The human—" Gloriana swallowed. "I can't believe it. It's been twenty years, Savin. And she just walked into your life?"

"Kind of like that."

"Oh." Again, Gloriana pressed her fingers to her mouth. "So she was there...with the...demons?" she whispered the last word.

Savin nodded. He'd described to his mother all he had experienced. And then she'd wrapped him in her arms. It might have been the first time he'd let out a breath and truly relaxed after that harrowing experience. It had been a long time coming.

"I'm keeping her safe," he said.

His mother nodded and grabbed a madeleine to nibble at the end.

"The reason I stopped by is Jett needs to find her mom and dad. She's alone in the world now and wants to reconnect. I figured if anyone had the smallest thread leading to either of the Montforts, it would be you. You were good friends with her mother."

"Josette and I were best friends. But, *mon cher*, you know she left not soon after the divorce. Just up and left her whole life behind. She didn't say a thing to me, and I haven't heard from her since. I can understand..." She looked aside. "You know she was angry with me?"

His mother had never told him that. But he could guess why. "Because I came back?"

She nodded, swallowed. "I understand, of course. Her daughter never came back."

"She has now."

"That's incredible. And you say she looks well?"

"She does. Do you think you can help Jett find her parents?"

"Well." She made the sighing thoughtful noise as her eyes traced about the kitchen. Then her deep blue irises brightened. "I'm not sure what good it will do…" She glanced down the hallway.

"What, Maman?"

"Sit tight. I have some things." She scurried from the kitchen and into the bedroom, where Savin heard her riffling through a large cabinet of craft supplies she ever fussed over. If she wasn't baking, she knitted and donated the sweaters to charity.

Savin downed two more cookies and another half glass of ice-cold milk. A man forgets about the comforts of home after living on his own for so long. If his mother were to invest in a food truck business, he would track her down daily for the treats.

"Here it is." Gloriana returned holding a rumpled brown paper envelope. She sat across from him and set the envelope on the table. "The Montfort house stood empty for a few months after Josette's departure. No realty sign, nor did I get a call from Josette. Finally, I decided to call the city and see what must be done. I was informed they would clean it out and take in hand all possessions, so I decided it would be best to sneak in and see if there was anything important left behind. Just in case Josette ever returned, you know?"

"Smart, Maman. You've always had a sneaky streak."

"And damned proud of it. Anyway, I found some family documents and important papers. Nothing much." She pushed the envelope toward him. "I haven't opened it since that day I took the papers out of their house. You give them to Jett. If they can help her, then I'll know my sneakery was worth it. I do believe there was mortgage info in there. Although the house has since been torn down. And there was bank account information. If those accounts still exist, Jett might be able to claim something for herself. Does she need money?"

"She doesn't have a job, but I'll help her out. You know I can." He didn't make the big bucks reckoning demons, but he did have a great financial investment adviser.

"You're so good, Savin. The two of you were like brother and sister. So close. I remember the day Jett told me she was going to marry you. I figured it would be the best thing that could happen to you. She calmed you. Kept you on course."

"You never told me that. Was I such a wild child?"

"Yes." She laughed. "Oh, yes, *mon cher*, you could never concentrate on a task for more than a few moments. What did they call it? ADD? I think it was that you got bored easily. You needed to feel the world against your skin, and sitting before a school desk all day drove you mad."

That was truth. There were days he'd cut out of school early just to rush home through the field. And yet another reason he'd dropped out in high school. "Music calms me now."

"It is good you have something to help you find peace. But never be afraid of your wild, *mon cher.*"

Savin nodded, smiling. He'd given ninety percent of the details when telling his mother of that harrowing trip to Daemonia. But he could never tell her that he harbored a demon within him. That was definitely his wild. And he wasn't afraid of the Other. Just wisely cautious.

He grabbed the envelope. "I'm sure Jett will appreciate this. No idea where her mother is living now?"

Gloriana shook her head. "Sorry."

"You got any more madeleines?"

"I've put a batch in the fridge, but I can see that was unnecessary. Need more milk?"

"Yes, please."

When the sound of the front door opening alerted Jett, she quickly pulled on her sheen. Oh, but that pinched!

With Savin gone, she'd given in to her desire to revive her energy. Wearing a sheen was so confining. But necessary. Once it was dropped, she had inhaled deeply. Standing in her natural state had allowed her to breathe and relax. She had needed that.

With a dash into the bathroom, she checked her appearance in the mirror. She had put on some lipstick and blush and was feeling more human with every second that passed.

"Looking it, too," she said with a wink at her reflection as she turned off the light and headed out to greet Savin.

When she walked right up to him, gripped him by the shirtfront and pulled him down to kiss, he didn't protest. Which she took as a good sign. But it was a quick kiss. Long enough to give her a taste of what she desired, but short enough to keep her wanting. When he pulled away, a confused sort of acceptance wriggled on his face.

"I like kissing you," she offered quickly. "Maybe it's that I like kissing in general. It is a good thing."

"Have to agree with that one. You can kiss me anytime."

"Really?" She planted another quickie on his cheek, right over that delicious dimple.

"Really. But before you get carried away, I stopped by my mom's place. The bad news is she doesn't know where your parents are right now. But the good news is she did have this."

Jett took the large manila envelope he handed her. It was thick and wrinkled with age. "What is this?"

"Apparently, my maman snuck into your parents' house the night before the city came through to clear out things before they placed it under lien. Maman took out whatever looked important to her. She thought your mother might return someday, and had intended to give her these things."

"That was thoughtful of her. So what's inside?"

"I don't know. I figured that was for you to open." He held up a brown paper bag. The bottom corner was glossed with grease. "I picked up some chicken gyros on the way home. There's a little place down the street that makes the saltiest *pommes frites*. I love them crammed into my sandwich."

"Sure." She sat at the kitchen counter, rubbing her palms over the envelope. "But no salt, please."

"No salt— Oh. Right. Sorry. The gyros aren't salted. It's just the fries. You've got to try something. Jett, you haven't eaten much since you've been here."

"I know. Don't worry about it. I haven't developed an appetite for human food yet."

She could hear his swallow. Wondering what demon food entailed, likely. He did not want to know. It had certainly taken her time to develop a taste for it. And by no means did demons go near salt. And she was not hungry, so she wasn't concerned.

"If I get hungry," she said, "I'll tell you immediately and make you run out for something. Deal?"

He nodded. "Does that mean I get to eat your fries?"

"You do."

He sat next to her and unpacked the food, which did smell delicious. But if those fries were indeed extra salty, she was not interested. And when she saw him pour white sauce over the sandwich, she decided there was no way she could work up a hunger now.

The envelope waited.

Inside was a stack of assorted papers. Some were neat and crisp, others folded, and a few were crumpled, having been compressed for years, and held a permanent fold crease.

"I don't recognize these company names," she said, glancing over the papers. The last time she'd been in this realm she had been nine. Adult responsibilities such as banks and bills had not been on her radar.

"That is the name of a bank, and that one..." He tilted his head as he read the paper. His hair brushed her cheek and Jett noticed a smudge of sauce on his mustache. "Looks like mortgage stuff. Must be for your parents' house. That, along with all the other houses in the area, was torn down last year to clear the land for the current construction."

"So, mortgage information is useless." She had to force herself to look back at the papers. How she wanted to lick his lips just now. To taste the flavor of the white sauce. And him. "The bank information might be handy," she said. "And this is...perhaps a list of phone numbers? No names on it. This might be important. Health insurance cards and my father's passport. Hmm, it's expired."

She tapped the small laminated photo inside the passport. It had been so long since she had seen her father, Charles Montfort. She'd never forgotten what he looked like. Yet now it felt as though she were looking at a picture of a stranger in a magazine. No attachment to the small portrait before her. Not even a skip of her heart in recognition.

But she couldn't let Savin know how alien the man appeared to her. "I got my black hair from him, yes?"

"I liked your dad," Savin offered. "He played catch with me more often than my dad ever did."

"If I recall correctly, your dad had a fabulous job jet-setting across countries."

"He was a pilot. And...a drinker. But he's dead now."

She hadn't remembered the drinking part. Strange, considering her own father had liked to tip back the whiskey. Had Savin's father turned to drinking after their kidnapping? And the way he'd dismissed the topic by stating he was dead. Jett wouldn't ask how he had died. She didn't want to stir up bad memories. Or try at empathy. She'd only just refreshed herself by dropping the sheen. Taking on human emotions could drag her down again.

"Those look like birth certificates." Savin tapped a yellowed paper. "What's that one?"

Jett turned it to read and sucked in a breath. "I don't understand this."

Savin leaned over to read the title on the page. "Certificate of adoption?"

"And the child's name on it is mine."

She met Savin's wide-eyed gaze. "You're adopted?" he asked.

"No. I mean, I don't think so. I'm not. I was… My parents never said anything of the sort."

She read through the document, her heart dropping with every word of evidence that claimed she had been born to a woman whose name was not her mother's and…there was no father's name listed, nor was it on the birth certificate.

And yet, even as her heart fell, the darkness within her nodded. Knowing. *You have always wondered…*

Besides the birth certificate, the certificate of adoption listed her parents' names, Josette and Charles Montfort, and a date of adoption. It was all very clear. And the documents were certainly official, to judge by the raised seal signed by a notary.

"I'm adopted," she said in disbelief. "I can't believe they never told me."

"Maybe they were waiting until you got older?"

She nodded, not comprehending, but also taking it all in, so deeply. There had been one thing she had wondered many times while in Daemonia. And to think on it now…

"I really was taken," she said with a gasp.

Because it had been said to her once—*you were taken*—but she hadn't wanted to believe it. No explanation had been given. Only that it hadn't been an accident that day she was sucked into Daemonia. She had been specifically targeted.

"Jett? What did you say? You were taken? Yes, I suppose you could call it that. We were both taken."

She collected the stack of papers before her and placed her palms over them. Now the salty scent of Savin's meal annoyed her. And she felt the immediate need for fresh air.

"I need to walk," she announced, and slipped off the stool and around Savin. Most important, she wanted to get away from the tug of the wards that now seemed to reach out toward her.

Savin caught her hand and met her gaze. Right now she didn't want his closeness, or the perceived compassion she suspected. This was big. Too big to take in while in the presence of one whom she must remain cautious of.

"You want me to walk with you?" he asked. "We don't need to talk."

It was a kind offer. The man cared about her. But... She shook her head. "I need to breathe for a bit. Alone."

"Got it. I had an extra key made today while I was out." He fished it out of his pocket and handed it to her. "If I'm ever not home, you'll need it. I'll try to remember to soften the wards when I'm out."

"Thank you." She clasped the key and left quickly.

Inside she was screaming and clawing at the darkness that had constantly surrounded her in Daemonia. A darkness she had welcomed and become. Because she'd had no choice.

She was beginning to get answers. And she didn't like them.

Chapter 8

Savin waited a few hours, but he couldn't sit around any longer and wonder if Jett would return to his place. She'd been upset by the realization she was adopted. He had to talk to her. And whether or not she wanted to talk to him, he could at least be there for her.

He grabbed his skull cap, pulled it on and left the flat. Wandering down the street beneath a fall of maple leaves, he decided that Jett could be anywhere.

When they'd been kids, their parents would take them into the city and they'd wander, mostly in the fifth and on the Île de la Cité, but they had visited and explored all the city parks and even the cemeteries. The best games were played in the creepiest of places. Would she remember? A graveyard held post down the way, so he veered toward it.

The Montparnasse Cemetery attracted Savin on those

occasions when he wanted to avoid the rush of tourists and traffic and get lost in his thoughts. Sure, there were plenty of camera-wielding tourists wandering about the cemetery grounds, but he knew the spots that were less frequented. Baudelaire's and Maupassant's graves attracted a lot of tourists. He avoided those sections and sought a back corner. The celebrities in Savin's ideal corner of the tombstone garden were long forgotten.

When he spied Jett sitting on an aboveground stone coffin, leaning against the headstone, her legs pulled up to her chest and arms wrapped around them, Savin smiled. She returned the smile as he approached, and patted the stone beside her as an invite to sit. He climbed onto the cool perch and stretched out his legs, then took off his hat and set it on his lap.

"Is it okay that I found you?" he asked.

"It is. How *did* you find me?"

"This is one of my favorite places to visit when I want to think."

"It's nice here. And it doesn't feel threatening. The dead tend to keep their secrets. If there even are any lost souls here. Feels…empty."

Indeed, Savin had never encountered a paranormal while here, not even a ghost. Surprising, considering the location.

He sat quietly beside Jett, figuring he'd let her bring up whatever she wanted to talk about. He wasn't about the third degree. Actually, it felt comfortable to sit beside her without speaking. In a manner, they were two alike. Together they'd been through some terrible things. They were bonded beyond childhood games and adventures. He liked that. Another person in the world he could relate to. The list was short.

After a few minutes, Jett leaned forward and said softly, "It was a weird thing to find out." Long dark hair fell over the side of her face and dusted her knees. "Adopted? I can't believe my parents never said anything. It's not like it's such a taboo thing nowadays. Is it?"

"Being adopted is nothing to be ashamed of. I haven't a clue why your parents didn't tell you. Although…your mother was a staunch churchgoer."

"Yes, Sundays were sacred to her." She smirked. "False gods and a controlling patriarchy. That's all religion is. There are demons far kinder than some religious zealots I've known."

Savin had to agree, but then, he was sure most of the major religions would pass on admitting him as a member. And yet he'd been trained by an exorcist, and their numbers were welcomed by the Catholic Church. And which institution was always claiming the most demon encounters? The Catholics.

He had to chuckle that most of those claims were unsubstantiated, yet they did get good press. The demons Savin knew were much smarter than to get caught in a human host. Most of them, anyway. And while exorcism was effective, a few rare demons were actually strengthened by the intrusion of the Christian rites. And such demonic strength from within utterly destroyed the human host. Tragic.

"This news doesn't change anything," he offered. "Josette and Charles loved you. They raised you. They are your parents."

"I know that. But do you know… It's silly to even wonder. I'm not an emotional person."

She tilted a glance up at him, and the Other inside Savin shivered. He pressed a hand to his chest but didn't think much of it. Or rather, didn't want to. The Other was cautious about Jett. To be expected from one who had just come from Daemonia.

Finally, Jett asked, "Were they sad after I was gone?"

"Of course they were. I only saw your mother the one time and she was in tears. My mom wouldn't let me near her after that. I upset her." He clasped Jett's hand. The simple movement worked like a squeeze about his heart. And yet the Other now cringed. Savin could feel it as a tightening in his insides that made him grit his jaw. What was up with her today?

"If I could change things," he said, "and make it so you had come back and I remained, I would."

"It is what it is, Savin. No sense in wishing to change the past. It's behind me now. Or I want to put it behind me. I need to move forward in this mortal realm. As a normal human woman."

"You are normal and human, but…I suppose it's going to take some time to adjust to this realm. Do you want to talk about it at all?"

Dare he ask her the burning question?

"If I did, it would only keep that horrible experience in my present. Can I put it out of mind, please?"

"Of course."

She dipped her head and Savin smoothed aside the hair from her face. It was soft and smelled sweeter than the shampoo he used. Chicks always smelled good without even trying. He figured it was an innate thing. When she turned to look at him, he thought he saw a glint of red in her pupils and pulled his hand away abruptly.

Jett's sudden smirk and soft chuckle softened his weird fear. "What?"

"Nothing." Had that been another alert from the

Other? He glanced aside. Ah. There. Outside the wrought-iron cemetery fencing a nearby streetlight flashed red. Whew! That was what had produced the strange illusion in her eyes. "You have beautiful brown eyes."

"Now you think them beautiful? You used to tell me they were the color of mud."

He shrugged. "I was an idiot when I was a kid. Now that I'm a man I've developed an appreciation for a woman's eyes."

"Just her eyes?"

"Eyes. Mouth. Hair. Everything else. It's all good." He cast her a long look but ended it with a smile. It was impossible not to feel happy around her. She was back in his life. And they were both grown adults. And the things he was feeling toward Jett right now could be a man's folly. Or an enticing dive into bliss.

"Your voice is so deep," she said. "It's sexy. You have grown to be quite the man, Savin." She turned over his hand and spread her fingers across his palm. "Your hand is wide and strong. Powerful. I bet you'd be a force in a fistfight."

"I try to avoid physical violence. Against humans, that is. I've had to punch a demon or two in my lifetime."

"Feels good, doesn't it?"

He lifted his chin at that comment. She'd said it with such conviction. The woman had punched a demon or two, as well. And she wasn't sorry for it, that was for sure.

Savin frowned. She should never have had to defend herself in such a manner. But thank the gods she'd had the moxie.

"You've seen horrors, Jett. I know that," he said

quickly, needing to get out the words so she knew how he felt. "But they do not have to define you. You can make your future anything you want it to be." He clasped her hand against his mouth and held it there. "I'll do everything in my power to help you rise."

She turned to press her other hand over the clasp he held at his mouth and leaned in to bow her forehead to his. "I need that. Thank you for understanding."

The hush of her breath over his skin scurried desire through Savin's system. She smelled like cool limestone with a splash of flowers.

"I'm still thankful it was you who found me that night I made my escape. It was meant to be. The two of us belong together."

"I believe that. Things will get better for you. I promise."

She nodded and kissed the back of his hand before breaking their clasp. And in that moment, Savin wanted to kiss her to show her how much he was attracted to her, to bleed her warmth into his skin and know her scent viscerally—but something stopped him. A tightening of his muscles that stretched up the back of his neck.

The Other was not into romance this day.

To break the spell of discontent that had fallen on his shoulders, he asked, "You hungry?" If he didn't turn this conversation away from the Other, he'd need to shoot up now, and he didn't want to do that in front of Jett. "You haven't eaten much since you've arrived."

"I haven't. And I think I am hungry. You know what I could go for? Roasted chestnuts glazed with sugar. Do they still sell those?"

"Hell yes. There's a vendor not far from here that sells

those and other sweets." He slid off the sarcophagus and offered her his hand. "Let's go get high on sugar."

The man was remarkable.

Jett couldn't stop from browsing over Savin whenever she had the chance. He led her to a trio of food stands selling various items and they each claimed a treat. Now they walked toward a bench beneath a yellow-leaved tree. Savin was taller than her by two heads and broad as a bodybuilder. So many muscles flexed and pulsed with his movement. Any shirt he wore seemed to struggle to contain all that man. And his deep voice. It crept inside her being and did things to her senses. Things she'd never imagined feeling. She felt a certain way when around Savin.

She knew what it was that coiled within her. Desire. The wanting and *needing* to touch the man, to kiss him. To do more than that with him.

Desire was a new experience for Jett. And it pounced upon her with an aggression that startled her. She wasn't sure how to handle it. She'd not known desire for another person. Not in Daemonia. Though the desire for things, safety and control had always resided inside her. And certainly she was no virgin who hadn't a clue what to do with herself regarding a man and sex. She had done things to survive.

No regrets, her darkness whispered.

No, of course not.

But now? Now she was free. And she wanted to explore the exciting feeling that warmed her from ear tips to toes. And everywhere in between. When gazing upon Savin and taking in his masculine build, she felt her breasts become heavy and full. Her stomach swirled.

And her pussy—well, she recognized the wanting ache for sex. For the first time in her life. Yet she also knew it sprang from the confidence she'd gained while inhabiting the darkness.

If she abandoned her dark side, would she also lose such feelings? She wanted the man. Dare she risk answering her sudden desperate desires when she knew the part of her that reacted in such a manner was not the part she wanted to encourage?

"My lady." Savin gestured to a bench under a tree just on the other side from a yard where children played. "You're almost finished!"

Guilty as charged. Her desire had manifested as a real hunger, apparently. Jett sat on the bench and licked the sticky sugar crystals from her fingers. She'd enjoyed this treat many a time when she was a kid. It was even better now.

"I think I finally got my appetite back," she said with a smile from behind another bite. More than one appetite, that was for sure.

"I guess so. Let me catch up."

He dug into the crepe he'd gotten at the stand next to the chestnut seller, while Jett was distracted by the shouts and laughter of the children behind them. So carefree and innocent. Unknowing of the dangers the world could present. Best they not wander too close to any demonic portals or—whoosh! Life would never again be innocent.

Adopted. Adopted?

Jett sighed, her shoulders dropping. She had never considered adoption, even though she had often wondered about who her father really was. As a frightened child, she'd dismissed the allusion to her real paternity as a mistake, a cruel trick to get her to submit and accept as the darkness had started to develop within her. Questioning her paternity had initially felt ludicrous, but she'd been so young. And had only wanted to be treated well. So eventually she had accepted that question as a real possibility.

"What are you thinking about?" Savin asked.

She glanced at him, unwilling to spill her secret pain. So she arrowed in on his upper lip, where his mustache was so thick and she knew the tickle of it during a kiss was the most exciting thing.

She touched his mustache. "You've got chocolate there. It's a lot." And then, without thought, she leaned in to kiss him. Tasting his mouth, the chocolate, and then dragging her tongue to lick the sweet treat. "Got it," she said, and sat back, crumpling up the paper her chestnuts had come in.

"That you did." He stared at her, his lips parted. She'd startled him? Good. She liked to maintain a certain amount of power, of control over men. Even if this was no longer her domain.

"If you don't finish that," she said, "I *will* go in for a bite. Just a warning."

He smirked, then offered the half-eaten crepe to her. She leaned forward and took a bite, and then another, her lips brushing his finger. The earthy taste of him combined with the sweet treat was the perfect tease to her appetite. She wasn't so much hungry for food anymore as she was for Savin.

A strange bell tolled, and as Savin pulled his cell phone from his pocket, Jett realized she'd like to have one of those. A telephone that had virtually all the information in the world on it with just a few taps of her finger? Hadn't he said he was going to pick one up for her?

While he spoke to the caller, she finished off the crepe and offered him a wink as she wrapped her fingers about his to get to the very last bits of it.

"I can come by soon," he said, then paused. When Jett looked up, the man was biting the corner of his lower lip, staring at her as she ate from his hand. "Uh… Yes, right. Sorry, I was distracted. See you in a bit, Malcolm." He tucked the phone away, then crumpled the paper and tossed it in the nearby trash bin. "You full?"

"Not even," she said. But it wasn't food that was going to satisfy her now. "What was the call about?"

"That was a friend. An exorcist. He's got a demon in a hex circle that needs to be reckoned. It won't take me long. But I should run."

"You are a very busy reckoner."

"Paris is a big city, and I'm the only one in town. I'll walk you back to my place?"

"Can I come along to the reckoning?"

"I, uh…work best without distraction." He waggled the finger she had licked, then winked at her.

"I like distracting you."

"I've noticed. I'll bring home something more substantial to eat when I'm finished, and wine. How does that sound?"

"Sounds romantic."

"You cool with a little romance?"

"I am. Are you?"

"I, uh…" He gave it some thought. "Yes, I am. I'm going to make this a fast reckoning. Come on." He stood and offered her his hand.

Once back at his place, Savin grabbed one of the

intricate brass instruments from his bedroom cabinet that Jett had puzzled over earlier. He called out that he'd hurry back.

Jett rushed to walk him out the door, then skipped around in front of him. Standing on tiptoe, she kissed him. The taste of chocolate lingered and the sudden, wanting clutch of his hand against her hip sent a thrill directly to her core. The man knew how to take a woman in hand.

"Just so you don't forget about the romance," she said.

"Oh, I won't."

"And you'd mentioned getting me a phone?"

"Ah, right. Sorry. I was so eager to get the envelope Maman gave me into your hands, I forgot about that. Stores might be closed when I'm finished reckoning."

"We can go out tomorrow and shop for one."

"We can. See you soon." He kissed her quickly, then walked out, closing the door behind him. The wards repelled Jett back a few feet, and so swiftly she caught her palms against the wall behind her.

The man was off to reckon a demon back to the Place of All Demons. And Jett's thoughts immediately tracked to the adoption papers. If she was adopted—and apparently she had been—then who was her father? Could those cruel taunts as she'd matured in Daemonia have been true? Which would mean…

If her father was a demon, that would make her half demon. Or whole? With things as they were right now…

Jett closed her eyes and shook her head. Things had to change. She wanted something good. She wanted Savin. But he'd never have her if he knew her truth.

Chapter 9

The exorcist John Malcolm lived in a tiny ground-floor apartment across the street from Notre Dame. The main floor would suit a tall hobbit with an interest in religious clutter. The man was a former Catholic priest. Former being key.

After shaking Savin's hand and offering him wine, which Savin accepted, John led him down into the cellar, which was a remnant from the eighteenth century when an artist once used the subterranean rooms for mixing volatile paints and practicing brush techniques. The walls gleamed here and there with gold leaf and streaks of fading cinnabar and egg-yolk tempera. Savin entered and inhaled the limestone and oily scent. And sulfur.

"Been over a year since I've seen you," John commented as he pulled aside a metal-legged chair that had been positioned before the salt circle on the floor and set it up against the wall. "You're looking rather clean-shaven, Thorne. Who's the woman?"

Savin could but shake his head. Had he seriously been looking so dreadful that a mere shave made people wonder about his sex life?

John picked up the wooden cross from the floor before the circle and kissed it. The demon standing inside the circle suddenly spun about to face them and hissed, revealing two pinpoint fangs dead center of its upper mandible. Its skeletal black structure stood hunched because its head was twice the size of a human's head, and the horns curled around its ears twice in glinting red.

"Beelzig demon," Savin said, recognizing the skanky thing with ease. They were insectile in true form, though this one looked half in and out of the sheen. Their principal reason for existence was to get inside humans and slowly drive them mad with a burning need to eat dirt. The demon fed on the worms and bacteria in the soil. A human, if not exorcised, would eventually die from eating more than his body weight of dirt in one sitting. "How'd it happen onto you?"

"I took it out of a teenager this morning. The boy is in Hôtel-Dieu right now with possible brain damage. He'd been eating mud contaminated with toxins from a nearby field that had been sprayed with pesticides."

John set the cross on the chair and joined Savin's side, where they stood facing the despicable demon contained in the warded circle. "So does that mean there isn't a woman or you're just not talking?"

"I thought I came here to do a job."

The demon inclined its head as if listening carefully.

"You did," Malcolm offered. "But you know my vows of chastity can be a burden. I need salacious details to brighten my day after seeing what this bastard did to that boy."

The man did not have to honor such vows, no longer being a priest, but for some reason Malcolm did. No judgment on Savin's part. But he couldn't imagine agreeing to not have sex. Ever.

"She's beautiful," Savin offered. "Long dark hair and sensual eyes."

John nodded. "Tits big?"

Savin's smile was easy. "Just the right size."

The demon hissed and jutted out its tongue at the two. "I will lick them for you, reckoner."

"Silence." John made the sign of the cross before him and the demon cringed.

But the beelzig didn't take its wicked regard from Savin. And he allowed it. Let the thing sniff him out, feel his presence. And know it had not long for this realm.

Savin shrugged off his coat and tossed it behind him, then rolled up his sleeves. This visit was business as usual.

"I can taste her on you," the demon said on a slithery tone. "In the air. On your skin. The earth she has trodden with bared skin is…" Of a sudden the demon stiffened and its eyes went wide as red beacons. "You must bow down before her!"

"Enough." Savin didn't need sex advice from a hideous demon.

Stepping forward, he began the reckoner's chant. It was something he'd devised himself, along with Malcolm's guidance. It had come from a deep and innate knowing. He hated it. But such was his life following his trip to Daemonia. It didn't pay to bemoan a situation he could never change.

He lifted his forearms and connected the sigils tat-tooed there, while keeping his palms facing outward from his face. And as the demon writhed and struggled and insisted he show his woman obedience, Savin fo-cused on getting the ugly bastard out of this realm.

The chant to call out to Daemonia to receive one of its own was repetitious and a mix of Latin and Dae-monic. Savin bounced on his heels, finding a visceral rhythm intensifying his focus. He needed to feel this weird magic in his very bones. The sigils on his arms glowed—and sometimes they sparked to flame. He was never harmed, beyond the mental toll of having to con-stantly deal with these bastards.

Could he find normal along with Jett? Was such a quest worth his consideration?

Halting his wandering focus, Savin shouted out the next few words to cement his vocal tones into the air and bring back his center to the task at hand. At his feet, the salt circle began to jitter and dance around the squirm-ing demon. And while the beelzig yowled, the salt took to flame, as did the sigils on Savin's arms. He winced. This pain was worth it.

Ten seconds later, the beelzig let out a wicked yip and its form was literally sucked out of the circle, leav-ing behind but a scatter of ashy residue. Savin swept out his arms to each side, which extinguished the flames. He tilted back his head, closing his eyes, and whispered a blessing.

John Malcolm sprinkled the salt and the floor with holy water, echoed Savin's blessing and nodded to the reckoner for a task well done.

Savin rolled down his sleeves and grabbed the re-mainder of the wine and tilted it down. It was too sweet for his taste, but the ex-priest wasn't big on the good stuff.

"What do you think the creature meant by his statement that you should bow down to her?" John asked in his careful but exacting manner.

"Stupid demon tricks. They're always trying to distract my focus."

"Sure. But it sensed something on you. *In* you."

"The Other," Savin said flatly.

John nodded. But it wasn't a convincing movement. "You want to talk about anything, Savin?"

Like reveal he was harboring a long-lost friend who'd spent the last twenty years in the Place of All Demons? He didn't have time for all the questions Malcolm would have about that situation.

"Gotta get home to those perfects tits," he muttered, and handed John the empty glass. "This one was on the house. Pray the kid survives with as little damage as possible."

"You know that I do. If I'm not exorcising, I'm praying. I owe you one, Thorne!"

"Never!" Savin called as he took the stairs upward. "Always willing to help you out." He paused at the top of the stairs. "Keep an eye out for more assholes like that one. Certainly Jones doesn't believe the rift is going to stay closed."

"Yes, I sense that. Won't be a picnic, that's for sure."

Savin sighed. "Nope. Not a picnic."

After stepping out of the shower, Jett pulled on one of Savin's soft gray T-shirts. It hung to her thighs and it smelled like him. Earthy and wild. He wouldn't mind. She had only a few items to wear and hadn't bought any night wear. She'd love to wander about the flat naked, but she wasn't ready for that boldness.

Yet. The darkness within her could easily get into a nudie walk. And a flirtatious wink or a crook of her finger. But she was keeping that part of her subdued as best she could.

It was growing harder, though. Her true self wanted to rise. To be known. To have. And to claim.

Jett hadn't been able to stop thinking about Savin since he'd left earlier to go meet the exorcist. He'd almost kissed her in the cemetery, but something had tugged him away. The demon inside him? She'd not been able to get a good read on her. The Other. Who and whatever she was, that demon had become deeply embedded inside Savin. If Jett were to touch him long enough, she'd touch the demon and know her.

It wasn't as though the Other provided Jett any competition in catching Savin's romantic interest. But still. The incorporeal demon felt like a rival, so Jett was going to call her that.

In the living room, she sat on the couch and picked up the envelope that contained the adoption papers and a few other items. A deed to the house. With the land cleared and construction under way, that was useless. Apparently, the lot had been claimed by the city years ago after her mother left.

There was a bank account number in her name, which Jett found curious. She'd not had a savings account when she was a kid. Had her parents set up an account for her in hopes she might someday return? Had it been a college fund?

Had they hoped for her return? It hurt her heart to consider what they must have gone through, especially

after Savin had returned. They must have hated him because he'd returned to his parents alive. Poor guy. She
hoped they hadn't said anything terrible to him.

These human emotions were so…difficult. She felt as
if she should perhaps cry, and then her darkness quickly
wrangled that silly reaction.

Her disappearance had obviously been tough on her
parents. Had the divorce been because of her absence?
Possible. There had been many a night when she would
lie in her bed upstairs and listen to the back-and-forth
arguments in her parents' bedroom below. Despite that,
she and her mother, as well as her father, had been close.
They'd been a good Catholic family who attended church
on Sundays, gardened, watched shows together in the
evenings and spent a lot of time doing things in Paris.
She'd been happy as a child. Could never have dreamed
of the horrors that waited on the other side of the lavender field.

That stupid spooky forest. If she and Savin had never
dared each other to approach it that day, might they have
been spared?

Setting the envelope aside, Jett pulled her legs up to
her chest and the T-shirt down over them, bowing her
head to her knees. She did want to cry, and she'd spent
her last tear a long time ago. Tears had not proved con-
structive in Daemonia. And they only gave one a headache. Nobody cared if you cried or that you might be
hurting, whether physically or emotionally. And those
who had cared?

"Dangerous," she whispered now as her memories
threatened to make her scream.

Lifting her head and putting down her legs, Jett shook
her head. And she summoned the power of denial that

she had learned to own. "I won't remember. It's behind me now."

But ever in you, her darkness whispered. That gave her a shiver.

The front door opened and Savin wandered in. Seeing her on the couch, he nodded and said, "Hey. I picked up some food, as promised. Sorry it's so late. It took longer than I thought with the exorcist."

"I don't expect you to cater to me all the time. You have a life. I'm just lucky you're kind enough to let me into it. So, was the exorcist unable to cast out a demon? Is that why he called you?"

"Sometimes an exorcism merely brings the demon out from the human host in corporeal form. And then it stays. The exorcist needs me to send it out of this realm. It was a beelzig. Stupid bastard."

Jett knew that breed. They were ugly and lived in the vile, rusted earth of Daemonia. She shook her head. *Not going to think about that stuff, remember?* "That smells great."

"Roast chicken and potatoes. The place down the street knows me and what I like. When I asked for a double portion, they didn't blink an eye. I don't know if I should be offended by that."

"Big, strong man like you? Not at all. I'll have a little. I'm still quite satisfied from the treats earlier."

"I'm going to wash up first. You, uh, okay?"

Jett stood and tugged at the shirt, which hung to the top of her thighs. "Yes. Why do you ask?"

"No reason. Just wanted to make sure you're adjusting well enough." He gestured down the hallway, then wandered toward the bathroom.

And Jett couldn't help thinking that had been a suspicious question. What did he think about her? Should she be worried?

She opened the food bag and pulled out the boxes. The man shouldn't spend too much time wondering if she was okay. Instead, the only thoughts he should have about her should mirror her own about him. He needed to see her as a woman, and not the child he had once known. She wanted him to want her.

Perhaps seduction would be on the menu tonight.

Chapter 10

It was late after they'd eaten, but Jett wasn't tired. Nor, it seemed, was Savin interested in sleep. He poured them both whiskey and sat on the couch, so she sat next to him and clasped his hand. After studying their hands together a few seconds, he gave her a look that said so many things. A little surprised, maybe pleased, unsure and perhaps excited. She could hope. But he seemed to struggle with their attraction, so she'd play him slowly.

"Tell me about all these guitars." She tilted her head back and settled against the comfortable leather cushions, catching her bare feet on the edge. "Do you play them all?"

"Most." He tilted his head back, too, resting the whiskey glass on his thigh. The man's intense heat warmed Jett and she alternated taking in the sharp tang of the whiskey and the alluring temptation of his scent. "That one there. The one that looks like someone went after it with a chain saw and then rubbed tar into the cuts?"

"It does look tattered."

"Used to belong to Steve Vai. One of the rock-and-roll guitar gods. I've never played it. The pickups are damaged. It survived a mosh pit and rain and mud. I salvaged it. The one next to it is Jessica."

"The guitar has a name?" Jett eyed the violet electric guitar that had a sparkly gloss to it.

"Most do. Jess is my sweetie. Her tones are so pure and the harmonics––whew! She treats me right."

"How does a guitar treat a person right?" Jett turned on the couch and rested her head on his shoulder. His hair tickled her cheek.

"She seems to have a lot of patience, that violet vixen. I don't have the longest or most delicate fingers, so some riffs are difficult to master."

"Interesting. And what's that one with just the single string? Does she have a name, too?"

"No name, and I don't think that one is a she. That's a diddley bow. Made it myself. It's an American instrument that came out of the blues scene. I spent some time in the southern United States a few years ago and fell in love with the sound and the use of the glass slide. It's what I use to practice musicomancy."

A shiver traced Jett's arms at mention of that magic. She knew nothing about it, but instinctually something warned her away from it.

"Musicomancy is all about using the slide to sing the single string," Savin said. "A way of drawing out a demonic song and then controlling the demon so I can ultimately perform a reckoning. It's a challenge for my big, rough hands."

He opened his hand against hers. It was so wide Jett felt delicate next to him. Not something she'd felt. Ever. She curled her fingers about his and stroked the side of his hand. "Your fingers are calloused. Is that from playing so much?"

"That, and from the metal and woodworking I do. But that's a good thing. A guitarist needs to build up that protection when strumming steel strings."

Drawing her finger along the side of his hand, she traced over the half moth tattoo that, should he hold his hands together prayer-style before him, would form a complete moth. The black lines were so fine; she marveled over the intricate artistry. "What is the significance of the moth? Is this a hex?"

"I don't wear hexes. Those are witch things. Me, I'm all about protections and wards. But the moth is special. The ink witch that pricked it into my skin attached it to my soul. It's sort of a get-out-of-death-free card. If I'm lucky. And if it should come to something like that. One use only. And I think it would change me."

"How so?"

He shrugged. "The ink witch wasn't specific, but anytime someone cheats death? Well."

Yes, she'd seen the results of that in Daemonia. Far too often. But she'd never seen it happen with a human. It couldn't be pretty.

"Do you often encounter situations that make you fear for your life?"

"Honestly? No. Demons don't scare me. Nor can they threaten me overmuch with all the protection wards I wear. But I'm not impervious. I am merely human."

That word was not something that should ever be

employed against Savin Thorne. "I don't think you're *merely* anything, Savin."

She let her hand drift from his and onto his chest, where she slid it across the hard plane beneath his T-shirt. The man was solid and hot, and she couldn't resist digging her fingernails in. Just a bit. He felt so good.

Savin hissed behind a sip of whiskey. "Jett…"

"Yes?" She lifted her head, but inches from his face, and studied his intent gaze. While she saw the darkness that inhabited his life every time she looked into those blue irises, now she also saw want.

Oh, yes, sweet, sexy man. The darkness inside her wanted, as well.

Jett moved up, clutching his muscled pectorals as she slid higher. Inhaling him. She smiled wickedly. Time to get what she desired.

She kissed his mouth, tasting the bite of whiskey that lingered on his tongue. He wrapped a hand across her back and lured her onto his lap to straddle him. Both his hands cupped her derriere and she settled against the firm hold. He squeezed at her with a wanton groan.

Bracketing his face with her palms, she dove deep into his kiss, wanting to fall as she had done that fateful day when she was a child. But this fall would not be dangerous; it could only grant her a delicious thrill. She wasn't afraid to seek Savin's darkness, because she could match it with her own. Together they could play in the dark.

Pulling her against him, he clung to her with greedy clutches. His kiss sought and teased and tasted her. He was at once playful yet also demanding. Jett willingly gave up her control to him. She had never allowed anyone or anything in Daemonia to kiss her. Not on the mouth. It was the most intimate and personal touch. Denying that contact had been her protection. And now she surrendered that carefully constructed wall of defense with pleasure.

"I want you," she gasped against his mouth, kissing him again and lashing her tongue against his teeth. "I need you, Savin."

She wouldn't dare to say it was because she wanted to know a real man. He would have too many questions. And really, the want was basic and feral. She simply needed right now.

He lifted her shirt and she raised her arms to allow him to slip it off. She wore no bra. That wasn't an article of clothing she'd ever worn or learned about. Her breasts were heavy and full and she pressed them against his chest. Savin groaned and cupped them both. When his thumbs brushed her nipples, she hissed a sharp, pleasurable gasp. Oh, yes, that was how a man must touch a woman.

Jett arched her back, which buoyed her breasts, and Savin's hot tongue seared about her nipple in the sweetest way. This was too much. And she wanted more, more and more!

She dug her fingers into his hair. Biting the corner of her lower lip, she closed her eyes and fell into the wicked, delicious sensations of him suckling at her breast. Her skin heated. Her system shivered. Her pussy grew wet. She pressed her hips to his torso, grinding, seeking the sweet spot that demanded attention, touch and oblivious surrender. Another place on her she had only discovered on her own; never had she allowed another to touch her there.

"Jett," he whispered as he switched to her other breast. "Oh, Jett."

Tugging at his shirt, she lifted it and he paused only a few moments to help her get it off. The man returned kisses and attention to her breasts as she dragged her fingernails down his hard, defined pectoral. For all her softness, he was her opposite in steely hardness.

With a nudge of her knee between his legs, she felt his erection. So hard, as if a shaft of steel confined within his jeans. Savin moaned as she pressed her knee harder against him. She wanted to unzip him, reach inside and wrap her fingers about his molten heat. Never had she so desired having a man naked beneath her. She needed to see him, to admire him.

To feel powerful here in this mortal realm.

Savin suddenly squeezed her upper arm. She looked up. Blew the hair from her face. He winced. Then he quickly kissed her on the mouth. But again, the squeeze about her biceps warned her against moving too fast. He pushed away from her.

Jett leaned in to kiss his jaw, along the line of his beard and up to lash her tongue at his ear. "Don't stop, Savin. Touch me. Everywhere."

"Want to." He groaned as he shifted his hips and she hugged her bared breasts against his chest. "Woman, that feels so good."

The hand he hooked at her hip held her firmly, and yet it almost seemed as if he were holding her back. Jett tested the hold by pushing forward and he increased pressure to stay her.

She tugged the flap of his jeans and released the button, but as she touched the zipper, the man slapped a hand over her wrist. "Wait."

"What? No. I want to see you, Savin. To hold you in my hand."

"I… Yes… Damn it!"

He pushed her roughly to the side and she slid off his lap. Standing, he gripped a thick clutch of his hair as he paced before her. His pecs pulsed and that six-pack rolled as if angry.

"What is it? It's her, isn't it?" Jett lunged for him, pressing her palms flat against his chest and closing her eyes. If she could make a soul connection with the man…

"The Other is screaming inside me," he said. "I can feel it more than hear it. Shit, I'm sorry. She's never done this before when I've been with a woman. It's like she wants out. Oh—damn! That hurts! I don't understand. Jett, I—"

She pulled her hands away from him and stepped away, setting back her shoulders and lifting her chin. "She won't defeat me. She has no right. I am her—"

She stopped from saying too much. But now darkness filled her. Suffused her being with her entitled power. She was in her element. What she had become. What she might always be.

What she wanted to run away from.

Or did she?

Savin exhaled heavily and gestured to the couch. "Put your shirt on. Please? I just… I can't do this with you. Not right now."

Jett picked up her shirt but didn't put it on. Instead, she stomped past him toward the bedroom.

"Sorry!" Savin called.

She muttered the word mockingly. But she wasn't angry with Savin. Instead, it was that incorporeal demon. Bitch.

* * *

Savin punched the thick wooden supporting beam in the center of the living room. His knuckles were calloused from previous punches. It was a reflex now. He no longer bled for his own anger.

He'd been cruel to Jett, shoving her away like that. He hadn't wanted to. Hell, he'd wanted to push down his pants and hers and get into it. The woman was incredible and her breasts in his hands had made his cock grow steel hard.

But that bitch. The Other. Why did she object to Jett? He'd had relationships and sex with other women and the demon inside him hadn't lifted a protesting finger. In fact, he sometimes got a creepy sense that she enjoyed the sexual experience as much as he did. Was it because Jett had so recently come from Daemonia? Had she remnants of that place on her that the Other couldn't stand to be near?

"You'd better get used to it," he muttered. Because he could not keep his hands off Jett any longer. He wanted her. He needed her.

Grabbing the diddley bow from the wall, he sat down and plucked out a few notes. She didn't deserve morphine tonight. That was a treat. If anything would suppress the Other, it was musicomancy.

She was not tired, and if she could not make out with Savin, Jett needed to get out of this place for a while. To breathe. To let off some sexual steam.

She pulled on a black dress that fit her curves tightly. The neckline exposed her breasts nearly to the nipples. They were both still so hard, and aching for Savin's mouth. Pressing her hands over her breasts, she closed her eyes—and heard a noise.

What was that awful screeching sound? It sounded like the worst death beetle dying over and over. It crawled over her skin and pricked into her pores. Body wavering, Jett clutched the cabinet for support. The brass devices on top of the cabinet wobbled. Her head filled with the racket.

Then she realized where it came from.

Staggering out to the living room, she saw Savin on the couch with the instrument he'd said he used to work musicomancy.

"What awful noise!" she growled. "Stop it!"

Savin's jaw dropped. He ceased—and then he did not. He plucked the single string as he wavered a glass slide over the neck. The sound cut down Jett's spine with an invisible blade.

She screamed and raced for the door.

Behind her, Savin stood and called, "Jett! What… what are you?"

Chapter 11

Savin let Jett leave. This time he wouldn't go looking for her. She needed some space and privacy.

And him? What did he need?

"Answers," he muttered.

The short riff he'd played on the diddley bow had affected her in a way he'd not expected. Only demons should have reacted so violently to the discordant tune. Jett had clearly been disturbed by it. So much so that she'd had to put herself away from it. And he had shouted after her…

"*Is* she demon?" he wondered with a sinking heart.

He slapped a hand over his bare chest, remembering the feel of Jett's fingernails sliding over his skin. Notching up his desire to new heights, fueling his need. Making her intentions perfectly clear with every kiss, every whisper, every sigh. His heart still pounded from their interaction.

Or was it because he might have been making out with a demon?

Any paranormal species that went to Daemonia— vampires, witches, harpies, sirens, whatever—could get in and out with few side effects. If the trip was quick. But it was known that anyone—paranormal or human— who stayed longer began to take on demonic traits. Some even changed to demon. It was like when demons came to the mortal realm. The longer they stayed, the more they risked developing human traits, and their demonic nature lessened, growing weaker until they were but shells that needed to return home or perish.

It would make sense that Jett, having been in Daemonia for so long, would have taken on some demonic traits. But.

"She can't be."

Why hadn't he had such suspicions immediately? A smart reckoner would have. He would have noticed that she wasn't right. Picked up the hum of her aura. Savin was ultra-tuned to their kind. Rarely did he miss one. And those he didn't pin as demon were masters of cloaking themselves with a sheen.

Had Jett worn an impenetrable sheen since arriving in the mortal realm? It seemed impossible to maintain for any amount of time. A demon had to be very strong to do so. Yet others did all the time. How many demons had Savin not noticed? And had innocent humans suffered because he had not?

He scruffed his fingers through his hair, tugging in frustration. Why hadn't she told him? There was no reason not to. Did she fear him?

"Of course," he muttered. "I am a reckoner."

He punched the air with a fist and a growl.

If Jett truly was part demon, he could well be her worst nightmare.

* * *

Arms swinging, Jett strode through the Paris streets. It was after midnight, but pockets of tourists still dotted the sidewalks. She passed over the river, drawing upon its natural power, infusing the strength of the flowing water into her system. Mmm… That was invigorating, most especially since the water was much cleaner than anything she'd ever drawn on in Daemonia. Now she marched onward with determination.

She'd unexpectedly revealed herself to Savin. And in that moment, he had known. He'd called after her as she'd fled his home, asking what she was. It might have been the wrong move to leave without an explanation, but her body had literally moved her over the threshold, despite the tugging wards, to get away from that place.

That terrible music! It had scraped inside her ears like the vilest insect chittering against her brain. Had she not been wearing a sheen, she suspected the sound might have brought her to her knees. The reckoner's musico-mancy was indeed powerful.

And too revealing.

As it was, the escape through the wards vibrating with the dangerous sound had affected her. Jett didn't feel as though she could hold on to the sheen for much longer. Not without a breather.

How could she go back to Savin now? The man had been her only hope for finding her family and getting back to normal. Could he accept her if she revealed her truth?

Did she want his acceptance? Was she fooling herself that she could go back to how things once were? She'd been a child then. Even if she could fully integrate herself back into humanity, nothing would ever be the same. Those hadn't even been her parents! Everything she'd once held as truth, as a means to survival, had been shattered.

Feeling her eyes begin to tear, Jett shook her head and chased away the ridiculous emotion. An inhale drew up a shiver of darkness from within, instilling in her the confidence she'd almost lost grasp of. She would not shed a tear over silly pining for a normal family life. Nor even the hope for a romantic entanglement. Even if Savin meant more to her than a few kisses and touches. He had offered to protect her and had allowed her to stay until she could find her place in this realm.

Right now she felt her only place was so far away and in another realm. But the option of returning wasn't on the table.

Crossing a busy street that flashed with bright head-lights and red and violet neon streaks, she veered away from a crowd that danced outside a noisy nightclub to the music drifting beyond the closed doors. Instead, she eyed a black metal door just ahead. She recognized the beefy bouncer standing solemnly with hands clasped before him. *Demon.* He needn't glance her way for her to pick up on his breed, but when he did, that confirmed what she knew. His red irises flashed with a glint from a nearby neon sign.

There was no name on the building before which the bouncer stood, but she could feel the vibrations of many demons, likely within and behind the door. Jett curled her fingers into fists. The pain of her fingernails digging into skin was acute. But it was a good feeling. That meant she was alive. A place of comfort was what she required right now. A dark, loud nightclub where she could release her sheen and scream like a banshee. And no one would know who she was.

Stepping up to the bouncer, she tilted back her head and met his gaze. Without a word, she delved through his skin and skull bone, needling into his feeble brain to work her influence on him. It was a handy skill she'd mastered while coming of age in Daemonia.

The bouncer's bottom lip quivered and his shoulders dropped in subservient acknowledgment. "My liege." He bowed, then pushed open the club door for her. "Enter, if you will."

Jett strolled into the pitch-black hallway. The utter darkness felt like a hug. The floors pounded with a frantic beat, pulsing up through her shoes and liquefying in her veins. The raucous beat led her onward. The darkness offered safety. And knowing this was a demon club decided her next move.

With but a thought, Jett shook off her sheen. The initial shiver of release was always orgasmic, and she sighed, which led to a satisfied growl. Her hair follicles tingled as the strands grew longer and spilled in long aquamarine waves down to her waist. All over, her skin prickled and took on a darker, dusky gray shade. Her fingernails grew to razor points and brightened to ruby. The demonic sigils that decorated her skin in violet and red lines, so fine no tattoo artist could achieve such, crisped to the surface with an exquisite sting that made her gasp. And her horns grew out from her temples in an obsidian curl that gently glided over her ears and tilted up to wicked points behind her head.

Smiling revealed canines that could tear, and even kill. Jett smiled with the utter pleasure of being back in the form she was most comfortable with. She entered the flashing red club lighting. One hand to her hip, she assessed the atmosphere with a regal lift to her chin. Ninety percent demon occupants. A sniff surmised the remaining breeds, which she determined were vampire or witch. Perhaps a few werewolves. No faeries. She didn't sense the weird energy of the sidhe species.

The club's décor was black and steel, burnished by red strobe lighting. A live band wielding guitars and a violin screamed to the masses from the stage. The crowd on the dance floor bounced as one, fists beating the air above their heads. Some of the heads were horned. A few tails whipped to the beat, their spaded tips slashing at skin and leaving in their wake fine cuts to spill black demonic blood.

The growls and rock-and-roll snarls coalesced into a wicked, thrilling welcome to Jett's innate darkness. She was demon. Or so she had become during her lengthy stay in Daemonia.

Survival? Sure, that had been foremost. But ultimately, she had grown into the form and had accepted it over any lingering human traits. And she would not be put back or disregarded in any way. The power she possessed gleamed in her sinews and tightened her muscles. Let no demon try to challenge her.

Striding toward the dance floor, she let the beat take her and bounced into the crowd. Head back and both arms outstretched, she reveled in the release of the confining sheen she'd had to wear to fit into this realm. To fool Savin. To win some time while she struggled to find her place.

Adopted? What the fuck was her father, then? She would find out. And whether she embraced him or punched him, who cared? Now was not the time for maudlin memory trips.

Shouting with the chants that surrounded her, Jett became the darkness she'd tried to ignore since arriving in the mortal realm. This was exquisite. And another lush, lung-deep growl felt appropriate.

When the dancers around her slowly stopped moving and the macabre merriness settled to a few drunken giggles, Jett spun to a halt and looked about. Glowing red gazes observed her with awestruck expressions and open mouths. Even the band ceased playing with a discordant scrape of the bow across the violin strings.

A particular male with small white horns sprouting above his ears and a switchblade smile stepped forward and bent to one knee. His hoarse voice held reverence. "My liege."

His actions were repeated by the circle surrounding her, and that waved back through the crowd until the entire club fell onto bended knee and bowed their heads, showing her their respect.

About time, her darkness whispered. *Screw hiding in fear. Let the party begin.*

Jett let out a wicked, throaty laugh and clapped her hands over her head. "We dance!"

And the nightclub burst into a frenetic collision of dancing bodies.

Chapter 12

Savin slept fitfully in the bed. He'd sat up drinking whiskey while waiting for Jett to return. After 2:00 a.m. he'd wandered toward the bathroom but had veered onto the bed and buried his face in his pillow that smelled of her. Sweet, dark and not at all like sulfur.

She was not a demon. She could not be.

He rolled over, and while his eyes were closed in the dark, he listened acutely. Nothing in the loft stirred. The distant noises of Paris's early-morning industry enlivened the air. Garbage vehicles rolled down the streets, collecting trash.

Had he been too trusting? No.

Maybe the musicomancy had malfunctioned? Very possible. He was so new at it and was far from a mastery of the magic. But he knew an incorrect spell should not have sent Jett fleeing with a painful scream.

Jett.

Jett.

He couldn't get her out of his brain. He'd invited her
into his life, and the place she filled had been swept free
of the cobwebs and welcomed her easily. She belonged
with him. It was an instinctual feeling. And that wasn't
because they'd been childhood friends. It was something
more. Something he couldn't put a label to.

"Jett," he murmured in his half-sleep reverie. "Come
back to me."

Jett stretched her legs out across the cool, sooted stone
capping the aboveground sarcophagus in the cemetery
she had wandered to last night after leaving the club. It
had become a weird beacon for her. A respite tucked
within the big city.

The sun had risen, but a nearby tree canopy provided
shade. A pair of sunglasses was in order for her next
shopping trip.

While standing in the center of the dance floor last
night, surrounded by sycophants, she had felt her power
rise. The inner strength and innate entitlement she'd
grown into while living in Daemonia had suffused her
system. She had been taken from this realm for a purpose, and she had fulfilled that purpose. She'd gained
subjects and minions, and with the snap of a finger had
decided the fate of so many.

And she had reveled in that power.

She still could. She did not have to forsake her demonic nature. She could keep it, hoarding it and using
it as she wished here in the mortal realm. It came naturally to her. It would be a pity to abandon it completely.
It had served her well.

And yet she shuddered now, so far away from the comfort of that dark club, and having successfully tamped down her darkness. Such power was a place she could not return to, did not want to return to. It had changed her. And that purpose? It hadn't been completely fulfilled. They'd wanted her for something more devious. It had been the last straw. She'd had to flee.

Jett tilted her head against the inscription that declared some long-dead woman a "considerate wife." Ugh. *Considerate.* She certainly hoped her epitaph would proclaim her wild, free and unabashed.

Or did she?

The shudder returned to remind her she wasn't the same Jett who had lived in Daemonia. A part of her had never left Paris and had only survived because she had clung to those roots of normality.

While she'd stepped into the exquisite feeling of control last night, today it saddened her that she had succumbed, if briefly, to that feeling.

She did not want to rule others. She did not require them to fall to their knees and worship her. And most important, she did not want to begin the next generation that would follow in her stead.

The only reason they had recognized her as a superior last night in the club was that she had released her sheen and allowed her demoness to rise. But now she again wore the sheen. It was the only way she could walk through Paris without turning heads. Wearing such a mask of humanity was tiring, but it also allowed her to stand aside and look over what she had been and what she could be.

She could be a woman, a human woman with goals and dreams and loves and hopes.

And Savin?

Would he still want to help her if she told him all? Dare she reveal the vile secret that had sent her fleeing to the mortal realm?

"Why?" she whispered, feeling the demoness speak up. "When I can have so much more by remaining as I am? What are these stupid thoughts?"

The stupid thoughts were what had brought her to this realm in the first place, had pushed her to escape. The need for more, for normality, for love and safety. But now that she was here, *could* she pull off human again? It seemed so...lackluster. Boring.

"No," she hissed at her dark side.

Whatever, the demoness inside her whispered dismissively. *You are a fool if you abandon me. Your kingdom asked so little of you!*

Bowing her head to her knees, Jett pushed her fingers through her hair and clasped them at the top of her scalp. No longer blue, nor thick and lush, it was simply black and wavy now. She preferred it blue—

"No," she groaned, and shook her head. "I am Jett Montfort. And I will not allow you to reign," she said to the darkness.

A pair of tourists wandered by, commenting in a language she did not know, and then shuffled past her quiet retreat.

When the next person, a lone walker, paused before the sarcophagus and did not move for a while, Jett looked up into Savin's deep blue gaze. No smile there, yet no accusation, either.

"Thought I'd find you here," he finally said. "May I?" He gestured to sit beside her and she nodded and slid over. "I didn't mean to scare you last night, Jett."

"You didn't scare me," the demoness insisted boldly. Then Jett bowed her head, reining in the dark. "I scared myself. Or rather, I reacted to your strange magic."

"I don't have any magic."

"You were invoking musicomancy."

"It's still a work in progress. But I told you it's only supposed to work on demons." He propped an elbow on his knee and turned to her. The brute stoicism she'd initially seen that first night he'd taken her to his home lived in his gaze. He was no man to mess with, to lie to or to attempt to trick or fool. And he knew about demons.

She knew what he wanted to hear from her. And even as she fought to maintain her secret, the dark inside her decided it was fitting and absolutely to her advantage to reveal her nature.

"A person can't survive in Daemonia for so long without taking on demonic attributes," Jett blurted out. How much dare she tell him? She'd feel him out and see where he stood regarding such a revelation. "I've been wearing a sheen since I escaped through the rift. I couldn't risk being seen in this realm. And when I learned you were a reckoner…"

"I only reckon those demons who have committed a crime against humans or have been determined to be a menace here in the mortal realm."

Which wasn't exactly a promise never to reckon her. And if he was attempting to send back all those demons who had entered this realm that night, wouldn't that include someone like her?

"I, uh…" Savin rubbed his hands together, then leaned back against the considerate wife's tombstone. "Okay. You're part demon. Nothing wrong with that. You were there so long. It was inevitable. And I mean, demons come in all forms, types and demeanors. Just like us humans. They can be benevolent. Even more human than some of the humans I've known. But—" he pressed his palms before him and against his lips, letting out an exhale "—you've still got human in you, right, Jett?"

She nodded. Maybe she did; maybe she didn't. She couldn't know one hundred percent. Without the sheen, she sported horns and dark gray skin. Entirely demon. Yet surely, her innate humanness would return to her now that she'd left that horrible place. With hope?

No, you mustn't abandon me!

She winced at the cry from her darkness, which was entirely her, not a separate entity like the demon who lived within Savin.

"I do have humanity," she said, trying to convince herself as much as Savin. "I think. I don't know, Savin. This is hard for me to talk to you about."

He clasped her hand, and that startled her. That he could still want to hold her hand after what she'd confessed. After witnessing her flee last night.

"I'm safe for you, Jett. You can trust me with your secrets. I promise. I'll do what I can to help make things right. No matter what happened to you in Daemonia? You didn't ask for it."

"I didn't. You're right about that. And everything I did while there was with the goal of survival. I always looked ahead to a moment when I might make my escape." And there was nothing her dark side could say against that. "But there's something you should know. Something I learned while there. I was tended by a cortege that catered to my every whim, took care of me, treated me well. One grew to be my confidante. And… she confirmed that I was taken because of my father."

"Your father? Your adopted father or…"

"I didn't know then that I was adopted. Well, there were clues. But I didn't know how to process some of the things I was told when I was so young. Anyway, I could only think of the man I've always known as my father, Charles Montfort. But who was he? He had no ties to demons or the Place of All Demons. It made very little sense. So sometimes I tossed around the idea that my mother might have had an affair with another man. Perhaps a demon."

Savin tilted his gaze at her. "Josette Montfort never seemed the sort to go in for dark and dangerous."

"I wanted to believe she didn't know. It was the only option besides believing my real dad, er, Charles, was demon."

"He wasn't," Savin said. "I just know that."

"Right. So the affair scenario. Demons can do that. Wear a sheen or a human costume. Humans never know who they are interacting with unless the demons want them to know. And, well, I know how demons are. They seduce humans. It is in their nature to do so. They constantly seek the human experience."

She was revealing too much, and yet why the hell not? The jig was up. The reckoner had discovered her. But just let him try to reckon her. He wouldn't know who he was standing against.

Foolish, Jett thought. She didn't want to be a threat to the man. She wanted him to admire her, not label her an antagonist.

"It doesn't matter now what I suspected when I was there," she said, "because I now know I was adopted. I got the answer I most desired. So perhaps one or both of my parents was demon."

"Whew." Savin rubbed a finger along his bearded jaw. "That's a lot to take in. But it is possible. Like you said, demons make it a game at seducing humans. And if your mother had been human but knew the father was demon? A good reason to give the child up for adoption. And I hate to say it, but it would make your kidnapping into Daemonia less random. Though why *I* was taken along with you..."

"You were not the target," she said quietly.

He turned to meet her gaze.

"I was told that," she said. "You were so close, though, and were sucked in along with me. I'm sorry. If I could have changed it so you would never have had to suffer..." She shivered and clasped her hands about her legs. This human emotion stuff was draining. But she refused to allow her dark to rise. Not now. Not when he sat so close and she could feel his comforting warmth. He needed answers as much as she did.

"Jett, don't blame yourself. Ever. I survived. And for a while there we were together. We took care of each other."

"For that I was thankful. I don't know what I would have done had I landed in that place all alone. You gave me strength, Savin."

"You're a hell of a lot stronger than I will ever be. So, about being kidnapped. What were you told? Do you think your father—if indeed he was demon—wanted you to live in Daemonia? Did you ever meet him?"

She shook her head. "What I've told you is conjecture. I was only told I was taken because of my father. No explanation beyond that."

Mostly. She did know the exact reason—it was what made her flee—but she wasn't ready to reveal that yet.

But why not spill all? Savin seemed open to listening, and perhaps even to accepting her. And she had no intention of committing a crime or becoming a menace to society, which would then require him to reckon her.

They could do this. She wanted that.

You want him, between your legs and in your arms.

"So you know things," Savin said. "Can I ask a few questions?"

In for the dive, Jett leaned back beside Savin and gave him the go-ahead with a squeeze of his hand.

"I know it's tough for you now, and you don't want to talk about your experience there, but the dark witch who put up a binding hex on the rift between Daemonia and this realm expects that to shatter soon. We can't let that happen. And while I'm no demon hunter, I don't relish having to reckon hundreds or thousands of demons after they've been caught, if it's preventable."

"Nor do I relish another single demon coming to this realm. They need to stay where they are." And far from her.

Last night she hadn't encountered any determined to send her back to Daemonia. But that only meant none there had come from the Place of All Demons, or if they had, they were being as stealthy as she should have been. What was it called? Flying under the radar.

"So, part demon," Savin muttered. "I'm usually spot-on with detection."

"I'm wearing a sheen," she said. "I have been since I arrived. Not to deceive you. It is a necessary mask to walk amongst those unknowing in this realm."

"I can't believe I didn't sense the demon within you. That must mean it is very weak. You're still mostly human, Jett."

She offered him a weak smile. It was difficult not to grip him by the throat and show him exactly how not-weak she was. But she had control over that side of her. For now.

"Is it difficult?" he asked.

"Very tiring. But I'm afraid of releasing it. And who knows, maybe it will become easier as the demon in me slips away? It's got to happen. I just want to be human again, Savin. To belong here in my home."

"What—" he dipped his head, and his hair concealed the side of his face "—are you like with the sheen down?"

Jett sighed. His curiosity annoyed her. And even if she did understand, she felt the prejudice in that question.

"You don't have to show me if you don't want to," he said. "I don't need to know. But, Jett, I mean it when I say I'm on your side."

He wouldn't be if he knew the complete truth.

Oh, she wanted him to trust her, and to help her. But her dishonesty would not make that happen. She had to tell him. To spill her truth. And if that scared him away, then so be it.

And if it made him come after her to reckon, then she would stand and fight to the death.

Because I am strong. The reckoner will bow to me as all others do.

Jett lifted her chin, feeling the dark energies infuse her system. She preferred him to know exactly what and who he was dealing with. "Savin…"

"Are you hungry? I'm hungry."

She slid off the sarcophagus and stood before him. "Sure, but I have to tell you everything. I need your trust. I need…" *Keep it innocent. He doesn't need to know how strong you really are.* "I need your help. I need…you."

"You have me, Jett. All of me."

"I'm afraid I'll lose you with my truth." Her darkness slipped. She quickly pulled it back up and used the power she owned to speak the next confession. She exhaled and spread her hands before her. "I was taken for a specific reason. To sit the throne," she said.

He cocked his head to the side.

"I'm the Daemonian queen."

Chapter 13

Savin stood abruptly.

A flock of crows pecking at a discarded bit of nearby food suddenly took to wing with an eerie chorus of caws. And Jett stood there before him, seemingly human and beautiful and so lost.

Or was she?

She held her head regally. Like a...

She'd confessed the most incredible and startling secret.

"You're..." He couldn't find the right words to express his mixture of dismay, shock, curiosity and downright revulsion.

"I had to tell you," she said. "I want you to know my truth, Savin. Then you can decide whether you want to help me or send me back to that terrible place."

He would never send her to a place she knew well yet did not belong in.

Or did she?

Who was Jett Montfort?

"Sit down," she said with a gesture to the sarcophagus. "I'll explain how it went down."

Savin crossed his arms high on his chest and did not sit. Then he realized he'd just closed himself off from her, so he dropped his arms and nodded, signaling his willingness to listen. It was the least he could do for her. Hell, what had just happened between them?

"I was brought into Daemonia by a queen," Jett said. Her voice was confident, modulated and precise. Chin lifted and hands hanging freely at her sides, she held herself with a regal air. "And then she fled."

Savin narrowed his brows. A queen had kidnapped Jett? And him, as well. Though, apparently, taking him had been a mistake. He'd been in the wrong place at the right time. Or had it been the other way around? Would his life have been different had he not been sucked into the Place of All Demons? Bizarre to even consider it now.

"It took me a while to piece together that she had wanted out of Daemonia," Jett continued, "but she had to find a replacement to take the throne in order to make that happen. In that legion of Daemonia they protect the queen greedily. Well, I imagine it is so in all legions. It is like here in the mortal realm with some of the countries. Royalty is not uncommon, and even revered."

The demonic legions were sections in the realm ruled by separate governance, a bit like countries or the states.

Savin nodded. "I know about the legions and royalty. I just never…"

He wasn't going to finish that sentence.

"As soon as the queen went missing," Jett continued, "there were cries of 'The queen is dead!' And then immediately after that, all gazes turned to me—shivering little nine-year-old me. And the shouts rose, 'Long live the queen!' I didn't know what to think of it.

"Well, you know what the conditions were like in that place. We were both near death and maddened by the experience. But I was sheltered and treated kindly amidst these strange creatures in a strange land, so at the time I thought it best to do as I was told. I was clothed and fed. My wounds healed and I began to think straight. I never stopped thinking of you, though." Her breath caught on those last words.

Savin swallowed. Alone and with no one to hold her hand, not a single friend… He couldn't fathom it. And yet. "Where did that queen go?"

"I don't know. I met her only the one time in the beginning when I was brought to her private chambers. It was right after I'd been scooped from the falls. I stood before her, tattered and shaking. She was vile and yet beautiful. Her skin was the color of a night sky splashed with indigo. She had a cackle laugh that I will never forget. Her red eyes seemed to burn my skin. She was the one who told me she knew my father and that was why I was there. I was so startled I didn't have the words to ask intelligent questions. You understand?"

Savin nodded. He would have been out of his mind had he been taken to such a place and told strange information.

"I was groomed and trained and coddled and dressed and taught how to be a queen. And as I matured, I learned that following rules was wise, but also that my newly gained title granted me power untold. I learned to wield it wisely, yet also always to protect myself. I never gave up hope of escaping. Someday."

A lift of her chin caught a glint in the corner of her eye. Was that a teardrop too proud to fall?

"So." Jett splayed her hands before her and said, "Throw me to the demons, I will rise their queen."

The tone of her voice held a wicked, dark edge and Savin felt he'd just heard the true queen. A woman who had grown into her power and embraced it. But for survival, or because she had learned to expect it?

"Call it my sad yet triumphant tale," she said. "I survived to escape. And yet here I stand before you, the one thing you have taken to task to destroy."

"Never destroy," Savin muttered. He did not do that. Reckoning did not harm demons; it only sent them whence they had come.

"Are you going to reckon me?" Jett asked in that same confident, and slightly challenging, tone.

Drawing in a breath through his nose, Savin straightened and met her defiant gaze. For the first time he saw a sheen of red in her irises. Barely there, but telling. He'd thought he saw it once before—in this same place—but had dismissed it as a reflection from a streetlight. What a fool. Yet he still couldn't sense her demonic nature as he could when around other demons. She wore the sheen well, and with an ease that amazed him.

"Reckon you? I don't know," he stated truthfully.

It hurt his heart to speak those three words. He wanted to know. He wanted to be positive that he would never harm her. He wanted only to protect her. But the situation had changed.

His alliances had been split.

"Thank you for your honesty," she said. "I've learned to recognize those who would lie to get close to me, only to ultimately betray me. Very few speak exactly as they feel and act. But you do. You are a good man, Savin."

He didn't feel so good. But he had spoken the truth. For right now. Ten minutes from now? A day or more? Everything could change. Like it or not.

Jett asked, "Do you want me to leave your place? If I could get a small loan—"

"You can stay, Jett. Nothing has changed between us. And…" A sigh was unstoppable. "Everything has changed. You've laid a lot on me. I have to think about this. We'll figure this out. I promise I won't play the diddley bow when you're around. And… I'll see what I can do about adjusting the wards on my place."

She lifted her head, her eyes smiling before she did. "That's very generous."

"I won't completely take them down. I'm not stupid. I've got to protect myself from all the other demons in Paris."

"I understand that. Do you feel you need protection from me?"

He shook his head. "My job is to send demons back to Daemonia," he said. "The dangerous ones. Are you dangerous?"

"No."

"I believe you."

Jett smiled. "You really want to help me? After all you now know about me?"

He did. Because…

Savin grabbed Jett by the shoulders and pulled her to him and kissed her. She went up on her tiptoes to meet his mouth in an intense, hard crush of desire and want.

She was his girl. They had been friends since childhood. They knew each other. And he wanted her back in his life. Demon or not. Queen or commoner. No matter what it took, he wanted to see if this could work.

He broke the kiss and Jett's sigh dusted his mouth. "I think that was a *yes*," she said.

"That was a *hell yes*. I'm going to contact CJ, the dark witch."

"What for?"

"He's keeper of the Archives. That place has an entire room on demons. And the book of all demons, the Bibliodaemon, is constantly updated. Maybe he can find us some answers, like where that queen is who kidnapped you, and even who your father is. Come on. Let's go home."

With Savin's adjustments to the house wards before he'd left on an errand to pay monthly rent, Jett felt more relaxed sitting in the cool evening shadows of the living room beneath the skylights. He'd been gone for hours, but she'd taken that time to close her eyes and go within. It was something she had done when alone in her rooms. She'd cross her legs and place her hands on her knees, palms up. And seek that deep and hidden part of her, the innocence that still lingered.

She had never been alone. Always the presence of a watcher was felt but never seen. After a while she'd stopped caring and had simply proceeded with her life, breathing, sighing, living, dressing, sleeping, without a care for that presence.

Focusing and moving inward was initially a struggle, getting past the darkness, but there, she touched it. That giggle. The long-lost smile directed toward the sunshine. The memory of Savin telling her she had a cotton-candy voice. But now the memory was strangely overlapped by the rugged, masculine tone of Savin's adult voice. One that had the power to glide over her skin and creep under her clothing on a tempting touch.

Jett sighed as she imagined him holding her with his wide, strong hands. His mouth sought hers and then explored her skin, gliding, skimming, licking and tasting. Her nipples hardened and she pressed her legs together to capture the giddy shimmy at her mons. It was a delicious fantasy. And before she realized it, the darkness in her moaned with pleasure.

She did not relent the fantasy. It was too rich and something she'd never had. A man willing to please her and not ask anything in return. Someone she had chosen and not the other way around. A man—not a demon—whose gaze could melt her and make her heartbeat race. A man.

She so desperately wanted that man.

Shaking her head out of the dream, she emerged from the reverie and looked about. This sort of fantasizing was well and fine, but she'd best target her energies toward Savin when he was here. She must do everything possible to make him forget where she had come from and what she was. It could prove a monumental task.

She was always up for a challenge.

In the meantime, she was bored sitting in this small place. She needed to start her new life. And the best way to do that?

Her gaze fell on the brown envelope with the family papers inside. Jett pulled out a few, and when she touched the bank statement, she nodded. If she could find this bank, then they might tell her if she had an account and, if so, some money. It was what she required to become independent.

her legs about his hips. He strolled through the living room but paused by the supporting beam and nudged her against it, holding her there as the kiss demanded all his attention.

The woman's legs tightened about his hips, urging him closer. The exquisite rub against his hard-on drew up a pleasurable hiss from him. He kissed her deeply, with an urgency that showed her his need. Hell yes, he craved. Jett knew who and what he was. As he did her. They were going into this with eyes wide-open. And he was good with that.

He pushed up her silky shirt and she clawed at his shoulders. The sweet pain gave the Other a shudder, but he ignored the bitch. She would not interfere this time. He would not allow it. To do that, he focused on the smell, taste and sounds of Jett. She was summer and flowers tinged with an edge of wicked. Her moans spurred him on. He rocked his hips against her.

"Take off those jeans," she said with a gasp and a demanding tone. "I want to feel you against me." She wriggled from his clutch to stand and shoved down her leggings. "I want you inside me, Savin."

It wasn't a polite request. Savin preferred his women bold and to know exactly what they wanted. And this one did.

Shuffling down his jeans, he hugged his stiff cock against her soft nest of curls and groaned at the exquisite contact. "Jett, you're so hot. Are you sure...?"

"Quit asking me that. I am very sure. Inside me. Now!"

Resisting the intense inward tug that cajoled him to step away from Jett, Savin leaned into her, putting

Chapter 14

Savin noticed as Jett paused before crossing the threshold into his home. He'd reactivated the demon wards upon returning home from his landlord's office but had forgotten to lessen them. It must take incredible energy for her to pass through without being torn apart or, at the very least, writhing in pain. Truly, she must be powerful.

A queen. Just how much of Jett was demon and how little of her humanity remained? It disturbed him, and yet it did not. And that realization worked to even further disturb him. Had he become so jaded to demonic existence?

"I can take the wards down," he offered as she closed the door behind her and stood in the cool afternoon quiet of the kitchen.

"That would be lovely for me, but not for you. You need protection from those who wish to harm you."

"Most demons know to keep a good distance between the reckoner and them. And I don't fear you."

"You should not," she said, meeting his gaze. Her smile was easy and so comfortable.

It was difficult to compare what she'd told him about being queen of Daemonia with the sweet, beautiful woman who stood before him now. Dressed in a soft red blouse and gray leggings, she exuded a feminine sexuality. He knew Jett was more human than demon. *She had to be.* He'd grown up knowing her. They had been best friends. And even now he couldn't push aside the need to protect her. To want to pull her close and know her. He desired her, no matter what species box she checked on a form.

Was that insane? She was *demon.* At the very least, part demon.

But if she spent enough time in the mortal realm, she would become completely human again. With hope.

"What are you thinking?" she asked. "Do you want me to leave? After all I've revealed I wouldn't be surprised if you wished to put up new wards specifically against me."

"I would never do that, Jett. Where were you?"

"Oh! I walked to the bank and asked about my account. It does exist and there's money in it."

"How much?"

"That's the problem. They could tell me I had an account but wouldn't give me access to it without identification. Driver's license or something with my current photo on it, like a passport."

"Both will take some time to get. I could—" Savin rubbed his jaw "—find a guy who would make a passport for you."

Her smile twisted. "That sounds sketchy."

Savin shrugged. "I'm a sketchy guy. What can I say?"

Her sudden laughter reminded him of better times. He'd once thought of her teasing voice as cotton candy, and the laughter that bubbled up was surely a treat. Savin couldn't resist crossing the room to pull her into his arms. He threaded his fingers through Jett's hair and kissed her hard and deep. He didn't want to hear any more of her truths. The reasons why he shouldn't have her in his home. He wanted only to feel her heat against his mouth and his body. He wanted her in him and all over him. He wanted to get lost in her hair and skin and sighs.

Jett's palms slid under his shirt, gliding slowly up his chest and then around his back. Her nails dug in, which sweetened the intense moment. With a lusty groan, he slipped a hand down her thigh and around to cup her ass. That sweet, rounded softness in his hand encouraged him to press his growing erection against her groin. He was rushing toward his wants. The moment demanded he show her how he felt about her.

And this was what he wanted.

"Savin, yes," she whispered at his mouth. "But are you sure?"

"I'm never sure of anything," he said. "Just following my heart right now."

"I can do that, too."

"You want this?" He moved his kisses over her cheek and to her ear. "Tell me this touch is okay. My kisses. And…more?"

"Yes, a thousand times, yes. I need you, Savin. Let's have sex."

With that permission, he lifted her and she wrapped

everything he had into moving toward her and never away. Screw the Other. This was happening.

With a grip of his cock, he glided inside the lushest, most delicious heat he'd ever known. The world changed. He groaned low and long against Jett's neck as he nuzzled his face into her hair. Closing his eyes focused all senses to smell and touch. Sweet, hot, wet energy. Lost inside her, he pumped slowly, then faster as her tight hug pushed him over some edge he didn't mind falling off.

This was his plunge into the lava falls. It had finally come to him. And he leaped freely and with arms spread wide to accept whatever dangers might come.

Gripping a hand at the back of his neck, Jett squeezed his hair tightly. "Yes, deeper. All of you, Savin. Don't stop. That is so… Ah!"

She shuddered against him. And he realized she had reached orgasm. How wondrous that she had. He normally had to work much harder to get a woman off. And that allowed him to release. With one firm, deep thrust, he came with a gasp—and then he had a sudden and intense need to pull out.

Savin pushed away from Jett, who clung to the wooden beam behind her. Had it been the Other? Or merely his better senses rising to the surface?

"Sorry," he gasped. "No condom. Forgot. Shit."

Jett nodded, huffing as she rode the lingering wave of her pleasure. Her breasts heaved within the dress. Her hair spilled messily across her rosy cheeks. "Right. That is something humans— Er, you have a condom?"

He nodded. "Bathroom."

"Then we're just getting started," she said in the most wicked and confident voice Savin had ever heard.

* * *

Savin had rushed to the bathroom and returned with a couple crinkly condom packages. It hadn't been a concern for Jett while in Daemonia. Demons had their own methods of birth control. Now, without missing a beat, they quickly returned to their frenzied lovemaking, this time on the bed. Gasps and moans were accompanied by the incredible freedom of skin upon skin, mouths tasting each other, heartbeats racing heartbeats.

When at the peak of orgasm, Jett felt the other demon inside Savin. When she sat upon Savin's hips, his cock fully hilted within her, and her body tremored with the most lush and unexpected bliss, a niggle of darkness shivered and tried to claw at her.

He called her the Other. She lived within Savin's body, inhabiting it, but not his soul. It was difficult for a demon to overtake a human's soul. Nearly impossible. However, if his soul had been occupied, then Savin would not even be Savin anymore. He would be whoever it was that was inside him.

Yet Jett wasn't able to delve deep enough to make that determination. And, honestly, she was too lost in the pleasurable moment to stop and attempt to dig deeply into Savin's being to learn that answer. She could do it. And she would. She wanted to know who and what lived within him. That was one determined—yet complacent—demon to have stuck around inside him for so long.

Lying down beside her lover, she kissed his shoulder and hugged him across the chest as the last delicious bits of orgasm pulsed in her belly. He smelled salty and fierce, his muscles tensing and relaxing in turns as his own orgasm played out. What an exquisite beast of a man lying beside her.

"That…was good," he murmured. The man panted, but his breathing grew more relaxed. How quickly he began drifting to a blissful sleep.

Would Savin let her step into his being and have a look around? Probably not. All manner of things could occur if Jett did such. She could learn things about him he'd rather no one discover. She could touch his soul, even. No human who knew what was up with such powerful magic would allow that. And Savin was a smart man.

And what would knowing prove? The demon was incorporeal. It could feasibly inhabit Savin forever. And, apparently, he'd developed a means to accept that, to even get along with the parasite. But the morphine he used so often could not be good for him. Even if most was sucked up by the Other, it was injected into his system. She hated that he had to use drugs to quiet the demon. He would be infinitely better if it were gone.

Jett would figure out who it was and, from there, could determine how to get her out. Because no other woman was going to dig her claws into her man. Savin was hers now. The sex had rocked her world and had connected them on a new level. They had moved beyond mere friends. She'd orgasmed…so many times. Never had she been brought to such a pinnacle. Treated as if a goddess. As if she was the one her lover had wanted to please, never mind his own pleasures.

And that was a good thing.

Savin's tight biceps pulsed against her arm as he moved a little. His deep, throaty exhale sent a delicious shiver over her breasts and ruched her nipples.

Eyes closed, he slid a hand over her stomach and his thumb smoothed the underside of her breast. The man's growl hummed in Jett's throat and lungs. It felt like a universal signal. One that she answered with an arch of her back and a nudge of her shoulder against his.

"You feel like everything I've ever dreamed about," he said softly. "This is good, Jett. The two of us."

Indeed.

He nudged his head against her shoulder and kissed her arm. Then he quieted, perhaps drifting into reverie once again. Lying beside him was the only thing she desired. Ever.

Chapter 15

Savin whistled while he dried off after a shower. Jett had gone out to collect something to eat for them. He had told her to take the credit card from his wallet. And he felt on top of the world. He wasn't going to make excuses for feeling this way, either. He hadn't felt this good in a while. He'd made love with a woman he cared about—who happened to be half demon. Life went on. If anyone wanted to argue against that, he dared them to stand up and show him their teeth.

Tossing the towel aside, he strolled naked into the bedroom and sorted around in the drawer for some jeans. His uncombed wet hair dripped down his back, so he pulled up his jeans, then sat on the bed and lay back, wriggling to wipe his back dry. He was a guy. So sue him.

The front door opened and he peeked around to see Jett. He'd left the wards down purposely, knowing she'd be gone only a short while. She blew him a kiss and he caught it.

And then he lay back again and closed his eyes as he listened to her sort through a bag and set things out on the counter. He'd just caught an imaginary kiss from a demon.

Half demon, his conscience corrected. And someone who had no intention of remaining that way.

She had been a queen, though.

What the hell are you doing, man? Do you know *what you're doing? Or are you love struck, following your cock instead of your brain?*

He honestly hadn't done that in a while. Hell, had he ever felt this way? Jett felt familiar to him, comfortable. Not like other women he'd met and had dated or with whom he'd had short-term relationships. She accepted him for everything that he was, including the Other within him. He could be open and honest with her. As she had been with him.

He sat up, wondering what the implications of a queen leaving Daemonia could mean. Did they know she was gone? If she had escaped, that would imply probably not. At least, not right away. Surely, they'd noticed her missing by now. Would they come looking for her? With the rift at a tenuous hold, what would a panic over a missing queen bring to this realm—and to Jett?

He rushed out to the kitchen and asked, "Are they after you?"

Jett set down a carton of apple juice beside a plate of fresh *pain au chocolat*. "They?"

"Your subjects. The inhabitants in the legion you ruled over. Did you...rule over them?"

She set a pastry on a separate plate for herself, then

walked around him to sit at a stool before the counter. With measured confidence, she poured a glass of juice and took a sip before speaking. "I ruled. In a manner. I was more a figurehead. Someone who represented our legion and whom the subjects could bow to. But I did have authority. And I was meant to…"

"Yes?"

She set down the juice and sighed. "I had to get out of there now because plans were being made. I'd been put on the throne for more than the purpose of a figurehead. I was to breed."

"Oh, fuck. Jett. I'm…"

She shrugged. "I didn't want to tell you that, but I trust you. And after last night…"

He kissed her temple and bowed his head to her, so thankful that she had escaped. "You're safe now. I promise."

"I hope so. Do you really think…they will come after me?"

"I'm not sure. It was a thought that suddenly occurred to me. Doesn't Daemonia *need* a queen? And if they wanted you to breed? You said the former queen took you as a replacement. Maybe that was her only means to escape. Ensuring that another queen was in her place. Who will take your place?"

"I don't know. And I don't care."

"I can understand that, but…maybe you should care, Jett. Was there a scion, someone who would take your place?"

"No."

"Well, I gotta think that the queen who took you did it for a reason. Maybe the same thing? She didn't want to be made into a breeding machine?"

"I know otherwise. She'd tried but was barren. She was not treated well after that fact was discovered. Which, I imagine, was her motive for making an escape." She took a few bites of pastry, giving it some thought. "You think I should fear capture?"

"You shouldn't. I will protect you."

"I am quite powerful. I can protect myself. But I won't disregard your offer of protection. Such a handsome man standing beside me as my champion?" She stroked her fingers down his bare chest and tucked two in at his waistband. "Will you be my champion, Savin Thorne?"

"Yes," he said without consideration. "I'm here for you, Jett. I…" He looked aside. The realization suddenly rose and it hit him hard.

"You?"

He clasped her hand. "I wasn't able to save you when we were young. I will not stop to save you now. I promise you that. I'm capable. And I'm strong. I know how to protect you. I am your champion, Jett."

She stood and kissed him, then pressed her hand over his heart. "I accept the offer, bold one. Now eat. And then? This queen desires more from you."

"More?"

She glided her palm over his quickly hardening erection. "Yes, more."

After a quickie on the couch that had led to a longer lovemaking session in bed, and then another against the bathroom vanity, Savin was feeling the champion. In a manner, anyway. Jett had asked if they could spend the day together, doing something—anything—that would not remind them of who they were, what darknesses lived within them. For they both harbored a darkness they'd rather not contain. And Savin had heartily agreed.

Now he and Jett stood at the top of the world, or reasonably close, as they looked down over Paris from within the Plexiglas-shrouded topmost level of the Eiffel Tower.

"I can see Sacré-Coeur," Jett pointed out with glee. "I love that domed cathedral. I want to go there. It's been so long. Can we do that next?"

"Of course. But, uh…it is a Catholic church."

"Yes. So? Oh." She wrinkled her brow. "Can I enter a place of worship now?"

"Generally? No. But to judge from your ability to wear a sheen with such ease, I believe you might be able to step on holy ground."

"Good. Then we'll go there."

Savin leaned against the window, the sights not as interesting to him as the woman who curiously gazed across the landscape and pointed out the landmarks she recognized.

He had dated many women in his lifetime. For a day or two, a few weeks, sometimes a few months. He'd never had a long-term relationship. Too difficult, considering his line of work. Yet he'd once yearned for simple domesticity with a former lover who had been a shoe model for a famous Parisian designer. She had left him for a stock-market trader.

Savin wanted a relationship. It wasn't a dirty word to him. When with a woman, he felt good. It wasn't that she filled him or completed him, but that she gave him a new outlook. And he needed more than his singular glance at life. He was a man who felt better when he could share his life and experiences with another.

But was Jett a person with whom he could hope to become involved? They had a history, and that mattered. But their history involved some pretty wicked stuff. And that mattered, too. They each knew what the other had been through. They understood each other.

Although he wasn't exactly sure what Jett's being a Daemonian queen meant. He felt sure she hadn't told him all. She'd been there twenty years. That was a lot of living. And surviving. He could be thankful she had risen as queen if only for the fact that they might have treated her far better than if she'd been forced to survive on her own and without any status. But to have been on the verge of being forced to breed? The thought of it made him shiver. He was so glad she'd gotten out of there.

She did have power. She wore a sheen right now, without seeming difficulty. So she must be strong. He'd felt her strength this morning while making love. He'd fallen into it and had luxuriated in it. And he wanted to do it again.

"What are you thinking about?"

He focused on her gaze and realized she must have been studying him for a while. Her smile was curious. He'd once wondered if her parents had named her Jett because her hair was so black. Not at all, she'd replied. Her father had suggested it, or so they'd told her, because he'd always wanted to fly in a jet.

A father who, apparently, hadn't been her birth father. Had Jett been sired by a demon? The implications were immense. Not least was the one that made him wonder who her demonic father could be. And was that unknown parent behind her being taken to Daemonia to replace the queen? What motives had been behind that move? Had he merely wanted his progeny to sit the throne?

"Savin?" she prompted. "Are you lost?"

"A little." He chuckled. "You want to know what I'm thinking about? Us," he confessed easily.

She blushed as she lowered her gaze and touched his chest.

He placed a hand over hers. "Will you be my queen?" he asked. "I don't want to worship you or put you on a pedestal. But I'd love to have you in my life. With me. At my side. In my bed. Here, holding hands, doing things we enjoy. Together."

She nodded.

"I realize you're only just getting your feet in this realm. Probably there's lots of guys out there waiting to meet you. And you'll want to explore and meet them, too—"

She pressed a finger to his lips to shush him. "I'm happy with where I am right now. With you. But are you sure you're prepared for whatever baggage I come with?"

He shrugged. "We've all got baggage."

"I'm going to wager mine's a bit heftier than yours."

"Probably. But I'm the strong one. I can lift a lot."

She smirked and gave his biceps a testing squeeze. "We'll see. I've been thinking about what you said about them coming for me." She glanced about, taking in the tourists around them, then lowered her voice. "I have to maintain my sheen. It'll keep them off my scent."

"Does it…wear you out? It must be difficult expending the energy."

"It takes a lot of work. But I'd never want you to see me…like that."

He stroked the hair over her ear and kissed her forehead. "Have more faith in me, Jett. There's not a lot that

I haven't seen. I promise I won't disappoint you. Deal?"
He held out his hand, which she clasped and shook.

"Deal."

"On to Sacré-Coeur?"

"Sure, but can we stop at the Louvre along the way?
Do they still have that éclair shop in the gallery?"

"I'm glad you're getting your appetite back. I'm not
sure, but we will find out."

They did still have the éclair shop tucked beside the
top of the escalator. Savin treated Jett to a green apple
and caramel concoction that had her swooning. She had
gotten back her appetite and her penchant for sweets.
Everything tasted so good. Was it because she'd had a
taste of Savin and that had opened her to all the other
delectable treats life had to offer? Most likely.

After the snack, they strolled through the Denon
wing, which was crowded with tourists struggling to
get a good view of the demure Mona Lisa.

"Remember when we got lost here?" Savin asked as
they strolled out from that gallery into the hallway. Jett
leaned against the wall to take in the crowd. "It was in one
of the galleries with the eighteenth-century furniture."

"Yes, I remember that daring escapade into the past.
We were firmly admonished by museum staff for hiding behind the King Louis XIV armchair. I thought for
sure my mother was ready to faint."

"We didn't get treats that day," Savin noted.

"No, but we did get to see the security office. That
was an adventure."

"Right, I remember that now. We played heist for
weeks following, plotting methods to steal the *Mona*

Lisa by hiding out in the guard's room until the perfect moment when we could make our escape."

His laughter rumbled and Jett clasped his hand, but of a sudden her attention was drawn down the long hallway to a crowd of teenagers dressed in black and chains. Someone brushed her shoulder, muttering "*désolé*" as he charged into the gallery. A definite feeling of recognition shivered up Jett's spine. Here, in this place that should hold only good memories, she could not escape the reminder that she was not the human she wanted to be. Would she ever be?

"I need to get out of here." She quickly strode off, knowing Savin would follow, and not wanting to converse when yet another accidental connection with a stranger could tease at her darkness.

The exit was just ahead. Even as Savin called after her, Jett picked up her pace. She fled upward, taking the twisting stairs to the glass pyramid aboveground, then exited out into the cloudy afternoon. Inhaling deeply the brisk air, she closed her eyes and caught a palm against her chest.

You are weakening, her darkness whispered. *You can stay strong if only you'll keep me at the fore.*

Jett shook her head. She didn't want to do that. She would not.

Why are you making this so difficult?

Savin touched her shoulder and bent to meet her gaze. "What happened in there?"

"Sorry, I had to get out as quick as possible. There were so many of them. I could feel them brushing my skin. It prickled intensely."

"Demons," Savin confirmed. "I sensed them. But

then, they are always near. I've become oblivious. I obviously don't feel their presence like you."

"It's like walking through a cloud of mosquitoes," she said, knowing it wasn't the best way to explain it. "I'd love to slap them away, but then my identity might be revealed to them."

"Why didn't they react to you as you did them?"

"I'm wearing a sheen, Savin."

"Right. I need to do a better job at keeping alert for them. I can steer you away when I know. I'm sorry."

"You have nothing to apologize for."

"I want to keep you safe, Jett."

"I love you for that."

He smirked behind her fingers, then kissed the tips of them. "Should we head to a cell-phone store and get hooked up?"

"Yes, it's time I started acting like the rest of the humans."

He clasped her hand and kissed it. "You are human. Don't forget that."

They strolled out from the Louvre courtyard, footsteps crunching the crushed limestone, but Savin's phone rang when they broached a tourist-crowded sidewalk. He answered and stepped a few feet away from Jett, slamming a hand to his hip as he spoke in low tones to the caller.

She tilted her head to listen, but it was too crowded to hear, and cars drove by, honking their horns at some emergency she couldn't guess at. From Savin's stiff posture and tightening jaw, she sensed whatever he was being told was not good.

Finally, he shoved the phone into a pocket and reached

out for her. She took his hand and he pulled her close. "They've broken through again," he said.

And Jett's heart dropped to her gut. She didn't have to ask what that meant. The rift had been reopened. They were coming for her. She knew without doubt.

Daemonia would not rest until its queen had returned.

Chapter 16

Savin wanted to go directly to talk to Ed. And when Jett volunteered to walk home alone again, he didn't argue. He needed the distance, actually.

She was, or had been, a queen. What were the implications of that? Would Daemonia send troops after her through the newly reopened rift? It was something he had to keep in mind.

The two of them...had something. It was a beginning. A new chapter to their lives. And yet a strange plot twist had been introduced. His best friend, survivor of the most heinous horrors, was a demon queen.

Those demons who escaped Daemonia and caused trouble in the mortal realm then became his problem. Not that Savin expected Jett to cause trouble. Ah hell, so he'd already taken the leap to believing she was dangerous?

He should probably tell Ed about Jett. But then, would

the man want to send her back? Even if she had taken on demonic attributes, she didn't belong in the Place of All Demons. Jett was an innocent. She belonged in the mortal realm. With him.

Up on the sixth floor, Savin strode into Ed's office. The clean interior boasted black marble walls and the entire outer wall was lined with windows. A massive conference table stretched half the length of the room. Ed's desk sat before the windows. On shelves along one wall were interesting objects that Savin knew were magical artifacts Ed had either collected or been given. Edamite Thrash's girlfriend was a witch and apparently he was smitten.

Ed stood waiting for Savin, leaning against his desk, arms crossed high over his chest. His slicked-back black hair revealed tattoos that crawled up his neck. On his hands he wore the ever-present half gloves, which exposed his fingers, but covered the poisonous thorns on his knuckles inherent to all corax demons.

"I just finished interrogating a bi-morph," Ed said.

Savin nodded. Those sorts were mighty ugly. But they had a strange penchant for lemons. He suspected, now that he got a whiff of the air, that Ed had employed that tangy treat as a means to twist the screws.

"The captive seems to know that there is only one means to securely close the rift to Daemonia."

"Which is?" Savin asked.

Sighing, Ed stood upright and splayed out his hands. "Apparently, one of the legion queens has gone missing. And until she's back where she belongs, upon her throne in Daemonia, the rift will never seal."

"A queen of Daemonia." Savin rubbed his jaw. What the hell? And Jett just revealing to him that she was once a queen? How to play this one? He wasn't going to lay out all the cards until he knew if he could trust Ed. But he hated lying to his friends. "Are you familiar with such royalty?"

"I know every realm has its various royalties. There are dozens of legions in Daemonia. Like countries here in the mortal realm. The Casipheans—whom I'm most familiar with—descended from angels. But they are a dying breed. And the bi-morph didn't think this specific queen was Casiphean."

"So there's many?"

Ed shrugged. "Dozens of queens, yes. But only one is missing with whom we need concern ourselves. I've put in a call to Certainly Jones. He knows everything. And if he doesn't, he can find the answers in that crazy library of demonic lore in the Archives."

Savin had been thinking the same: to ask CJ what he knew.

"For now," Ed continued, "I'm going to call it and put out a hunt for a demon queen. There certainly can't be many running about Paris. In fact, I'm sure there can be but one."

And right under their noses. Shit. This was not how Savin wanted things to go down. But… "You need my help?"

"Thought you didn't hunt demons."

"I don't, but I can do whatever you need."

"For starters, there's a bi-morph in the basement waiting for reckoning."

"Will do." Savin rubbed his jaw, considering the information about Jett.

"Female problems?" Ed asked.

"Huh?"

"You've got that look. You got a woman that's making you smile and frown at the same time."

"Isn't that what they're supposed to do? Drive us men crazy?"

"In theory. But the good ones will do it with relish and make you love them even more for all the ups and downs."

"You and your witch have ups and downs?"

"Once in a while. She wants to travel and I'm happy right here in Paris. I've got a city to look after. Not that I'm doing a very good job of it lately."

"The demon queen will be found," Savin said. "And until she is, we'll have to batten down the hatches and keep a close eye on the rift. Can CJ put another hex on it?"

"Yes, but it's like slapping a flimsy plaster over a fatal wound."

"Right. Maybe I can do some asking around."

"About what?"

Savin shrugged. "You never know. I'll talk to people I know. See what information they might have on the local demon scene and if there's a queen wandering about we're unaware of. If she's powerful, she could put a sheen over herself that would—" Hell. Was he really going to lie to Ed?

"That would what?"

"Huh? Oh. Well, I just think she could walk right by us and we'd never know."

Ed's cell phone rang and he turned to answer it. He spoke to someone with half his gaze toward Savin. "Really? All bowed down?...Thanks. Did you get a description?...Yes, do that. Bye."

"What's up?"

"News on the queen already. Apparently, she showed up at l'Enfer last night."

L'Enfer was the nightclub owned by the Devil Himself. It was frequented by demons, mostly, and a few brave vamps and werewolves. Jett had gone there?

"My source said she walked onto the dance floor and everyone bowed before her. Started calling her 'my liege.' Most had never seen her before, but they all instinctually knew."

"Did they get a description?"

"No."

Whew! Of course, any description would be of Jett sans sheen. He wondered now what that looked like. She didn't want him to see her in her demonic form? He needed to see her truth.

"I'll head out to l'Enfer tonight," Ed said. "We've got an escapee queen wandering this mortal realm, and it sounds like no one will be safe until she's sent back where she belongs."

Savin nodded, swallowed. "Stay in touch, man. You said the bi-morph is downstairs?"

"In the holding cell. You are billing me for all these reckonings?"

"Hell yes." Savin nodded and left the man's office. As he stepped into the elevator, he blew out a breath. He did not like concealing the truth from Ed. He was a friend, and his loyalty to him ran deep.

His alliances were now sharply divided.

After reckoning the bi-morph back to Daemonia, Savin returned home with his mind at once racing and wanting to shut down. To help Ed and his efforts to keep Paris safe from hundreds, possibly thousands of demons coming into this realm? Or to stand beside Jett, a woman he cared about, yet who might prove his greatest enemy yet?

Jett wasn't the enemy. She hadn't asked to be queen. In fact, taking on the role might have been the very thing that had kept her alive all those years. In an odd way, assuming the throne had been a blessing for her.

But how to work for both sides? He couldn't stand back and *not* reckon those demons he was called to send back. But he would never reckon Jett. It was unthinkable.

There had to be another solution. And until he discovered what that was, he couldn't tell Ed he harbored the queen in his home.

He tossed his keys onto the kitchen counter but didn't call out for Jett. Due to their intimate connection, he sensed that she was not here. She was inside him in a way the Other never could be. And he wanted her there, racing through his veins, tickling over his skin and sighing against his heartbeat.

A glance revealed a torn piece of paper on the counter next to a pen. She'd left a note?

He read the words that were scrawled in that rounded style he recalled she'd used when they were kids. But no heart dotted the *i* this time. *Ran out for something to eat. Back soon!*

Savin's cell phone rang. It was his mom. She sounded excited.

"You'll never believe who just touched base with me."

He couldn't imagine—but then he tried a guess. "Josette Montfort?"

"Yes!"

He smiled at his mother's enthusiasm.

"I had put out a call to a long-lost friend I missed

dearly on my Facebook page, and she messaged me. Said she was doing well and missed me."

"You spoke to her?"

"No, just the online back-and-forth. I didn't know how to tell her that her daughter had returned. I didn't want to do it online. You know? I asked her if we could meet for lunch and she's in the Bahamas. What should I do, Savin? She needs to know about her daughter."

"She does." But how to explain everything Jett had been through to Josette? "Maybe that's something that Jett should get to decide about. Yes?"

"Yes, certainly. You'll tell her I corresponded with her mother? Perhaps I can be a liaison to hook the two of them up on Facebook."

"Thanks, Maman. I'll tell her and see what she wants to do about it. How are those madeleines?"

"At this very moment Roxane and I are filling out forms to apply for a loan for the food truck!"

"That is awesome. Remember, your first stop has to be the fourteenth."

"Of course, Savin. But we've got a long way to go before we start baking. If the loan happens, perhaps next summer will see our maiden voyage. Oh, I'm excited about the possibilities! I'll talk to you soon. Let me know what Jett decides."

"I will. Love you."

He set the phone on the counter and exhaled. Was this good, bad or ugly news? How could Jett tell her mother what she had been through, and what she had become?

And yet would her mother have information about her real parents? And if so, would that lead them to a father who could very well be demon? Did it matter? Savin wasn't sure what knowing the father's identity would provide in Jett's quest to assimilate to the mortal realm.

On the other hand, if the demon was someone so important his natural daughter had been taken from the mortal realm to rule in Daemonia, then Savin would like to have a chat with him. He couldn't possibly know the hell he'd put Jett through. Or worse? The bastard knew exactly what he'd done to an innocent human girl.

Chapter 17

Getting a haircut and manicure was a strange luxury.
Jett had been attended by many while ruling as queen.
But she'd never simply relaxed into a chair and trusted
the outcome. She allowed that to happen today. She'd
needed this after telling Savin what she really was.
Something to distract from reality.

Her long black locks that had previously hung to her
waist were now trimmed to her elbows. Her hair felt
so glossy she bounced as she walked down the street.
A flash of silver in a retailer's window caught her eye
and she went inside. Five minutes later, she wore black
ankle-high boots studded with silver spikes on the toes.
They went well with the black leather mini and red silk
shirt, over which she wore a black lace vest that spilled
long fringes about her waist. A pair of sunglasses kept
everyone from noticing a red glint in her eyes.

Because she needed to drop her sheen. And soon. She was tired, and it was becoming harder to concentrate. The sheen was growing thinner. She could see that when Savin looked at her. He saw the red in her irises now. He hadn't before.

She considered finding an abandoned building and releasing her human shroud, but there weren't a lot of places in midcity Paris that would offer such privacy. And doing it at Savin's place? She'd done it after first arriving, but only after he'd left the place for a while. And now that he knew everything about her, it should be all right. But to reveal herself to him would not be wise. The man might believe he was okay with her being part demon, but she could imagine his reaction should he see her with horns, blue hair and gray skin.

That was not a party she wanted to attend. At least not with a man with whom she was growing intensely infatuated.

On the other hand, he hosted a demon within him. He was not so different from her. That was something that bonded them.

A short man wearing thick black-rimmed glasses walking toward her swept her with a look from legs to face and down to her breasts. As she passed, Jett heard him say, "Sexy."

Being called sexy made her feel good. Better than good. Never had she turned a man's head. At least, not a human man's head. Demons didn't count. Not here they didn't. Such attention could go straight to her heart.

With a wink over her shoulder to the man, who returned the wink, she strode on toward the river. Savin's place was a long walk off, but these boots were comfortable. And she intended to shine in the sun today and meet every wanton gaze with a flirty smile of her own.

Savin plucked out a chord on the diddley bow. It was the same chord that had sent Jett fleeing the other night. He'd just gotten off the phone with Certainly Jones. The witch was heading out to the rift to assess the damage. Savin had said he'd meet him there, with diddley bow in hand. Maybe combined with the witch's dark magic, the two could do something to slow or even stop the influx of demons.

He placed the instrument in its soft zip-up case. The body was convex and shaped like a turtle shell. It had a Bluetooth pickup so he could play the thing and amplify it over his phone. It was freaky crazy, but he wouldn't have an electrical outlet for an amp out in the field, so he was glad for the app. Jett had yet to return, but it was only early evening. She must be shopping. She deserved the freedom, so he decided not to worry about her.

Besides, when he saw her, he'd have to tell her about what had gone down in Ed's office this afternoon, and he did not relish having that conversation with her.

He opened the front door to a woman with her hand lifted to knock. Jett's smile beamed and she lunged up to kiss him. Shopping bags crunched against his back as her kiss opened his mouth and she tasted him as if she were starving. She tugged him toward her, so he stepped across the threshold and into the hall.

He wrapped an arm about her back and pressed her against the wall, not wanting to leave the kiss. The woman was delicious. And dark and mysterious. And so eager to meld to his touch and mouth. Yet she was demanding and took what she desired from him. A confident woman who would not be put back for any request.

A queen.

Shit.

Savin broke the kiss. "You're in a good mood."

"And I must have caught you on the way out?" She looked over his shoulder where he'd slung the case. "Have a concert to perform?"

"Kind of." He winced. No time to have the big discussion right now. That was an excuse, but he was happy for it. "I'm meeting the dark witch out by the rift."

"Right. Opened once again. That explains the annoying feelings of demonic presence I've felt all day." Her shoulders dropped, as did the shopping bags, landing on the floor. "You're going to use musicomancy?"

He nodded. "I'm still not so sure I can invoke it properly, but I mean to give it a try."

"It has been proved effective on me."

"Sorry about that."

"You should not be. You didn't know then what you now know. I'll let you get off to that adventure."

He sensed her unease. "I'd invite you along, but you're better off as far from that place as possible."

"I am a big girl. I do very well on my own. And I've got to learn self-sufficiency sooner rather than later. I might even attempt to cook a meal."

Savin's eyebrow quirked. "You ever cook before?"

"No." She chuckled, then waggled a teasing brow. "Don't worry, I won't burn the place down. I do recall helping my mother with her pies and cookies."

He'd forgotten about his mother's call with the information about Josette Montfort, but CJ was waiting.

"I look forward to whatever you create." He kissed

her on the forehead. "Remind me we've much to talk about when I return."

"Sure," she said as he started toward the stairs. "Uh, will you let down the wards for me?"

"Right. Sorry." Savin backtracked and spoke the Latin words that would release the protection wards. To his side, Jett noticeably shivered, as if shaking off a chill. "I'll leave them down while I'm gone."

"Thank you." She kissed him on the cheek. "I'm going to try on my new things!" She skipped into his loft and he closed the door behind her.

And Savin exhaled heavily. Could he trust CJ with the information about Jett's demonic nature?

Chapter 18

Watching the dark witch conjure a spell was mesmerizing. CJ stood in the center of a black salt circle poured on the tire-trampled grasses that edged the lavender field. He'd been speaking Latin for a while, and every so often punctuated those words with a good pull at the whiskey bottle he held in his left hand. In his right, he brandished a crystal wand, and when he drew sigils in the air before him, the magical symbols glowed green and lingered for minutes.

Savin stood before the truck hood with the diddley bow strapped across a shoulder. He put up a foot on the tire so he could prop the instrument on his knee. He needed to lay it flat to play it properly. The Bluetooth was activated. The phone app that would broadcast the musicomancy was set to play with the volume tuned to High.

Even though the rift was open, there was no discernible wavering in the sky to demarcate the tear as they'd seen that first night. It was apparent it was open to another realm. Savin felt the evil, cool vibrations pricking at his bones. He'd picked up the first tingles when he was about a mile away from the site. They hadn't seen any demons come through since arriving, but that didn't mean the incorporeal ones were not slipping into this realm. They could be ghostly figments that traveled about in search of a human host to fully achieve corporeality.

It was the corporeal demons Savin most wanted to catch. More often than not, they were assholes. They looked like monsters, acted like monsters, and not only did they scare the shit out of humans, but they tended to not care if they were seen. Very few bothered with a sheen.

CJ turned to him and nodded. As the dark witch spread his hands wide above his head, stretching out a magical green static of energy, Savin played the first lick in a series that he'd learned could incapacitate a demon.

Pressing the glass slide across the single string, Savin made his instrument sing a sorrowful cry that he at once loved to create and despised for the wickedness it was required to control. And then he took great satisfaction in knowing he could annihilate that wickedness and slam it back to the realm from whence it had come. A waver of the slide across the string teased up Savin's own brand of innate magic. It birthed in his soul and swelled in his bones. The sigils tattooed on his forearms glowed. That brief time he'd spent in the Place of All Demons had infused this skill within him.

And he would wield it relentlessly.

Sustaining a long and moaning note, Savin searched the sky. A flicker of red sparked above CJ's head and embers scattered over the ground.

"That was one!" CJ called.

Their combined magic had worked like a bug zapper to an incoming demon. Nice.

Savin slid another note into a commanding cry. Now, this was a weapon he could wield all day.

The cell phone Savin had picked up remained in the box. Jett ran her fingers over the smooth matte-finish box, marveling at the utter beauty of it. Just the box! It would be too complicated to figure out how to operate the phone, she suspected. And it didn't feel right to open it without Savin to help her with it. And really, she had no compulsion to walk the streets of Paris gabbing as all others did. Besides, she had no one to gab to.

She set the box aside, and with a preening gaze over the mess of Savin's amps and sheet music stacked beside the couch, she noticed a small radio.

"I do know how to operate a radio." She picked it up and played with the dials until a slow sensual tune sung by a woman with an incredible, longing voice captivated her. Shivers traveled over Jett's arms at the intense visceral connection she felt to the tones. Setting the radio on the wooden chair arm, she swayed and closed her eyes, turning about in the living room beneath the skylights.

Lifting her arms over her head, she whispered the release that dropped her sheen. Her hair thickened and grew blue. Her skin prickled as it darkened. And the horns at her temples stretched out and over her ears.

"Ah..."

Respite.

* * *

Savin bumped fists with Certainly. The witch hadn't managed to close the rift, but they had cleaned up dozens of incoming demons. And that had seemed to put up a warning beacon. They hadn't witnessed any new arrivals in the past half hour they'd stood by, waiting, sharing the dregs in the dark witch's whiskey bottle.

"You know they'll start coming through as soon as we leave," Savin commented.

"I'm going to mark a blood hex on the ground that will, at the very least, give them pause. It's not much, but it's all I can do until we find that queen. Ed tell you about that?"

Savin nodded. "Yep." He picked up the diddley bow from the truck hood and opened the passenger door to place it inside on the seat. "I should head out. I'm drained. Gotta go home and recharge."

CJ waggled the empty whiskey bottle. "This didn't do it?"

"That makes me tired after a reckoning. I can barely keep my eyes open as it is. I'll check in with you tomorrow."

"Thanks. I have to hit the road, too. Vika complains when I'm out too late. The twins are a handful."

CJ and his partner, Vika, had twin boys. Savin figured they were toddlers, but hell, who knew, they could be rowdy teenagers. He nodded and climbed in behind the steering wheel. The witch cast ash and salt across the ground and began to stomp out a ceremonial chant as he pulled an athame across his palm. What kind of father was that to have?

Savin drove out of the field and onto the gravel road. He led such a weird fucking life. The whole idea of having children, of being married and *domestic* teased at him. And yet it felt wrong to fit *ordinary* into his lifestyle. But the dark witch did it. CJ worked at the Archives, cast out demons and dealt with magical shit all day; then he headed home to the family—for all Savin knew—to have cupcakes and tell bedtime stories. So weird.

Yet maybe not. Maybe the weirdos were the humans who had no clue what paranormal crap was going on right under their noses.

"Hell." Savin turned toward the city. He was the weirdo, no *ifs*, *ands* or *buts* about it.

Despite being weird, he didn't aspire to normal.

Now he wondered if two weirds—he and Jett—could make a right. Or even a family. He wouldn't mind having a child or two to deal with and love. Someone to read a bedtime story to? He could imagine doing such a thing. And he would never make his child feel unworthy or insignificant, as his father had done. Blame it on the alcohol, but Jacques Thorne had taken a drastic one eighty after Savin's return from Daemonia. Not a day had gone by that he hadn't fallen asleep on the couch with a whiskey bottle in hand. Rarely had he time for Savin, and when he did, it had been to berate him or tell him he could have done whatever it was Savin had been doing so much better.

Savin didn't miss his dad much, and that was a shame. A man should have a strong father figure to look up to, to mold his life after.

Jett was lucky to have been adopted. He couldn't imagine what would have come of her had her real mother and demon father raised Jett. Would she have grown up in Daemonia? That was too fucked to consider.

Half an hour later, he parked and jogged up the stairs to his place. He was exhausted from all that reckoning, but knowing a gorgeous woman waited for him lifted his spirits and gave him renewed energy. He strode inside the apartment, strengthening the wards behind him as he closed the door. It was dark, but he heard the music immediately. So she'd found the radio?

"Don't look at me!" Jett called out. She dashed out of the living room.

And Savin immediately knew he'd caught her unawares. Must have taken advantage of his absence to release her sheen. He flicked off the radio and tightened his fist. He'd just spent the evening vanquishing so many demons.

Demons were assholes. He hated them. He hated the Place of All Demons. And he hated…

He didn't want to hate her. He did not. Did he?

Why couldn't he sense her demonic nature? Closing his eyes now, he concentrated, focusing, searching for that hum in his bones. Nothing. A man should consider that lacking sense a good thing, but he wasn't sure what to make of it.

Jett spun around the corner from his bedroom, casting him a shy glance. She looked human. Was human. *For the most part.* She had pulled on the sheen. "Everything go well?"

He set the instrument case on the kitchen counter and nodded, sure if he spoke right now that his voice would quaver with the anxiety of walking in to find a demon dancing in his own home. Had he been mistaken to not tell CJ and Ed about Jett?

"Uh, were you…?" he started.

"I'm sorry," she offered, rubbing a palm up her bare

arm. "I shouldn't have done that here. It tires me to keep up the sheen."

He put up a hand. "I understand." He did. But he didn't want to.

"I attempted to make a meal, but…" She glanced toward the kitchen and for the first time Savin picked up the scent of something burnt. "Can we order out?"

"Sure. I can run out and get something. Give you more time to yourself?"

"No, I'm good. I don't want to be alone now. Can you just make a phone call?"

Whatever demon had been dancing in his living room had retreated. Jett was now that sweet, innocent, frail woman he'd found by the side of the road. And all he wanted to do was wrap her in his arms and make everything safe for her.

Savin tugged out his phone and pressed the speed dial for his favorite local restaurant. The girl who took his call knew his usual, and he doubled it. It would arrive within the hour.

Jett sat on the couch, stretching her legs before her as she sat sideways. Her arms on her knees and chin resting on one forearm, her hair spilled…not so far as usual.

"You cut your hair?"

"Needed a change. You like it?"

"I do. But it doesn't matter what I think about your appearance. That's all for you."

"Is it? You don't care if I'm a mess or a glamour doll? What if I didn't comb my hair for a week?"

"I'd still find you attractive."

Her lip wobbled. "You find me attractive? Even knowing…?"

"Even knowing." Though truthfully, a part of him still

couldn't wrap his mind around the fact that his girlfriend was part demon. "I'm sorry you feel that you have to hide your true self from me, Jett. I wouldn't be upset if you wanted to drop your sheen more often."

"But it's what you work against. Things like me."

He sat on the sofa and lifted her head by her chin. Her brown eyes were glossy. "You are not a thing. You did what you had to do to survive. I know that."

"Oh, Savin, I need your trust so much right now."

"You have it."

She moved onto her knees and glided to him, pressed her hands to his cheeks and kissed him. He didn't protest, because he didn't want to. He wasn't going to allow his brain to process the fact that he was making out with a woman who was also part demon.

Sliding a hand up Jett's hip, he slipped it under her shirt and groaned as her incredible warmth seemed to heat him to the boiling point. Her body hugged his and made everything on him instantly hard. She'd never been kissed before he had kissed her? Hard to believe. Or maybe he was that good a teacher. Heh.

Jett made quick work of removing his shirt, though it got hung up on his biceps. "How do you get such hard, big muscles from reckoning demons?" she asked.

"Reckoning requires a strong body, so I lift weights. Whew! But I am tired out from this evening's work. CJ and I managed to extinguish a few dozen incoming demons."

"Extinguish? I thought when you reckoned them you merely sent them back to Daemonia. Do you kill them?"

"I said that wrong. Well, yes and no. CJ and I combined our forces and—yes, it kind of worked like a bug zapper to the incoming. But no, I don't generally kill them. Reckoning sends them back, all in one piece."

He winced. Why did he feel as if he were reassuring her of something that could happen to her in the future?

"I see. You said you're tired?" She kissed his forehead. "Then let me do all the work. You sit back…" Her fingers danced down his abs and unbuttoned his fly. "And let me take care of you, lover."

Not a single protest came to mind. Savin lifted his hips as she unzipped him and pulled down his jeans. Felt great to let his shaft out of its confinement and… Yes… The woman curled her fingers into a nice, firm grip.

Jett dragged her fingertips over her tongue and winked at him, then placed her wet, hot fingers around him and began to work him up and down. Slow, and then faster. And then so slow he wanted to grip her hand and make her go faster. But… No, that was good. The tension she used was just right. Then she torqued her grip to the left and then…

Savin tilted his head back against the couch and groaned deep from his chest. Not a thing wrong with this situation. And when he felt her lips on the swollen crown of his cock, he nearly lost it. It was only when she tongued him that he had to grip at her hair and the couch and began to shudder as orgasm dashed up on him much quicker than expected.

The door buzzer rang and Savin shouted as he came, then swore because he was in no condition to answer the door. Damn, the woman had hit him hard and fast.

Jett stood. "Food is here. You want me to answer?"

Lost in some kind of wild and delicious high, he was capable of reaching into his back pocket to pull out his wallet. "Credit card is in there."

She took it and approached the door. "Wards?"

Breathing out a few exhales, Savin stood and pulled up his jeans. "I got this." She handed him his wallet, then cupped his cock through the jeans. "Mercy, Jett."

"I did okay, then?"

"Okay?" He grabbed the doorknob. "I don't think there's a rating high enough for that performance."

She mocked a bow and then climbed onto a stool before the counter.

He winked at her but opened the door and took the delivery from the man, promising him the usual tip. Closing the door, he joined Jett at the counter.

"Ribs?" she guessed.

"There's a place that makes them like I remember my dad used to cook on the grill. Whew!" He shook out his hands and then found his place. Segueing from the high of orgasm to answering the door was weird as shit. "Okay, I'm cool."

"You're not, really. And I'm happy for that. Your cock is so big. I like it." She winked.

And he would be hard again in no time.

Jett took a tin container and peeled off the foil cover. "I remember eating at your house. Often. Your parents were so good to me."

"We had good times when we were kids." He set plates and forks out and joined Jett on the next stool.

"We can have good times as adults."

"I thought we already were."

She kissed him and handed him a sauce-laden rib. "That we are."

Chapter 19

Jett licked her fingers and then stuffed the empty food containers in the garbage bin. Savin had wandered into the bathroom for a thorough wash. He'd eaten all but one of the ribs. For some reason the meat hadn't appealed to her. But she'd eaten the Gouda potatoes after testing them to be sure they hadn't been salted.

Demons and salt. Gave her a shudder. Though she was half demon, so she couldn't know how some things would affect her here in the mortal realm. Like knowing that her eyes could give off a red glow, even when sheened. Or that if she wasn't careful with her sheen, her skin might darken and look ashy. Gray ashy, not a normal skin tone. And oh, if she let even a portion of her horns out. On the other hand, it could be considered by some as body modification. Humans did a lot of weird stuff to alter their appearances nowadays.

It was late, nearing midnight, but the day had been good. Because even after almost catching her without a sheen, Savin still had wanted to have sex with her. The man desired her. And he did care about her. She felt that.

"There's a few things I need to tell you," he said as he wandered back into the living room.

The man was a walking advertisement for sex. Those jeans hanging low on his hips revealed all the many tight, hard muscles on his abdomen and chest. His arms were solid and big. And that tousled hair gave him a wild, virile look that made Jett weak in the knees. She wanted more of him. Inside her, filling her, tasting her and owning her.

Never had she had such a thought about a lover while in Daemonia. She had not considered them lovers, actually. Merely things to entertain her. Things she had not allowed to kiss her. She was glad for that caution now.

Refilling her whiskey glass, and one for Savin, Jett walked over to the couch, handing him the glass as they both sat. He downed the two fingers of whiskey, got up and retrieved the full bottle.

"Might need this," he said.

"Is what you have to tell me that terrible?"

"I, uh… I'm not sure. I'll start with the maybe-good thing first."

"Okay. But first." Jett held up a finger to pause him while she downed the swallow of whiskey. With an exhale, she held up her glass for him to refill it. "Okay, go."

"My mom is on Facebook," he started.

"A book of faces?"

"Huh? Oh. Right. The internet has really exploded and become this sort of social hangout since you've been gone. There's a thing called Facebook and everyone is on it. You can post about your life and see what other people are doing."

"Like a means to spy on them?"

"No. Well. Maybe." He gave it some consideration. "Normal people use it to stay in touch with friends and relatives. I'm sure there are creeps who use it for nefarious means. Anyway, my mom, after I'd talked to her about your parents, decided to try to contact your mother on Facebook. And…she did."

Jett clutched the glass to her chest. "Where is she? How is she? Did she ask about me?"

"My mom didn't know what to say about you, so she didn't mention your return. We both feel it's up to you how, or if, you want to make contact with Josette. Apparently, she's living in the Bahamas."

A much-admired vacation spot. Jett recalled her mother cutting pictures of the island from magazines and pasting them in her dream scrapbook. The memory loosened a tear at the corner of her eye, so she quickly swiped it away.

"How is that possible?" she asked. "How could your mother have learned these things about my mom without actually talking to her?"

"Through the internet. It's like email, but Facebook messaging is instant. What matters is that Josette wrote back to my mother that she was in a good place and didn't foresee coming back to Paris. That was all the contact my mom had with her. But she has Josette's Facebook information if you want to contact her."

"I do. I mean…" Jett sucked in the corner of her lip.

What *did* she want to do? Her mother was alive, and apparently well. Living in her dream getaway. That was good to know. She must want to know about her daughter. Yet Jett had been gone for twenty years. Had her mother believed she was dead all that time? How would it impact her to know she was still alive?

And no longer completely human.

"Right." Jett tilted back the rest of the whiskey. "I have to think about that one."

"She's as close as a computer message," Savin said. "But I'm sure you'll want to weigh the pros and cons about contacting her."

Jett took the bottle from him and poured herself more. "Do you think I should contact her?"

She handed him the bottle, and this time Savin drank directly from it. "I can't tell you what to do. Your mother will most likely be elated. But it would be weird for her, too. Might take her some time to figure everything out, as it has taken for you. She thinks—well, you know— she thinks you're dead."

Jett toggled the glass on her stomach.

Savin leaned over and kissed her on the shoulder. "You just need some more time to adjust to being here."

"And to forget about the past."

"And…" He sighed heavily. "CJ and I managed to destroy and/or send back dozens of demons this afternoon. But there's something you need to know."

She turned to look up into his deep blue eyes. She trusted those eyes. They would not hurt her. "Tell me."

"Edamite Thrash interrogated one of the demons he captured and the thing told him how, exactly, to close the rift and seal it."

"Which is?"

"They want their queen back." As he met her gaze, Jett saw the stoicism return to his demeanor. "We send her home to Daemonia, and the rift can be sealed."

A stunning revelation, issued with a cruel calm that shouldn't surprise her. The man did do that for a living. And he was trying to protect innocents. She had no qualms about that. Save that she was also an innocent. In her core, she was. Despite the darkness that clung to her.

"I'll never reckon you, Jett. Promise."

"But I'm their queen. You have to send me back."

Jett stood up from the couch. She paced toward the kitchen, keeping her back to Savin. He got up and pulled her into a hug from behind. She initially struggled, but when he wrapped his wide arms about her and hugged his head aside hers, she could no longer resist the need for the safety he offered.

"I promise you," he reiterated. "My word is good. I will not reckon you to Daemonia."

"But so many could suffer if you do not send me back. The people of Paris…"

"We're keeping things under control. For now. CJ's fix on the rift should slow the influx, but…I'm going to the Archives early tomorrow to see what CJ has found in the demon room."

"The demon room?"

"They have a room for every paranormal being that exists. Filled with source materials, documents, histories, artifacts. There's got to be something in that room that can help you."

"Make me completely human again?" She turned in his embrace and her wide eyes pleaded with him.

He hadn't considered that option for her survival. Daemonia would not want back a queen who was merely human. That could be a way to save Jett. And…

He nodded. "And maybe we can find the other queen.

The one who took us in the first place. If she's still out there, we can send her back."

A twinge at his insides gripped him like a vise about the spine. He let go of Jett and stepped back from her. She stood before him, seemingly weak and defeated, an innocent woman. Looking so frail. He wanted to hug her again, to hold her tight to make her know what he said was the truth.

But something kept him from doing so. And then he realized what it was. Or rather who—the Other.

Bitch.

What did she have against Jett? And why had she allowed him to make love to her without interference, yet at moments like this it was as if she cringed in horror at their closeness? It had been a few days since he'd given her morphine, and he wasn't about to shoot up again so soon. The bitch could go through withdrawal for all he cared.

"What did the dark witch say when you told him I was the queen?" Jett asked quietly.

"I didn't tell him. Wasn't sure how. Also, didn't feel he had a right to know. Yet."

She nodded. "Yet." He reached for her, but she turned a shoulder to him. "I'm tired."

Right. This was too much for both of them right now. Savin grabbed the whiskey bottle and nodded toward the bedroom. "You should get some rest. In the morning I'll head to the Archives. I don't think I'll sleep much, but I'm going to try."

"You need to be strong." She bowed her head. "Thank you, Savin. For telling me the truth. You could have kept it to yourself."

"Secrets only grow. I want you to trust me, Jett."

"I do. I'm going to think about my mom. I'm not sure it would be a good idea to contact her right now."

"Give it some thought." He started to lean forward and kiss her on the forehead, but the Other turned him toward the couch.

Just as well.

"Good night," Jett said softly. She padded into the bedroom.

He listened to the sheets rumple as she climbed in, and her sigh as her head hit the pillow.

Savin tilted back another swallow of whiskey. He'd once told a friend this stuff had been brewed by trolls. He'd like to punch a troll right now. A big, blocky bit of stupid that could take a punch like a sand-filled punching bag.

He wanted to beat out his anger and frustration on something, that was for sure. But how to attack that which lived within him?

He eyed the tin of morphine of the shelf beside the couch. "Bitch," he muttered.

Jett woke from what felt like a refreshing slumber. She stretched out on the bed, then immediately noticed that Savin had chosen to sleep on the couch last night. The information about her mother and the subsequent heart-wrenching decision that had to be made—to seek her out or not—had not lended to a sensual snuggling session following. Nor had the fact that the queen was needed to close the rift.

Just as well. She was thankful that he'd been truthful with her.

Now to figure what should happen next.

She did not want to go back to that literal hell. No one could make her take a single step toward that realm.

But no matter if she planted her feet firmly, Savin did have the power to send her back. He was a reckoner. He could send any demon back to Daemonia.

He'd said he wouldn't reckon her. And she did believe him. But it pained her to know she would be forcing him to go against his loyalties to the job he performed. Reckoning was all he knew. What would the consequences be if he refused to do that job?

Surely, the man hadn't reckoned all the demons who had come to this realm from Daemonia. Some were smart, and perhaps others blended easily into society, becoming a part of the human race. They might not present harm or a danger to humans. No need to send them back from whence they'd come.

She hadn't harmed anyone. And didn't want to, either. Yet she had worn the crown and still felt that power within her. A power that was stifled too much lately.

Sliding out of bed, Jett wandered into the bathroom and twisted on the shower. Checking her reflection, she sneered. Her skin had gotten pale and her hair wasn't as glossy since she'd escaped that place. If she were in her demonic form, she would glow. Literally. And she would feel her strength so much more.

Keeping up the sheen was growing more difficult. And yet she sensed it was also getting easier. Was that because some of her demonic nature was changing, going away? Could she ever become completely human again?

Savin had said he'd look into that today. Something about a book on demons. And now, when she took a moment to slip through the bedroom and glance out into the living room, she didn't see him on the couch. It was late, around eleven in the morning.

"He must have left for the Archives."

She hoped he could find what they both desperately needed.

Chapter 20

Savin wandered into the demon room behind Certainly Jones.

"Must be freaky working here with all these strange artifacts and—" Savin bent to peer into a glass cylinder container that was about two feet high and filled with clear liquid. Inside floated what looked like a jellyfish, but it was thorned and its eyes were red. "Hell fish."

"Got it on the first guess. This is not one of my favorite rooms." CJ led him toward the Bibliodaemon, the Book of All Demons. "The witch room is comforting to me. And, not surprisingly, the unicorn room is fascinating."

"Unicorns exist?"

"Everything fucking exists. Don't you know that by now?" The dark witch wandered ahead.

Savin could but shrug. He knew all the myths and

legends did exist, but he hadn't seen them all. He'd love to see a dragon soaring through the clouds. And hell, he wouldn't mind throwing those much-desired punches at a troll. But for some reason the unicorn still challenged his sense of reality and fantasy. Couldn't there be one legend that really was made-up? A fantasy that people could entertain and not have ruined by reality.

"If you tell me unicorns are assholes, you're going to shatter a childhood fantasy," Savin said as he joined CJ before a large book on a dais.

"Never met one. They are fierce, is what I know. There are always assholes in every species, most especially humans, yes?"

"True enough. So what have we got here?"

CJ stepped onto the steel dais and, using two hands to grip the thick leather cover, opened the book randomly. The tome was massive, stretching about three feet long and two feet wide, and it was a good two feet thick.

"The Bibliodaemon." CJ rubbed his hands together with more eagerness than his dislike of the room should have warranted. "This is the book that records all demonic happenings, spells, hexes, possessions and exorcisms, heritage, and breeds. Most species have such a book."

"What about us reckoners?"

"You're not exactly a species, more a rare tradesman. And humans have enough books recording their antics, do they not?"

"Most history books are often proved inaccurate."

"Perspective," CJ said. "It changes as we grow and learn, and uncover and disprove the falsehoods that were generated by the past." The witch threaded his fingers from both hands together before him and flexed them outward. "Now, what are we looking for?"

"Information about the queen of Daemonia."

"There are many."

"Yes, but the one from the particular legion where the rift opened up. Is that possible to locate? An identification can only help to catch and send her back."

But would a search show Jett's face? What Savin wanted to find was the former queen who had taken him and Jett, who had also ruled over the same legion. This was going to be a tricky search, no matter the outcome.

"I'll take a look." CJ closed his eyes and held his hands, fingers spread, over the book as he murmured in Latin. The thin pages began to slowly turn, whispering across one another, then picked up speed. CJ said over the flicking pages, "It's like an internet search. Only, you know..."

"The old-fashioned way." Savin leaned against the dais, the sweep of the pages brushing his face with a cool breeze. "What part of Daemonia did you, uh, visit?" he asked, just for conversation. But also, if the dark witch had been there when Jett was queen...

"Probably this same area we're searching now. I didn't mark down the territory. It was...eh, a spur-of-the-moment decision to do some reckless magic. I paid for it. In spades."

CJ had told him that he'd been possessed by a dozen demons upon his return to the mortal realm. One had been a pain demon and, upon his return, had forced CJ to harm himself. That hadn't been nearly so terrible as the grief demon, though. Savin couldn't imagine. Well, he could. He didn't know what kind of demon lived inside him, but for the most part she was quiet. Unless, of course, he kissed another demon.

Was that it? Could the Other be jealous? It didn't make sense. It wasn't as though he and the Other could be intimate in any way. More intimate than him wearing her inside him, that was. Whew!

He really wanted to unload her, but there didn't seem to be a way to do it. Not without a supreme sacrifice. That was something he had never wanted to face, and would not.

"Here's something." CJ leaned over the book and read while Savin peered over the edge of the page. The dark witch's long black hair fell over the paper, and his fingers, heavily tattooed with all sorts of spells, drew a line down the page as he silently took in the information. Finally, he stood and tapped his lower lip. "It seems one queen disappeared a while back and was replaced with a half-breed. That's the one who is currently missing, the half-breed by the name of Jettendra."

Savin muttered the name, thinking it could easily be an elongated form of Jett. She'd not told him that. Not that she would. "And the former queen's name?"

"Fuum."

"Fuum? Sounds like a bad rash."

CJ chuckled. "Apparently, Fuum went missing and the half-breed was left in her place, already designated to take the throne."

Savin knew that much from what Jett had told him. "So where is the former queen?"

"Why? Shouldn't we be focused on Jettendra? It says she escaped recently to the mortal realm, but there are no dates. It always takes these books a while to update the details, but when they do, they are incredibly accurate. I wonder if it was the night the rift first opened."

It had been. And hell. "But why veer focus from the former queen? I mean, it's always good to have options. More choices will ultimately make it easier for us, yes?"

CJ studied Savin with such a delving gaze, Savin felt sure the witch was tapping into his soul. Something witches could do without a guy even knowing it had happened. He crossed his arms over his chest and met CJ's gaze with as sure a stare as he could manage, though he wasn't feeling at all confident with the stuff he was not telling CJ.

"You know something," CJ finally said. "And I need to hear it."

A knock at the door lifted Jett up from her inspection of the diddley bow Savin used for musicomancy. She didn't dare to touch it but wondered how easy it might be to cut the string.

Another knock sounded. Had Savin forgotten his keys? He would have told her if he'd expected company, and surely he wouldn't have left her to greet that company on her own.

From outside the front door a woman called Savin's name.

Company? Jett hustled out to the kitchen. She'd donned black leggings and a silky red sleeveless shirt that hung below her hips and sported a few rhinestones decorating the low-cut scoop neckline. She looked presentable. And the wards were loose enough that she could leave and return on her own, so she was good.

Gripping the doorknob, she tried to get a sense for

who—or what—could be on the other side of the door, but her senses didn't twitch.

Opening the door, she was surprised to find an older, glamorous blonde woman holding a plate of something that was wrapped with cling plastic.

"Oh?" The woman peered beyond Jett, searching the kitchen. "Savin isn't home?"

"I'm afraid not. You've missed him."

"Oh, but you must be Jett."

"I…" Jett narrowed her gaze, wondering who the woman was.

"I'm Gloriana Thorne, darling. Savin's mother. And you have been away a very long time."

Chapter 21

Savin stepped back from the steel dais and turned about, taking a moment to weigh his options. He could walk out the door, but he never ran away from a threat. And CJ was no threat. The witch simply wanted the truth. Which Savin had and should share with him. But…could he trust the dark witch wouldn't go to Ed with the information? Why keep the info from Ed? Perhaps if he told him everything, the corax demon would agree that Jett should be protected and not sent back to the Place of All Demons.

Like that was going to happen.

"Thorne?" CJ prompted. He jumped down from the dais, his bare feet landing on the cool limestone floor. The witch stood as tall as Savin and was formidable, but Savin knew, were it a battle of might and muscle—without magic—he could take the witch. With ease.

"I guessed right, didn't I?" CJ said. "There's something you haven't told me. Has it to do with the rift and the demons?"

"It does," Savin finally said. "I didn't think telling you and Ed what I knew was necessary. Initially. And I've been protecting her..."

"Her? Protecting who?"

Savin toed the base of the dais. He had to be honest with Certainly. His loyalties to his friends were paramount to him. "You know all about me being kidnapped to Daemonia when I was a kid."

"Yes."

"Remember I told you about the girl who was with me?"

"You said she died. Fell over a cliff into some sort of lava falls?"

"That's what I thought. Until I found her wandering the roadside that night we first closed the rift. She'd been living in Daemonia all this time, CJ. Has done everything she possibly could to survive until she had the opportunity to escape. Her name is Jett Montfort. She was my friend then, and she is now. She hasn't lived in the mortal realm for twenty years. She has nowhere to go, no one to care for her. I've taken her in."

CJ blew out a breath and hooked his thumbs at his pants pockets. "Wow. For a human to survive so long in Daemonia..." Then he met Savin's gaze. "She must have become demon. At least part."

Savin nodded. "She has. I'm not sure how much. I know she's still human. But demon, too. Except she can pull on a sheen even I can't detect."

"That's a powerful demon." CJ's gaze grew more discerning. "I've been there. I can't imagine surviving so long. And I'm a dark witch. How did she, a mere human, manage such a feat? A ten-year-old girl? All alone?"

"She was nine. And…she still hasn't given me all the details. I haven't pressed her for information. She's been through a lot. She did what she had to do to survive."

CJ nodded. "Smart girl. But what you're telling me raises a lot of questions."

"I know. But I don't think it's fair to treat her like a criminal or even a target that needs to be sent back to Daemonia. She doesn't belong there, CJ."

"She *didn't* belong there. When you were kids."

That comment bit. Hard. Where did Jett belong now? Was she more demon than human? *Could* she exist as a mere human now?

"So now she's back in the mortal realm," CJ said. "And she's living with a demon reckoner."

"I probably wouldn't have been her first choice for a roommate, but it's how things played out. I was there at the right time. I have to believe we were meant to find each other."

"There are no coincidences. The universe knows exactly what it is doing." CJ nodded. "Yes, you were meant to help her. Or, at the very least, to have her in your sight so she was accounted for."

Savin winced at that explanation. He didn't like CJ's manner of seeing things in more than one way. And not always the best way, either.

"So…you didn't tell Ed and me because you thought she wasn't a problem. She's not a threat to humans."

"She's not. Jett wants to live a normal life. But there's something else you need to know. She just told me. It changes things. I don't want it to change things. And maybe it doesn't have to if everyone involved has all the information and we look at all the options rationally and with Jett's best interests in mind."

The dark witch lifted his chin. "And that is the 'something else' I need to know?"

Savin pressed his lips together and squeezed his eyelids shut. This was not a betrayal against Jett. It couldn't be. He only wanted to help her.

He opened his eyes and said, "Jett is the missing queen."

Gloriana Thorne strolled into the kitchen and set the plate she was carrying on the counter. She turned and, with an assessing summation, took in Jett from head to toe. Jett remembered Savin's mother as always smiling and friendly to a fault. She'd eaten over at their house often and had even stayed some nights when she and Savin would watch a movie, popcorn in hand, and fall asleep on the couch.

"You've grown up," Gloriana finally said. "You're beautiful, Jett."

"Thank you." She lifted her chin. The darkness within loved to be complimented. "You haven't changed at all. Very glamorous. Savin always called you his movie-star mama. Did he…" She worried her lower lip, but again, her darkness would not allow her to cower or feel less-than. She was who she was, and damned proud of it. "Did Savin tell you everything?"

"He did."

"Even about…"

"The demon place?" Gloriana sat on a stool and patted the stool next to her, which Jett slid onto. "I always took everything Savin said about demons and such with a huge grain of salt. But I've watched him over the years.

He was not a boy, nor is he now a man, who lies with any sort of ease. I can't imagine he made it all up. Even knowing how he loved to play those silly make-believe games about dragons when you two were young."

"He didn't make anything up. I swear it to you."

Gloriana shook her head. "I believe you. Because for you to suddenly appear after twenty years? There's something to all those tales Savin told me. I've known it since he first told me when he was a child. Here." She shoved the plate toward Jett and peeled back the plastic wrap to reveal delicate fan-shaped madeleine cakes. "We have a lot to talk about."

"Your Jett—the little girl you were once friends with—is the queen of Daemonia?" CJ leaned back against the dais, taking in that information. The witch looked flummoxed, and Savin could understand that feeling.

He was still out of sorts about the whole thing, and yet not. He knew where his alliances stood, and they were with Jett. She needed him. End of story.

Or was it a continuation of their story?

"Then all we need do is send her back to Daemonia," CJ said. "Close the rift, seal it and all is well. But I'm suspecting that is not your first choice in this problem-solving endeavor."

"I won't reckon Jett. She escaped that place, CJ. She was taken there against her will and forced to survive. Now that she's free I will do everything in my power to ensure that freedom."

The witch nodded, yet Savin did not release his clenched fists. He wasn't angry; he was feeling his power. Let no man stand against him.

"Then Paris will be overrun with demons," CJ stated simply.

"We can find another way. There's another queen," Savin said. "Jett told me that she—we—were taken by the queen and then that queen disappeared, leaving Jett behind to assume the throne. What was her name you read in the book?"

"Fuum. You think that queen escaped to the mortal realm, as well?"

"Possible. We have to search for her."

"How? Where? If Jett has been there twenty years, that means Fuum may have been here twenty years. She may no longer be in Paris. She might be dead. Who knows?"

"It's a long shot, but I owe Jett that much. I have to search for the other queen. You've got spells to track demons. I've seen you do it before."

"Yes, but to locate a specific one? Do we even know who she is?"

"What does the book say about her?"

"Right." CJ returned to the Bibliodaemon and read aloud, "Fuum. It says she did escape to the mortal realm by transforming herself into an incorporeal demon. I would assume she's taken on a human body since. But there's nothing more on her after that." CJ tapped the page. "Ed needs to know about this. He's assembling troops as we speak, Savin. I don't think it'll be long before the humans notice demons, perhaps even get hurt by them. The influx is increasing."

"Then I've got my work cut out for me. As do you. I need a tracking spell for the former queen. Can you fashion something using the info in that book?"

"I...might be able to." CJ jumped down again to stand

before Savin, and this time his gaze wasn't so much delving as compassionate. "Are you sure this woman is worth it?"

"She's my best friend, CJ."

"Is she really? She's lived in the Place of All Demons for twenty years. Hell, a lot longer according to how time works there. Are you sure she's the same person you once knew? You were kids then. And she is, at the very least, half demon now. If I were her, I'd use every trick in the book to maintain a rapport with the reckoner who rescued me. To keep him from reckoning me. And to stay under the radar until…"

"Until? CJ, she's one tiny human woman with an unfortunate past and a huge desire to step as far away from that past as possible. I promise you, she's not a threat to anyone. I will personally take the blame if she does become a nuisance. And I can say that because I know and trust her."

CJ put up both hands in surrender. "Very well."

Gloriana had suggested they go outside for a walk in the subdued fall sunshine while they talked. So, with a madeleine in each hand and sunglasses in place, they walked beneath the shade of chestnut trees creeping over the chain-link that surrounded a public garden.

"You're quite remarkable," Gloriana offered. "To have survived what I can only imagine are incredible horrors. I never wanted to think too much about the place Savin described to me, but I confess it was difficult not to imagine…things. How are you, Jett? Here." She tapped her temple.

"I feel fine. I mean, I know I'm not fine. I know it's called having baggage. And I have a lot. But all I want is to get back to normal. To be a regular woman and to forget all about that time away." She finished off the last madeleine. "I've been thinking about contacting my mom, but I'm not so sure it's the right thing to do. If she believes me dead, maybe that's better."

Gloriana heaved out a sigh. "She was devastated by your loss. And then with the divorce… Well, she's been through a lot. But it has been twenty years. She might be able to face this new trial. And it's not a trial, is it? She'd be getting her daughter back."

"Gloriana, did my mother ever tell you I was adopted?"

"No. I'd forgotten about that. Oh, dear, I must confess something to you. Your mother had never mentioned anything of the sort to me, but when I was looking for things to rescue from your abandoned house, I did happen upon the adoption papers. It was a surprise to me at the time. And I haven't looked in the envelope I stuffed all that information into for…well, over a decade. You just reminded me of that now. Is that the first you learned, when reading those papers?"

"Yes. It was a surprise."

"I'm sorry. But you must know your parents loved you so much."

"I do know that. And I can accept it. But I'm still not sure it would be wise to contact my mother. And if I did? How to tell her the truth? She would never believe I've spent the past twenty years living amongst demons," Jett said plainly.

"Most certainly not. I think it best you maintain the story Savin initially told the police about being abducted."

"Perhaps. I'd have to invent some details. I'll think about it. I want you to know, Gloriana, that Savin can trust me. I promise you. I'm not…evil." At least, she hoped she was not.

"Yes, well, I hadn't considered that until you brought it up." She angled across the street toward their departing point. "Do you know Savin once told me something when he was nine? He said he was going to marry you when he grew up. And he might even consider kissing you, too."

"He did?" Jett felt a blush ride the back of her neck. Well, she'd felt the same way then. Yet it hadn't been an adult longing, a sensual kind of attraction between them then. Kid stuff.

Things had changed. He'd kissed her. And so much more.

"Yes, and I would pat his head and tell him he should go right ahead and do that. But to wait until he got a bit older." Gloriana sighed heavily as they neared the front door of Savin's building. "But now?"

Jett brushed her palms together to disperse a few cake crumbs. "Now?"

"I have to be honest, Jett, I certainly hope you don't attempt to sway my son's head toward his ridiculous childhood fantasy of marriage. I could not condone it."

Jett's jaw dropped open.

"If what Savin has told me is true, you're a…why, you're a creature."

"I, uh—no," Jett said on a gasp. Tears pooled at the corners of her eyes.

"Oh, *cherie,* I know you didn't ask to be taken away and kept amongst those nasty creatures, but it's the truth. And my son has only ever fought to keep the streets of Paris safe from your sort."

The way she said *your sort* hurt Jett's heart.

Gloriana ignored Jett's obvious dismay. "You have to look at things from his perspective. He rids the city of demons. You are one of those...awful things."

Over Gloriana's shoulder Jett noticed a figment of black mist forming. Her senses immediately picked up demon, and the sulfurous scent spilled into the air and her nostrils. Along with that she could only think, *Danger.*

She grabbed Gloriana by the shoulder. "You need to get inside now!"

"Unhand me!" The woman shook off Jett's grip and clutched her purse to her chest. "You see? You're wild. A thing!"

"It's coming at you!" Jett lunged to push Gloriana against the brick wall.

As she did so, she heard Savin shout from down the sidewalk, "No!"

Chapter 22

At sight of Jett attacking his mother, Savin charged forward. He managed to shove her away and wrapped an arm around his mother, moving in front of her to block her from Jett.

"What the hell?" he blasted at Jett.

"Didn't you see it? The mist demon?" Jett protested.

He had not seen anything but Jett attacking his mother. And if a demon had been that close to Gloriana, he would have seen it, no matter its speed. Savin turned his back to Jett and slid his hand down the side of his mother's head as he inspected her face. "Are you okay?"

She was startled but smiled up at him. "Yes, I'm fine. I'm glad you arrived when you did." She glanced over his shoulder to Jett. "What's wrong with her?"

"It wasn't me," Jett insisted from behind him. "There was a demon."

"I didn't sense anything," Savin said. "A mist demon? Those are obvious, Jett."

Jett dropped her mouth open, at a loss for words.

"I'm going to take my mother home. All right, Maman?"

"Yes, please, Savin. I'm feeling shaken. I was only being nice to her."

"It's okay. Where's your car?"

"I didn't drive here. I took the metro."

"My truck is in the lot. Come on."

With an arm around his mother's shoulders, he walked away from Jett without looking back. He couldn't bear to look at her after watching her bodily fling herself at his mother. And a sniff at the air did not scent sulfur. Mist demons were smelly. And even after they'd gone, their scent lingered. And if not for a noticeable scent, he should have felt the thing's hum before even getting close.

"She came at me so angrily," Gloriana said. "Why would she do that?"

"What did she say to you?" he asked as he and his mother turned the corner.

"She didn't say anything. She just lunged. I think I might guess why. I had told her I didn't want her involved with you. She reacted. She's a wild thing, Savin. Jett Montfort is not the same girl you were friends with twenty years ago."

After witnessing the attack, he had to agree.

Even if his mother had said something so inconsiderate to her, Jett had no right to attack. In broad daylight on the sidewalk with so many walking by.

Had he missed something? *Had* there been a demon?

He stopped before the passenger door of his truck and helped his mother up and inside. She clasped his hand, still shaking. No matter what had gone down, he would find out.

* * *

Jett watched Savin walk away with his mother. He'd yelled at her. Had believed she had been trying to attack his mother.

Her chest ached and her throat grew dry. She wanted to cry out for him to please listen to her, and that she would never harm his mother. Not anyone. But if he hadn't seen the mist demon, then she had no proof of her innocence. It certainly must have looked as though she were attacking Gloriana.

Without a glance back at her, Savin turned the corner.

And Jett kicked the door to the building. "Damn it!" Had she just lost Savin's trust?

She had reacted. Thinking to grab Gloriana and pull her away from the demon, which was gone now. Why had it dared to materialize like that in public?

The darkness inside Jett straightened. She knew. It had wanted her to see it. To challenge her to act out in public. Did it know she was the queen? Had they already sent minions to find and retrieve her?

"Let them try," she said, curling her fingers into fists. "They will have a fight."

And then she dropped her tight pose and bowed her head. She didn't want this. Not here in the mortal realm. Would she ever be free from what Daemonia had made her?

Savin returned to his place after nightfall. His mother had still been shaken when he walked her up to the front door, so he'd sat with her awhile. When she'd begun to sweep the spotless kitchen, he knew she was getting back to herself. In that time, his anger had settled. And he'd given the incident some thought. Jett would never have purposely tried to harm his mother.

He wanted to believe that.

Finding a half-full bottle of whiskey on top of the fridge, he then sat on the couch and picked up the diddley bow. A slip of the glass slide across the string would send out wicked vibrations to any nearby demons. Jett was not here, so he didn't worry about how it would affect her.

Did he care?

A mist demon. He'd seen them before. They were exactly as they sounded: a swirl of insignificant black mist. Red eyes seemed to bobble within the figment about head level. Sometimes they possessed a sharp tail that could snap around and slash across flesh, searing through blood and bone as it cut deeply.

He'd not seen it. But had it already fled by the time he'd noticed Jett lunging for his mother? Had the shadows created by the overhang from the building disguised the ghostlike creature? They could be fast, misting out of sight as quickly as they had a tendency to appear.

He wanted to give Jett the benefit of the doubt. And he should talk to her, listen to her side of the story. But she wasn't here. He'd not expected her to be here. If she didn't return tonight, he figured it was because she truly was guilty and couldn't bear to face him.

He grabbed the whiskey bottle and took a long swallow. He fitted the glass slide on his middle finger. Time to dally with some demons.

Jett returned to Savin's home well after dark. Despite knowing she was probably not welcome here now, she had nowhere else to go. She hadn't money to stay at a hotel. And while the cemetery might have provided a private place to snuggle up against a tombstone for the night, it had begun to rain. She was finding it difficult to keep her sheen on with the fresh water falling from the sky.

She hated feeling so dependent on another. *It is beneath you.*

She nodded in agreement as she took the stairs upward. How easy it would be to simply let go and be and look the way she really was. But worry over Savin's opinion of her appearance aside, she still had to think about the reactions from other humans. Not a wise move.

At the front door, she paused with her palm facing the demonic wards. She felt them more acutely than she ever had. She was growing weaker. She had to either drop the sheen to get past the wards, or else suffer a wicked pull to cross the threshold.

She glanced along the floor and to the corner of the hallway not five feet away. The idea of settling in for the night curled up in a ball did not appeal. And besides, she was not one to give up and hang her head in defeat.

With a heavy sigh, and an inhalation of bravery, she gripped the doorknob and turned it. It wasn't locked. But as she crossed the threshold, her body felt the electric prickles and vibrations that fought to keep her out. She was still too strong for expulsion, but oh, that hurt. Right in her heart. It thudded loudly and her nerves twinged, curdling a moan in her throat.

Stepping inside and closing the door shut off the wards. Jett pressed her forehead against the wall, breathing in deeply to work through the lingering pain. Savin had not loosened the wards as much as usual. And she could guess why.

It was time she figured out how to survive, how to

get money and to support herself. She had a way to get in touch with her mother. Would she help her?

Creeping in through the kitchen, Jett paused in the living room. Savin lay on the couch, a whiskey bottle not far from the hand that was splayed out over the floor. His legs stretched across the hardwood.

"Savin?" she whispered. "Is it okay that I stay here tonight?"

With a grunt, he rustled, obviously sleeping, or had been very close. "Jett? Was worried about you."

"You were?"

He made a come-here gesture with his fingers. Jett approached, smelling the whiskey and sensing he'd probably used the alcohol to drown his apprehensions about her. Warranted.

"I'm sorry," she said softly. "I wasn't trying to hurt her. But if you didn't see the mist demon, then I understand how it was difficult to believe me."

"It's over," he muttered, still teasing sleep, for his eyes were closed. "Sit here."

She sat on the edge of the couch, and his torso hugged up against her derriere. He was so warm, and beyond the whiskey he smelled dark and delicious.

"I should let you sleep," she said.

"Yes. Long day. Tired," he muttered. "Kiss me? Good…night?"

That was either the whiskey talking or— Jett wasn't going to overanalyze the request. Any chance to kiss the man would be met. Always.

She bent and kissed Savin. The arm he'd had outstretched wrapped across her back, but not possessively. He was sleeping and dreaming or maybe in a half-wakeful reverie. So she would make it the best dream he'd ever had. Straddling him on the couch, she deepened the kiss, diving into his whiskey sweetness and tasting his throaty growl. The man's body was solid and hard beneath her legs and chest, and she pressed her breasts against him. Her nipples hardened, stirring her need for pleasure.

He didn't seem awake enough to want to have sex, but when his hand slid up under her shirt, she pulled it up higher to give him access to her bare breasts. Mmm, that soft, not-so-focused touch giddied her. And then she felt him resist with a slight shove against her rib cage. The demon within him?

"Shh…" Jett kissed him again, lulling him toward sleep. "Let's just hold each other."

She didn't need to make love to him. And right now she had a more important goal. She wanted to dig in and see if she could read the demon lurking inside her lover. And she might be able to if Savin agreed, or…if he were not fully in his senses. Taking his slight nod as a signal he approved of her suggestion as permission, she glided her fingernails down his chest. A kiss to his firm mouth. A brush of her lips over his beard. She nuzzled her cheek against his. He was like a big cuddly cat whose purrs were more like wanting growls.

His hand at her breast dropped the clutch as he drifted into reverie.

Fine with her. And much better if he wasn't fully aware.

Jett bowed her head and focused within on her darkness, summoning her demon. She would not shift, but she would use the skills she had learned while sitting the throne. Reading others was a necessity for survival and everyday rituals such as assessing work tasks and punishments. Incorporeal demons were tricky and liked to hide out in human bodies or even another demon.

The only way to tap into them was to send her detection senses through skin and bone, moving like an invisible finger to touch the demon's essence.

Digging in her nails, but not so firmly that they drew blood, Jett pressed her fingertips about Savin's left pectoral, right above where his heartbeat had slowed to a relaxed pace. Whispering a word to command obeisance, Jett connected.

The Other within him jerked and lifted her head. She knew Jett was coming in but was not so subservient to allow it with ease.

Jett had to move quickly. She forced out her influence through her fingers and swirled it in through Savin's skin and muscle and felt the tug as she entered him and saw the Other. With her eyes closed, a figment of the one who inhabited Savin formed in Jett's mind. Tall, lithe, long hair and…so ancient. She had served…something. It wasn't clear to her yet. Yes, a female…

…that she recognized.

The Other growled and Savin's body jerked. The incorporeal demon inside him fought back at Jett's intrusion with a remarkable power of her own. Jett's fingers left Savin's chest as she was bodily flung away and off the couch to land on the floor in a sprawl. She lifted her head and eyed the sleeping reckoner. Thank goodness, he hadn't woken.

And yet she knew exactly who she had seen. That bitch!

Understanding emerged. What a foul and wicked plan the Other had taken. Her name was not Other, though. It was Fuum.

"Very tricky," she muttered. "Now the game has changed."

Chapter 23

Savin shut off the shower and heard his cell phone ring. Hand dripping, he reached out and grabbed the phone. "Ed, what do you got?"

"A news report about the sudden, strange increase in demonic possessions. It's on France 24."

"What? Humans don't believe in that crap. Well, you know. The smart ones don't."

"In a perfect world they would all believe it myth. Apparently, exorcists are getting a workout. And the possessions are focused specifically here in Paris."

Savin blew out a breath. He hadn't heard from John Malcolm. Was it because he was too busy?

"CJ was able to work out a tracking spell for the queen," Ed said. "We're going to activate it as quickly as possible. I'd like you to be there."

"I can…"

Could he walk in and watch as the guys attempted a spell that would ultimately, if it worked, lead them to Jett? Savin stepped out of the tub and slapped the dry towel over a shoulder. Had CJ told Ed about Jett and the fact that there was another queen out there somewhere?

"How about in a few hours?" Ed said. "At my office."

"Sure. I'll see you soon."

He set the phone on the vanity, then pulled the towel off his shoulder and used it on his hair. He'd woken on the couch this morning and had snuck past Jett, lying in the bed, and into the bathroom. She was probably still snoozing. It was only around 7:00 a.m.

He remembered her coming in late last night and he'd asked her for a kiss. He might have been swimming in whiskey and half-asleep, but he'd felt the intensity of their touch and could not deny he'd needed it. And then something strange had happened that he wasn't too clear on. Had Jett been disgusted by their kiss? She'd pulled away from him so quickly. And...he had dozed pretty fast after that. He didn't have a clear memory of what had gone on.

Whew! He never overdid it on the whiskey like that. What the hell was wrong with him? He had to get it together. Had his whole life suddenly turned upside down because of a woman? While most men would find that fact strangely welcome, he wasn't sure how to take it. Because was the woman in his scenario even human?

Wrapping the towel about his hips, he opened the bathroom door to find Jett sitting up on the end of the bed, waiting for him. She was naked. Looking every inch a human. It didn't take long for his erection to rise and salute beneath the towel.

"Morning," he mumbled.

"We need to talk." She patted the bed beside her.

"Sure, but, uh, it's going to be mighty hard for me to concentrate with you doing your Venus thing."

"My Venus thing? Oh. Sorry." She grabbed a T-shirt from the pillow and pulled it on. "But what about you, looking all Greek god and glistening with water— Ah, shit, Savin, I have to tell you this. I can't get distracted by all that…candy."

"Candy?" He smirked. Never heard his abs called candy before.

All right, so he was on board with the woman fucking up his life a bit. But she was right. They did need to talk. And both were aware of how far that talk would progress if they were not fully clothed.

He pulled up the blanket from the bed and wrapped it about his shoulders. "Better?"

"Sure. But not really. Just sit." Impatient, she got off the bed and paced before him as he sat on the end. "I know we're still not okay with the thing that happened to your mother. You may never believe me—"

"My mother wasn't hurt, just more scared by your sudden need to grab her. For now, let's pretend it never happened. I think that can work for both of us. Okay?"

"If you say so. But your mother hates me now."

"We'll leave that for her to worry about. So what do you want to talk about? Is it about last night? Sorry, I was in my cups, as they say. If I said or did something wrong…"

"No. It wasn't you, it was me. I was bold. I shouldn't have— But I had to know—"

He grabbed her hand, stopping her pacing. "I don't know what you're trying to tell me, but you need to know what's going on out there. Ed reports the influx of demons is growing. Incorporeal demons are taking up residence in humans. The exorcists are busy."

"I suspected as much. My skin crawls with recognition of so many demon entities," she said, meeting him with a direct and defiant look. "You need to send back the queen."

Savin nodded. "That seems to be the fix. Ed wants me to meet him this afternoon. The dark witch has developed a tracking spell for the queen. I'm hoping it can locate the old one, but we don't even know if she is in Paris."

"She's right here," Jett said.

"I know that, but I still haven't figured a way to avoid the spell zooming in on you."

"I'm not talking about myself. When I said she's right here…" Jett pulled her hand from his clutch and placed it over his heart. "I mean, she's right here. Inside you."

"What?"

"Savin, last night when we were making out on the couch…I sort of took advantage of you. You were… I needed to get answers, so I looked inside you. I was able to briefly connect with and see the demon within you. And I recognized her."

Stunned that she'd done such a thing, without his permission, Savin wanted to charge out of the room. But something kept him on the bed. A shiver inside him. The demoness knew that Jett had seen her. What did the Other fear?

"You *know* her?" he asked.

Jett nodded. "She's the one who had us brought to Daemonia. Savin, the demon who hitched a ride in you is Fuum, the former queen. The one who kidnapped me and put me in her place so she could escape. I know it. I felt her and she felt me."

"Fuum." The same name CJ had read in the Bibliodaemon. The former queen who had disappeared from Daemonia.

The shivering inside Savin turned to a jitter. His arms and hands began to shake. A piercing burn stretched from throat to gut. This was not a nervous reaction to hearing the uncomfortable truth about his latest romantic entanglement. Savin had experienced this before. And it never ended well.

"Leave," he said curtly.

"What?"

"Just get out of the apartment. She's going to blow."

"She's—" Jett nodded. "You can't control her?"

"Not when she gets angry." He stood and stretched out his arms, the blanket dropping behind him. "Oh, man, it burns inside me."

"Unhand him!" Jett cursed. "Or I will make you regret it!"

Savin gritted his teeth. His body moved toward Jett, and his feet felt as if the Other controlled them as he tried to stop the movement. The Other was pushing him, commanding him.

"Get the morphine," he managed through a tight jaw.

Jett searched the cabinet top. "Where is it?"

"In the living room."

She ran out and he heard her collect something. Savin punched the wall and shouted because his knuckles opened and blood ran out. "You're the queen?" he said to his disgruntled passenger. "I will send you back!"

Bodily, he threw himself against the wall. His shoulder

crunched upon impact and he dropped. His entire body shook as the darkness within him went on a rampage.

Jett plunged to the floor beside him, and the stab of the needle entered his neck.

Savin swore at the pain. He grabbed Jett by the shirt and whipped her across the room. It hadn't been him! She landed hard against the cabinet, toppling the demonic devices. With a shake of her head, Jett said something in the Daemonic language and then…she shifted.

Chapter 24

She had never wanted to drop her sheen before Savin. But now was no time for vanity. Or to be ashamed of her true nature. The demon inside Savin was powerful, and the Other was determined to hurt him, and Jett, at all costs.

Even as her horns grew out and over her ears, Jett lunged forward and gripped Savin by the shoulders. The connection, her hands to his skin, shocked her influence into him and jolted the demoness. Savin yowled, but it wasn't his voice that sounded, but rather the former queen's.

"You can't make me harm him, you nasty bitch," Jett said firmly. "But I will make you regret ever hitching a ride in my best friend."

Focusing her will, she seared a vicious hex through Savin's body and felt the demoness within shudder and jerk. Jett was more powerful than the one who had stolen her so many years ago, and she would make her know that now.

Savin's head rocked backward, hitting the wall. Jett held his shoulders firmly, exercising her strength over her enemy. Her lover slapped a hand through the air, landing it on Jett's waist. He gripped but did not clutch her for long. His arm dropped weakly. He couldn't take much more of her influence coursing into his system. Two powerful hosts of darkness battled within him—and only one could win, rendering him incapacitated.

No. This wasn't the way. She did not want to hurt Savin.

Jett released him and stepped aside. Spreading back her arms, she drew in her vita from the prone man on the floor, retracting what darkness she had put out in an attempt to defeat Fuum. It came to her in sparks of crimson that electrified her system upon reentry.

The Other's vibrations shivered to nothing. Savin let out a gasping exhale as his demonic passenger relented. Fuum had been subdued thanks to Jett's intervention. And likely the morphine had kicked in. Savin's eyelids fluttered, but he managed to catch his palms against the wall so he did not drop to the floor. He glanced to her, mouth gaping.

Satisfied, Jett nodded and then was sweeping her hands over her head in preparation to pull up the sheen—when Savin grabbed her by the wrists.

"No. Don't put on a sheen," he said. "It's getting harder for you, isn't it?"

Suddenly humiliated to be standing before one she wanted to see her in only the best light, Jett bowed her head and nodded.

His eyes took her in, gliding along her dark gray skin and up over her face, which she knew altered slightly, narrowing, the flesh clinging to the bone. And then the horns that she'd learned to take pride in captured his attention.

"You're beautiful, Jett. It doesn't offend me to look at you like this."

"You might want to believe that. And speaking it sounds good to both you and me. But now that you've seen my true appearance, you'll never forget it." She sighed. "I am this thing, Savin."

"You are Jett." He reached to touch her horn, but she flinched away and he retracted his hand to his chest.

"I'm sorry," she said. "I didn't mean to hurt you."

"You didn't. Just zapped the strength out of me for a bit there. I know you were fighting her."

"She knows who I am," Jett said. "And she knows that I know who she is. I've subdued her, but she takes her strength from you. You are a strong and mighty man. She'll rise soon enough."

"I know. But I think the morphine kicked in. I know when it does. I feel her make a sort of giddy shiver. It's...weird."

"I'm so sorry you need to do that. You shouldn't have to."

"The drug used to affect me, but I've become immune to it over the years. Either that or she sucks it all up before it can even influence my system. I don't miss getting high, that's for sure."

"Have you tried to expel her?"

He nodded. "Yes, it won't work."

"But exorcists—"

"John Malcolm has tried to exorcise her. No go. And

I can't reckon her out of my own body. It's just not possible. And…well, some sacrifices aren't worth it. Like I've said, I've learned to live with her."

"But now you don't have to. If we can get her out of you and you can reckon her back to Daemonia, then I won't have a thing to worry about."

"That sounds great. In theory."

Jett lifted her head but remembered her horns. No matter what he said, she knew he could only ever see her as *not human* from now on. She swept her hands over her head and pulled on the sheen. Her body segued from tight and muscled to firm and pale skinned and the horns receded with an inward tug.

And Savin pulled her to him and kissed her, drawing her body against his and pressing into her as if they could become one. His mouth tasted her slowly, deeply. The feel of his body, so commanding and strong against hers, weakened her need for shame, to believe that he could not adore her. Dare she hope they could have a future together?

"That's how much you offend me," he said as he withdrew from the kiss. "I know that's what you were thinking. But don't waste your well-being on such thoughts. We're good."

His words brought tears to her eyes. "How can we be?"

"I know a lot about demons, and where you've come from. And I know you, as well. Oh, sweetie, don't cry."

She sniffed and wiped at a teardrop. "You only know the nine-year-old me. I've changed, Savin."

"Have you?"

"Of course, I—I've matured. I've changed! And I'm not an innocent."

"Never thought you were."

"I really do want to be human again. And oh, when you kiss me. Savin." She stepped out of his embrace and crossed her arms over her chest, immediately regretting the distance from him, but feeling she had to tell him her thoughts or risk losing him forever. "I've been with… others. It was a means to learn and experience— Well, I am a woman. I couldn't ignore my changing body or my growing desires."

His expression softened, but he didn't say anything.

"I thought that sex was what pleasure was. You know? It's what I received and I knew nothing else. But now. Here. With you. When you touch me and kiss me. Oh. I know now that what I had then was never true pleasure. Only you have shown me that. And when you look at me, I see in your eyes such honesty and…is it admiration?"

"It is, Jett. And I'm glad I've been able to make you feel good. But I wish when you looked in my eyes you could see that I trust you, too."

"Be honest, Savin. We stand on opposite sides. How can we each ever truly trust the other will work for our best interest?"

"You can trust me because I give you my word. I… wasn't able to protect you when we were kids. That kills me. And I've atoned for that ever since. But now? I will protect you, Jett. You have my word. And we'll find some way to send the Other back to Daemonia. I promise you."

She nodded, still not willing to completely trust him. He believed he could do such a thing, but was it possible? That be-damned conniving queen! She was to blame for all this. And all this time Fuum had hidden away inside

Savin, him not being the wiser that he harbored the very demon who had irreversibly changed both their lives.

"I need to go meet with Ed," he said. "He and CJ have a tracking spell for the queen. Maybe it's time you come along and I introduce you?"

"So you can offer me as a sacrifice?"

"Never. I just want Ed to understand that you are no threat to any in this realm, and that our focus needs to be directed on the other queen."

"I am not a threat." Jett shivered and wrapped her arms across her chest. Was she? Every day she felt the darkness within her recede. And that was a good thing. Now to fight for her right to remain here, as a human. "If you think it will help, I'll come along. And if it's a trap, then so be it."

He kissed her. Hard. Then bowed his forehead to hers. "How do I make you trust me?"

"You earn it."

He nodded. "Then I will."

Chapter 25

When Jett and Savin walked through the door, Edamite Thrash turned abruptly from his position standing before the windows at the end of his vast, ultrasleek office. He pulled his hands from his trouser pockets, and his fingers flexed into claws.

Jett felt his gaze go right to her and she sensed his discomfort and recognition. She also recognized him as a fellow demon, but his vibrations were cool and quite different from what she was accustomed to. He was kind; she knew that. But also leery of her. He wore an aura of restrained power and she guessed he would not hesitate to wield it against any who betrayed him, or who had done wrong.

A corax demon, she knew, could shift to an unkindness of ravens and fly off, then shift back to human shape, clothing intact. The demonic sigils visible on his neck above the white dress shirt resembled a black raven's feather. As well, sigils decorated his hands, but most were covered by the half gloves that must conceal the thorns she knew grew on all corax demons' knuckles.

"Ed, I want you to meet Jett Montfort," Savin said as they stopped in the middle of the marble-floored office. He still held her hand, which provided her the added courage she required because she hadn't known what to expect from this visit. But now that she had read Edamite, she knew she could control him. If need be.

Ed crossed the room and shook Savin's hand, and then the demon with the slicked-back dark hair looked to Jett. He didn't extend his hand to shake, and his brows quirked. "Demon."

Savin nodded. "She's my friend. I've known her since we were kids."

Further consternation crimped Ed's brow.

"I need to catch you up on things," Savin said, "and I ask you to listen without judgment. I told CJ about her yesterday. I want you to have the same information."

Ed crossed his arms high on his chest. His eyes did not waver from Jett. And she held her gaze firm, yet softened it, not intending to throw out any defensive vibes. But she held her sheen on tight. For now.

Savin laid it all out. How Jett had escaped to the mortal realm that night when the rift to Daemonia opened. How she'd been staying with him since then, and how he'd just learned she had been their queen. A title she had assumed for survival, he made clear.

"She is not a threat to anyone in the mortal realm," Savin finished. "Nor to you or me."

Ed, who had taken to leaning against his desktop, stood now and wandered to the marble-topped bar along the wall. He poured a shot of whiskey and drank it. Then he offered Savin a drink, but he refused. The corax demon let his gaze fall slowly over Jett. He didn't offer her a drink, but she wouldn't expect it, either. He didn't trust her.

If this man had taken it upon himself to protect Paris and police the local demon population, then he was doing a good thing for the humans. And it ultimately protected him and those demons who simply wanted to exist and not ruffle feathers. Without knowing her personally, Jett could only be a threat to him.

Unless she could prove otherwise. And she hadn't a clue how to do that.

Ed let out a hefty exhale and approached them. Now his demonic vibrations felt a bit stronger. Jett lifted her chin, forcing out her influence as a warning. The demon stopped and nodded, sensing her challenge.

"This fucks things up," he finally said.

Indeed.

"It doesn't have to," Savin said. "What if we can exorcise the demon from inside me and send her back in Jett's place?"

Savin had also told Ed that she recognized the Other as the former queen, Fuum.

Ed nodded, finger to his lips in thought. "Possibly. But I thought—"

"Yeah. Exorcism is out. How easily I forget that." Savin now walked over to the bar and poured himself that shot of whiskey. After tilting it back, he turned to Jett and silently inquired if she wanted any. She shook her head. "So that's what we've got to work with right now."

"A mess?" Ed posited.

Savin shrugged and poured another two fingers, quickly making work of the amber liquid.

Should she sacrifice and go back to Daemonia? It was the sure way to close the rift. And as Ed had mentioned, humans were beginning to notice the outflow from that realm. Possessions were occurring frequently. The news media were reporting exorcisms on the rise. And in Paris specifically. They could not let the rift remain unclosed for much longer.

But she didn't suggest she be the sacrificial lamb. She desperately did not want that to happen.

"How can we get Fuum out of you?" Jett finally asked Savin. "There must be a way, beyond exorcism. The dark witch might know a way."

"I've talked with him about it." Savin poured another shot. "There is a way. And you know it." He and Ed exchanged glances that Jett could not read. They knew something they were not telling her.

"What is it?" she asked. "If you need my help…"

"There is one way to scrub the demon out of Savin," Ed offered. "And that requires his death."

Jett tugged Savin's hand, forcing him to turn and look at her. "Is that true?"

Savin shrugged noncommittally.

Ed said again, "Yes, it is true. He's gone over this with Certainly Jones. Years ago, the witch found an expulsion spell for Savin's situation, but it'll kill Savin to remove the demon within. And now I figure it is because she was once a queen. Very powerful. I assume she's been able to root into him."

"It's nothing," Savin said to Jett, and he looked away.

But Jett wasn't about to let him dismiss it so casually. "It's not nothing. It is your life."

"Sending the Other back to Daemonia will close up the rift and save you," he said.

Jett dropped his hand and crossed her arms. "There will be no sacrificing of one's life today."

"Then we'll do it tomorrow," Savin said coolly.

"I'm not going to let you do that," Ed said. "There's got to be another way to get that bitch out of you, Thorne. And I'm siding with your girlfriend. No sacrifices."

"Yet you would sacrifice me," Jett said defiantly to the corax demon.

His smirk was more evil than he might have wanted to display. "I don't know you enough to trust you. And you *are* their current queen."

"What if I can find a replacement? Such as the one inside Savin did with me? As long as there is a queen to sit the throne, then that legion in Daemonia should be appeased."

Ed shrugged. "There is a time element here. Your kind are flooding the mortal realm."

"My kind? They are your kind, too, Edamite Thrash. More so, because I assume you are full demon. I am not. Do you forget that?" She beat her fist against her chest. "Half of me is human. And I can feel my demon side growing weaker every day."

Ed approached her, hand out and palm facing her. Jett backed up, and when her shoulder nudged Savin, he put an arm around her waist and held her protectively.

"We're not going to sacrifice Jett, either," he said to Ed. "What are you doing?"

"I'm just trying to get a read on her." The demon did not relent.

And so Jett would give him what he wanted. She pulled out of Savin's grip and pressed both her palms to Ed's temples, forming a connection that would open them both to each other. She saw his life, his triumphs and failures. His love—he loved a beautiful witch. And she touched his raven core that squawked and beat its wings frantically at her unwelcome invasion.

At the same time, she gave him her truth. Her fall into the lava, which had burned and iced at the same time. Her hurried and bewildered ascension to the throne, and her desperate need to do as she was told for survival. She showed her ability to put a vile demon to heel, her ease at reading all others and her unrelenting power.

When finally Ed was able to push away from her, he stumbled backward, catching himself against the desktop.

"What did you do to him?" Savin asked.

"I gave him my truth. And I showed him who his queen really is."

"You are never my queen," Ed said with a sneer. "I am not from Daemonia. They are all...filth." Jett lunged, but Savin caught her about the waist. "But...you are right," Ed continued. "Your human half is growing more prominent. Should we send you back to Daemonia now, you may not—"

"It's not happening," Savin interrupted. "Jett stays in this realm. Done deal. So let's come up with another plan."

Ed eyed Jett and she saw in his eyes defeat and a reluctant submission. He nodded. "Yes, another plan. CJ should be here by now. He mentioned tracking the queen. But if we know where both are...?"

Savin rubbed his chest. "Right. Hmm..."

"What if there is another?" Jett suggested.

"How many queens are there?" Savin asked.

She shrugged. "I don't know. How many queens does the world have? Many, yes? Fuum and I cannot be the only ones."

"I believe the specific queen for your Daemonian legion is the fix," Ed said. "There's CJ."

The glass office doors opened and Certainly Jones strode in. He took one look at Jett and slashed his hand before him. The sigils on his left hand glowed a bold emerald.

The repulsion spell pushed Jett off her feet and she landed in Savin's arms.

"CJ, this is Jett!" Savin said as he helped her to her feet. He charged toward the witch, who held his ground with palm extended and wards glowing. "Stand down!"

The dark witch thrust a glinting green hex toward Jett. She managed to dodge it and put up her palm in retaliation.

Ed called, "No! You cannot practice your demonic magic inside my wards!"

A second round of hex from the witch was this time caught by Savin, right on the chest, as he jumped to stand before Jett. Savin yelped and clutched his stinging chest.

The witch swore and reversed the spell, drawing back the magic into his hand, where he crumpled the hex and dropped it over a shoulder.

"What the hell? She's not going to harm anyone," Savin insisted. "Man, that hex hurt! Jett, stay by me." She clutched his hand, but he could feel her rage in the tight grip. "Settle," he cautioned her quietly.

"He was going to hex me!" she protested.

"Sorry. I may have rushed to a conclusion—" CJ started.

"This is ridiculous." Jett tore her hand from his grip and marched past the witch toward the door. "I am out of here!"

Savin took a step after her but then stopped. She needed to get out of here, away from the wicked energy of the lingering hex. One that still burned in his lungs. Whew! He glared at CJ.

The witch shrugged. "I didn't realize it was *your* Jett. It would have only shackled her, had you not taken the brunt."

"The brunt." Savin pressed his fingers to his chest and winced. All in all? That had been a mere tap. "You're slipping, witch. Didn't even knock me off my feet."

"It wasn't designed to—" CJ silenced himself with another glare from Savin.

"I told her she could trust the two of you," Savin said. "Good going. Now we've a Daemonian queen wandering the streets of Paris. And I'm going to wager she's pissed."

Jett charged across the street and raced blindly forward. Sure, Savin had tried to protect her. Feebly. The dark witch had actually blasted a stream of magic at her! What kind of hello, how are you, had that been?

She'd trusted Savin. Had he walked her into a trap?

Much as her darkness cajoled her to believe just that, Jett fought to remain on Savin's side. He'd been just as surprised as she when the witch walked in with hell blazing in his eyes.

She'd had to get away from them all. They needed to send a queen back to Daemonia to end the influx of demons into this realm, and she was an easy target.

Yet they had another option. The demoness who clung to Savin's soul. If he had so many friends like witches

and other demons, surely between them they could figure a way to oust Fuum from Savin's body and send her
back. It couldn't be that difficult to accomplish for men
who were demon, or as a reckoner whose sole task required him to have an intimate knowledge of demons.

However, to do it without killing Savin was key. She
didn't want that. Never.

Shoving roughly past a man talking on a cell phone,
Jett sneered when he flipped her off. If he only knew
how easily she could take away his voice.

Should she?

She paused at a red light and turned back to listen
to the man who walked a circle on the sidewalk. Some
kind of business chatter about stocks peaking. To buy or
sell? He talked so loudly. Was he not aware that everyone could hear him? Did no one respect personal boundaries anymore?

Jett muttered a few words that began a spell, but the
laughter of children interrupted her. Two kids, probably
around ten years old, ran down the sidewalk with kites
in hand. The moment curled into her chest and lessened
her anger. The darkness receded and she turned to face
the crossing. The light was green. She crossed without
concern for the noisy businessman.

Turning down a narrow alleyway, she rubbed her
palms over her arms, whisking away the tension. A walk
in the fresh air was what she needed. A few raindrops
splattered her cheeks and she actually smiled. Yes, she
really did want to exist in this realm. And to do so, she
had to get control over her darkness.

Or find a way to remove it from her completely. Could
the dark witch help with that? No, she didn't trust him
as far as she could spit.

A left turn and then another left lured her close to the scent of a river. She wasn't near the Seine, but she remembered a canal that jutted out from the river on the right bank where she walked. Had to be close.

The sudden sensation of another nearby—demon—slowed her pace. No. She didn't care. She must not. Let them be wary of her. If they were smart.

Venturing forward, she heard voices and slowed. Now the shiver of recognition shook her shoulders. A demon was just around the corner. He was powerful and... speaking to a human, if she guessed right. His sensual voice and promising words would appeal to any woman who wanted to be praised for her beauty.

Darkness rising, Jett tightened her fist. "There is only room for me in this realm." She rushed around the corner.

The human woman saw her and fled. And having lost his prey, the demon, who sported long dark dreadlocks and a furrowed brow, turned to growl at her. Fangs lowered and glinted. And when Jett sensed he would lunge for her, instead the demon cracked a smile and shook his head.

"It's about fucking time," he said. "You, my lovely bastard child, have been very naughty."

Chapter 26

Arms held slightly away from her body and fingers curled to ready as weapons, Jett walked a tight half curve about the demon who had just called her naughty. And… his child. Her entire body was tight and ready to defend. Yet as she took in the demon's arrogant grin and assessing gaze, she saw so many similarities between the two of them. Her breath left her in a hush.

"I heard you'd come to the mortal realm," he said, propping a hip against the brick wall and assuming a cocky pose before her.

He was lanky and his wrists were wrapped with leather straps and buckles. His arms, revealed by a sleeveless shirt, were blackened with so many tattoos Jett could not determine where one sigil began and another, possibly a skull design, ended. His hair was as dark as hers. And his nose long and…so much like hers. Eyes glowed red now that the human had fled. Jett could not determine if they had been brown, like hers. The one thing that drew her interest the longest was the glowing sigil between his brows that formed a symbol denoting his rank and heritage. Only demons of royal birth wore such, in various places on their bodies.

Jett absently touched her hip, where beneath the silk shirt a sigil to match the one on the man's forehead heated and glowed.

He noticed and nodded. "Yep, it's me. Daddy dearest! Sorry I didn't stick around for all that child-birthing stuff. Cramped my style. But look what I did for you. A queen! And then you flee the throne, you ungrateful bitch."

Jett lashed out and slapped his cheek, dragging her fingernails across the human skin he wore. Dark runnels of blackest blood oozed down his cheek, and she wiped the thick substance from her nails across her pants.

"Ah, that's sweet." He lashed out a very long tongue, licking away the blood even as the slashes healed. "So, you going to speak to me, or do I have to narrate this little tête-à-tête? One way or another, it's going to end with me kicking your ass back to Daemonia where you belong."

"I do not belong in the Place of All Demons," Jett hissed. Her body shivered, and she knew it was nerves, and fear. She mustn't cower before this vile man, father or not. She lifted her chin, assuming the regal mien she had grown to accept. "How dare you speak to me with such disrespect!"

The demon laughed in a low rumble and shook his head. "Fair enough. My girl knows how to play the queen, that's for sure."

"I am not your girl."

"Beg to differ, Jettendra. You've got my blood in your veins."

"And who else's? Did you rape a frightened human woman? Is that how I was conceived?"

He swiped a dismissive hand between them. "Rape is boring. I prefer seduction. And…" He blew out a breath. "I don't remember them all."

"You are despicable."

She stood before her demon father. And she had never felt more repulsed. Not even in the twenty years she had lived in Daemonia. He was vile and idiotic and— Hell, *this* was her father?

The demon held out his hand to shake. "Drav," he offered. "Seventh underlord of the clan Tratch."

Tratch. Yes. That was the legion she had ruled.

Jett considered his hand, and when she did not shake, he grabbed her arm and pulled her to him, chest to chest. His gaze held her speechless, and…she had not felt so helpless since that day she was tossed into the falls and taken to the throne.

"That's right," he said. "You grew to become a powerful half-breed, but you'll never be full demon like Daddy. Cocky is good. But you watch yourself, youngling. I can eviscerate you with a sweep of my hand. But I won't." He shoved her away from him. "Because we are going to get you on your way back to Daemonia so whoever is in charge can seal that damned rift and keep all the deplorables out of my territory."

His territory? Jett guessed Edamite Thrash might have qualms about such a bold statement.

"No one is going anywhere until I have the answers to the questions that have haunted me for years," Jett said. "And you may wish to believe you are stronger than me...but I have a reckoner on my side."

Drav mocked a shudder, which shook his dreads. "Yeah, I noticed. Disgusting. Why the hell did you hook up with him?"

"I don't owe you any details regarding my love life."

"Ah. It's a love life, is it? So you've fucked him. That is some kind of ill shit. Cripes. But hey, just means you're as fucked-up as your daddy. Good going!"

"Who are you?" Jett insisted, because she wasn't certain she could endure standing in the demon's presence for much longer without flaying him to a heap of demonic sludge. "Royalty? Why are you not in Daemonia sitting the throne yourself? And why me? Why kidnap an innocent child and force her to such servitude?"

"Servitude?" His laughter sounded like stones clacking against wood. Jett clenched her fists. "You were treated like the queen they made you, sweetie. Don't deny it."

"I was stolen from a safe home in the mortal realm and forced to another land to learn ways unfamiliar to me. I was a frightened child! They insisted I breed for them! I barely escaped becoming a broodmare."

"Yeah. Well. Had to be done. Fuum was getting antsy."

Jett gripped her father by the throat and squeezed. She pushed some of her influence in through his skin, and she could feel his skeletal structure shudder. "Fuum?"

"You are good at exerting influence," he managed through his compressed trachea. "Pain gets me off, sweetie."

Jett shoved him away from her, and his shoulders hit the wall so hard the brick cracked. The demon slipped on that malicious grin again and clapped slowly as he nodded in appreciation for her display of power.

"Enough with the dramatics," Jett said. "Tell me about you and Fuum."

Drav exhaled, his shoulders dropping. "Fine. We'll get the catching-up shit out of the way, and then down to the real nitty-gritty. Fuum. The worm bitch. I was having a fling with her at the time—"

"In Daemonia?"

"Sure. I used to go back and forth between realms all the time. The advantages of being born into legion governance. As a Tratch I was privileged and have always had the ability to move from one realm to the other at will. But you know that. You didn't need any special release to get here. You just had to wait for the right moment, eh?" He winked.

Jett sneered at him.

"Right. So we were getting it on, and Fuum wanted to come to this realm, and I was willing to help her. The best way to do that? Replace her seat at the throne with another queen."

"But I was not a queen," Jett protested.

Drav swiped a finger over a lingering trace of black blood on his cheek and showed it to her. "You had the royal blood, sweetie. And I had the influence. So I searched for my by-blow—uh, that would be you. You were an easy find."

"Your— How many half-blood children do you have?"

"Truth? Not a hell of a lot. Surprising, considering my frequent copulation habits—"

Jett put up an admonishing palm between them. "Just stick to the details."

"Right. I located my daughter who had been adopted because, well, your mom didn't survive the birth. That's kind of a side effect of having a demon's baby, if you're a human. Can't be avoided. Anyhoo. I found you and had you brought to Daemonia. Stupid little boy got taken along with you, though. That wasn't part of the plan. But then again, he did serve Fuum as a vessel to get to this realm. All in all, it worked out swell."

"I hate you."

"Yeah? That feels so good." He slid a palm over his chest, and Jett could not look at him any longer.

She turned away, crossing her arms and sighting the nearby canal. Moonlight glinted on the water. Silver and clean and not at all like anything in Daemonia. She had never expected to meet her father. And she would never have guessed it would go down like this. What an utter asshole.

"I heard that," he said. "I'm good at picking up thoughts from my blood kin. Asshole. Idiot. Whatever you want to call me, I'm still your daddy."

And here she had been troubled to learn she was adopted? Not anymore. Josette and Charles Montfort had been the best, and only, parents she'd ever had.

"Why didn't Fuum leave Savin's body after they arrived in this realm?" she asked.

"That was the annoying glitch to the whole plan. Bitch tricked me. She didn't really want to come here and set up house with me. She just wanted a ticket out of Daemonia, so she used me to get you to sit the throne. Grabbed the boy and headed off on her own sweet way."

"She dumped you?"

Drav shrugged. "No big loss. Hey, I got to claim a daughter as a queen out of it. Do you know the privi-

leges that grants me now? Man! I can waltz into Daemonia with armloads of illegal morphine and toss it
around like candy and no one is going to stop me, the
queen's father." He lifted his chin and pressed a hand
to his chest. The entitled mien did not look half as good
on him as it did on her.

"How come you never visited me the entire time I was
there?" Jett asked. "I should think you'd have a care to
thank the one who gave you such privileges."

"I'm not into family reunions."

"You're lying."

"And you can read thoughts, too."

So she could. Must be the family blood. Ugh. Jett did
not want to know what was going on in the man's mind.

"I never visited because I didn't want to get tangled
up in the royal mumbo-jumbo stuff. If they had inducted
me into your court, I would have been stuck there."

"Just like me?"

"Oh, come on, enough with the pity parade. I don't
care what your reason for leaving the place was. You
needed a vacation? Fine. You've had it. Beautiful Paris.
Rendezvousing with your lover. A reckoner. Really?" He
again dismissed the statement with a sweep of his hand.
"Whatever. Women always have such strange taste in
men. Now it's time to skip back to the throne and be a
good little queen for our legion."

"So Daddy's privileges will not be revoked?"

"You got it, sweetie."

Jett thrust out her hand, forcing a vile hex at her father. It slammed him into the brick, this time fitting
his body into the hard structure in a spume of dust and
painful growls.

"I am not your sweetie." Jett turned and walked toward the canal.

As far as meeting the father for the first time went, she'd mark that one as Avoid All Future Contact. Now she was walking away from him. For good.

When an arm hooked about her neck from behind and her throat constricted, she instinctively bent forward in an attempt to toss off the attack. But Drav clung to her, and everywhere his fingers touched her skin, she felt his wicked influence seep inside and begin to take control.

Savin walked the streets for hours. This time he was not going home without Jett. The sun had set and the sky was dark, for the moon was new and no stars could ever breach the illumination of Paris. He'd held such intense focus during his walk, senses focused toward any demon he neared, that his temples now ached with a burgeoning headache.

He stopped by the steel guardrail that edged a stairway leading down to the canal. He picked up vibrations from a few demons in the distance, but none felt familiar to him. Not that he'd ever detected Jett. And why was that? Why could he not know—had he never known?—what she was?

Was it because it was better that way? Better for his heart and soul. No matter what makeup she now was, she would always be his girl. And if that meant he had to love a half demon, then he was in for the fall.

When he heard a sniffle below near a patio edging the canal, Savin looked over the balustrade. And saw the lush black hair that glittered without moonlight. Because she always shone to him.

"Jett!"

He rushed down to the patio and she turned and plunged into his arms. He kissed the crown of her head and felt an instant release of the head pain as her warmth melded against his. It never felt wrong to hold her.

"I'm glad I found you," he said. She nestled against his chest, silent save for tears. "I had no idea CJ was going to react that way. I'm sorry."

She didn't speak, only clung to him tighter.

"I love you, Jett."

She nodded against his chest. "I...I wasn't trying to hurt him. Maybe...maybe I was."

"Huh? Jett?"

Then Savin noticed the dark figure sprawled at the edge of the canal, his head tilted back and long dread-locks swept by the water. His mouth was open and black blood drooled out into the water.

"What happened? Demon?" Savin asked.

Jett nodded against his chest. She tucked herself up even tighter against him and he wrapped his arms across her back. Much as he wanted to inspect the body, he wanted even more to hold Jett.

"He tried to hurt you?"

She nodded.

"I'm sorry I wasn't here for you. Damn it," he swore softly. "I can never seem to be in the right place when you need me most."

And that fact hurt him more deeply than anything ever had. Even the sour looks his father had given him or the vile interactions he'd had over the years with those demons he'd reckoned couldn't match the utter devasta-tion at not being able to protect Jett.

"His name was Drav," she said, and lifted her head

to meet his gaze in the darkness. "He was my demon father."

Savin didn't know what to say. How could she know that? Had he come looking for her? Had she sought him? What was going on?

"He told me everything. And then he insisted I return to Daemonia. He was going to take me there at any cost. And… I almost fell victim to his influence. But you know, men are men, no matter their form and physicality."

Savin wasn't sure what she meant.

"I kicked him in the crotch and that bought me the few seconds I needed to pull up everything I had within me. I ripped out his heart and tossed it in the canal."

A matter-of-fact recitation of a truly nasty encounter. Yet Savin was only glad she had triumphed. He kissed her forehead and tasted her sweetness.

"I don't want the darkness to win," she whispered. "Help me?"

"Always. Come on, I'm taking you home."

They stood and, upon considering Drav's body for a moment, Jett suggested Savin shove it into the canal. The demon would decay quickly and become but a thick sludge in less than a day. It was the way of those born completely demonic. Death in the mortal realm did that to their bodies.

They walked hand in hand in silence. No words were necessary. Savin understood she was helpless regarding the demon inside her. Her darkness? Now that her greatest threat had been extinguished—the father who wanted to send her back to Daemonia—he would do what he could to help her rise above the demon she still wore within her. He'd read all the books, master all the spells, even consult witches, wizards or warlocks, if that was what it took to save Jett from her darkness.

At his place, he took down the wards and then left them down after he'd closed the front door. He knew it drained her to have them activated. He'd risk it for tonight.

Jett wandered quietly into the bedroom and pulled off her clothes. Savin stood by the wall, watching as she undressed. With no moonlight sifting through the clouds, shades of gray filled the room, but he saw the shape of her against the bedclothes. So beautiful. A match to the darkness he held within his soul?

When she turned and held out her hand to him, that was the only invite he needed. Savin pulled off his shirt and unbuttoned his jeans. He crawled onto the bed and kissed her.

Chapter 27

The next afternoon, Jett walked into the living room, which resounded with acoustic guitar music. Savin did not play the diddley bow, thank whatever gods for that. Instead, it was a classical piece that featured rapid arpeggios and some high notes that sang to her inner desire for all things beautiful. She lingered by the wooden support beam, not wanting to interrupt and hoping he'd continue through to the end.

He was a dichotomy of dark and light. As was she? Perhaps. But did their opposing sides balance each other out when needed? Or when they were both at their darkest, would they be hell to deal with? Maybe that was what was required to see this current situation to a resolution? Both mining their darkest powers to fight it back?

It was an idea. But she wasn't sure Savin would get behind it. She had exercised her greatest skills last night to defeat Drav. So easy to rip out a demon's heart. To hold it in her palm and feel the beats that had given her life. That had marked her as not completely human. An outcast in the mortal realm. She hated him for that, for his callous decision to use her as a means to get Fuum out of Daemonia. And for what? Fuum had ditched him immediately and remained in Savin. And Drav had walked away. Just another failed romance.

Jett closed her eyes. She had been a pawn. Who had risen to queen.

She did not want that. She wished to shuck any part of Drav from her body and bones. This morning she felt the exertion as an all-over muscle ache. Every day she grew…lesser. The sheen was getting easier to keep up because… Was she losing the demon inside her? There was less and less to hide now.

The music ended abruptly. "Didn't see you standing there."

"I didn't want you to stop," Jett said. "It's beautiful."

"Some Scarlatti. I like the classic stuff as much as the blues."

"I remember you started taking guitar lessons that summer before we…" She didn't need to finish that sentence. "You wanted to be a rock star."

Savin set the guitar aside and patted the couch beside him. Jett joined him and he wrapped an arm around her shoulders and brought her in to hug against his chest. "Doesn't every kid want to be a rock star?"

"I don't remember what I wanted to be."

"A nurse," Savin said easily. "Don't you recall all those times you'd bandage my wounds after our adventures? And that time I actually broke my arm?"

"Oh hell, I do remember that now. Your mother was

so freaked that I'd splinted your arm with branches and your torn T-shirt."

"I think the emergency room doctor was impressed. I was."

She snuggled her head against his chest and listened to his calm heartbeat.

"How are you today, Jett? After…last night."

"I'm tired, but not upset. It was either him or me."

"I know that. You did what you had to do." He kissed the crown of her head. "I think I've always loved you, Jett."

She closed her eyes, letting the words flow in, but a little unsure how to process the confession.

"You're my friend, my confidante," he said. "My partner in adventure. You know me."

"I *knew* you," she clarified. "We used to be those things, Savin. And…much as I would like to continue the way we once were…can that be so?"

"We just have to get through this mess with the open rift and the queen," he said. "Then it can be. If you want it to be."

"I do. I mean, I think I do. I'm not sure I know what love is."

"You loved your parents. You loved that mangy cat that used to hiss at me every time I'd come over."

"Oh, Snoodles! I forgot about him." Memory of that ginger cat dashing up and down the carpeted stairs after a piece of string warmed her heart. "I really did love that stupid cat. He hated you."

"I put up with the scratches because I wanted to be near you. I didn't know it when I was a kid, but you were my world, Jett. And it feels like now you've stepped back into my world for a reason."

"What if that reason is to challenge you? To make you stand up to the darkness I am and send me away?"

He sighed and hugged her tighter. "I hope not. I really hope not. But if anything were to happen to me, just know that I love you. From my heart. In every way possible."

She pressed her lips to his hand and kissed it. She didn't know how to say she loved him. Wished she did. But for some reason the word didn't feel right. It could be her darkness. It could simply be that she had so much learning and growing yet to do.

"Do you remember when we would sing?" she asked.

Savin chuckled. "Oh yeah. All those Saturday-morning-cartoon songs? Ha! We knew every single one."

"And we'd sing them at the top of our lungs while perched in the massive oak tree in your backyard."

"Those were good times."

"Savin." Jett swallowed and lifted her chin to meet his gaze. "Those songs kept me alive. When I needed to not lose hope and remember that I was human and that I might someday escape the terrible place, I'd sing one of those songs. Only in my thoughts, mind you. But I'd hear your voice singing along with me. You were always there with me."

He bowed over her and hugged her tightly. And Jett thought she heard him sniff at a tear. Her heart warmed and she clung to her sexy lover. She never wanted to let him go. His heartbeats buoyed her. Maybe she did love him.

Jett sat before the laptop computer that Savin had placed on the kitchen counter and inspected the screen. After his mother had refused to help with further liaising between Jett and her mother, she did forward Josette's email address to Savin. He'd sent Josette an email stating he had some information about Jett, and Josette Montfort had replied with a desperate plea to learn more.

So now Savin suggested she send her a letter online. This email program would enable her to write to her and send it. Her mother would have the letter as soon as she clicked Send. And then it was in her hands to reply or not.

Heartbeat thudding, Jett closed her eyes. She needed this to erase the lingering foulness of meeting her demon father from her very soul.

Savin leaned in and kissed her on the cheek. "I know. Give it some thought. You don't have to tell her all the details."

"I can't lie or make something up. You said you told them we were kidnapped by humans?"

"That's what I decided I needed to tell the police and our parents so they wouldn't think I was crazy. Later I told my mom the truth."

"But my mother only knows that original lie?"

"Yes."

So she must have concluded that her daughter was harmed, maybe even abused or tortured, and very likely dead by the hands of cruel humans. What a terrible mistruth to have to live with. Yet it had been twenty years. Surely, her heart had healed and she had moved on. "I don't know how to do this."

"Maybe just start with a hello. I'm going to head out and scavenge up some food. Give you some time to yourself. When you're done typing what you want to say, just hit the send button and then I've shown you how to close the program."

She nodded. Her fingers shook over the keyboard, so she pressed her hands together and tucked them between her legs. "Thanks, Savin. Pick me up something sweet?"

"You always were a sugar freak."

That made her smile. Would they ever get back to the way they were twenty years ago? She didn't want that childhood friendship anymore. She wanted them as adults, in love and sharing their lives. And he'd said he loved her.

Did she—*could* she—love Savin Thorne?

The front door closed behind him. And she missed him already.

He'd lied to Jett. He would pick up something to eat. But first a detour was in order. There were things he needed to take care of. Much as every mile he drove farther from Jett killed him, Savin pressed onward until he arrived at the field where it had all begun.

Savin walked out into the field beneath the rift. A man couldn't see the tear between the two realms, but he felt it. The air was still. Quiet. He didn't sense any demons lurking or coming through. But it wouldn't remain so for long. The afternoon was growing into evening. He'd left Jett before the laptop, knowing she needed some time alone for such a momentous thing as contacting her mother. He didn't know how to help her with that. It had been difficult for him, as a ten-year-old, navigating his own return and concocting the story about being kidnapped.

Yet here he stood. He'd survived and thrived. And he'd walked a path he hadn't chosen but had been led toward. Never would he have purposely sought to reckon demons. But really, what other choice had he? And he did the job well. But he didn't take pride in it. It was just the thing he did. To survive. To move along with life. To exist.

Just as Jett had done for so long.

Was there something else out there for him? Could he have a real life? What was that to him?

Family was the first word that popped into his brain. Yet the image of green grass, a picket fence, a puppy and a backyard swing set replete with one or two children made him shake his head. A foolish notion. Who was he to believe he could father a child and take care of it and teach it morals and values when the only example that child would have was a man who sensed, talked to and reckoned demons?

No life for a child. Nor for a wife who just wanted to be normal. Because a wife was necessary for a child. Savin had never looked at a woman in such a manner as future wife potential. He had promised Jett when they were kids they'd get married. Stupid kid stuff. But...not really. He'd meant it last night when he told Jett he loved her. Now, as she was. As the person—part demon—she had become. He could imagine spending his life with her. They got each other. And they each had secrets that only the other could understand. She fit him.

But there was only one way to keep her safe in this mortal realm. And that decision suddenly became less tough than it had been years ago when he first learned the only way to get the Other out of him. He knew what he had to do. And he would do it for the woman he loved. Because if he couldn't have the picket fence, she deserved a chance to live as a human and to have that opportunity at building a family.

Behind him, a white hearse pulled onto the grassy off

road and parked. He'd asked Certainly Jones to meet him out here. Meeting at the Archives only raised red flags. And he knew the director of Acquisitions, Ethan Pierce, would question him if he got wind of his frequent visits. He didn't want to make trouble for anyone. As well, CJ had wanted to check out the rift.

The witch wandered over, his tall, lithe figure moving the air with a wicked vibe. Always dressed in black, and that long black hair and so many spell tattoos marked him as the dark witch he was. Savin did not fear him. Yet, much as he didn't trust witches, he respected CJ's power. Always good to have such an ally.

On the other hand, the witch was on his list after yesterday's fiasco in Thrash's office.

"Surprised you contacted me," CJ said as he approached.

"You're the only witch I trust. And that's a tough one to admit after what you did to Jett."

"I apologized. I reacted. I do shit like that sometimes."

"Yeah." Savin heaved out a sigh. Didn't they all?

CJ handed Savin a corked glass vial sealed with black wax. Savin sniffed the seal and jerked away from the vile smell.

"You don't smell it," CJ said. "You drink it. Preferably fast. Or it'll come back up on you." He dug out a folded paper from his coat pocket. "This is the incantation. But, Savin." He laid a hand over Savin's, enclosing the paper between the two of them. "Give me a few more days, will you? There's got to be a better way. I can find the answer in the Archives."

"I asked you about this years ago, CJ, and you looked then. What's changed?"

"Maybe my determination? There's a hell of a lot of information to go through in the demon room. My search last time wasn't focused, or as motivated as it is now. You know what enacting this spell means. I am only giving you this stuff because I also know what it can do on the other side. Sealing this rift is paramount."

As if on cue, a sudden flash in the sky spit out a black cloud. Both Savin and CJ ducked to avoid the onslaught. And while the dark witch called out a Latin incantation and cast a hex into the air, the demons escaping into the mortal realm seemed oblivious, quickly spiriting away from where the men stood.

The sight left Savin with a foul taste in his mouth. "I'll give you one more day. But I've seen the news reports. The demons are growing bolder. We'll have a disaster on our hands sooner rather than later."

"Ed and I are doing our best."

"I intend to, as well." Savin stuffed the vial and paper in his coat pocket. "Thanks, CJ. Can I ask you another favor?"

"Always."

The witch walked closer to the edge of the field and Savin followed, standing side by side with him. They looked out over the twilight, which cast purple and red across the tree-jagged horizon.

Savin swallowed but then summoned the courage required. "If all goes as it should in a couple days…promise me you'll keep an eye out for Jett. I've already called the bank and had her name placed on my accounts. She now owns everything I own. I wouldn't have it any other way. But she needs guidance. The demon she still wears is power-hungry and, well—"

"I got it," CJ said. "Will do. Promise." He held out a

fist and Savin met it with a bump of his own fist. "But it's not going to come to that," CJ added. "I hope."

Savin wanted to have as much hope, but he could not stand by and idly wish for the best. He'd made plans and was ensuring Jett's security. Now to let the chips fall where they may.

Chapter 28

Savin sorted out the takeaway meal on the kitchen counter. Jett, looking gorgeous in a soft, floaty red dress that resembled something a woman would wear to a wedding, climbed onto a bar stool, knelt and watched him.

"You going dancing?" he asked.

"No. I love this color and I wanted to look nice for you when you got home."

"You always look nice. I can't imagine you looking un-nice."

"What about with horns and gray skin?"

"Still pretty."

"Liar." She picked up a fork and tested the peppered potatoes, sans salt, at his request to the chef.

"Nope. Not lying. Did you send an email to your mom?"

"I did. I told her I was in Paris. Didn't know how

to tell her what I've been up to the past twenty years, though. I mentioned you'd taken me in and I've been relying on you for strength. I asked her if we could exchange emails to get to know each other again. She hasn't replied."

"It's only been a few hours."

Jett bowed her head and stabbed her food.

"It could take days for her to find the email," Savin encouraged. "Some people don't check their account that often. It'll be okay." He kissed her, then sat beside her. "So tonight is for seduction, eh?"

"Why do you say that? Because I'm in a red dress?"

"Yes. Red wilds me, Jett. Especially when it's on you."

"It does? Like a bull?"

"You'll have to find out for yourself."

They exchanged winks, and that made getting through supper all the harder for Savin. Because if his plans went well, then there would be very few teasing winks they would again share.

After dinner, Jett picked up the acoustic guitar from where he'd set it beside the couch and held it out to Savin. "Will you play for me? I want to dance."

"Yeah? I might have some dance music in me." He took the guitar and sat on the couch. Anything to keep his mind from impending doom, right? Strumming a few chords, using the *rasgueado* flamenco technique he'd once tried to master, Savin lit into a slow E minor run.

"I recognize that," Jett said as she twirled before him. "You and your mother used to listen to it when we were kids."

"This is like soul stuff."

"It's what the Spanish ladies dance to. Your mother

used to do a dance for us, if I recall. Yes?" She stretched up an arm and performed a delicate wrist curl and then stomped her feet. "So the bull is rising already, eh?" She winked and turned, doing her best impression of a flamenco dancer.

Indeed the bull inside him, if there was one, pawed at the ground, wanting more. More Jett, always Jett, stop the world and make this moment last forever. Savin strummed a series of chords and slapped the guitar body in punctuation of the call to a free-spirited dance. He'd never been to Spain, but he'd love to visit.

That dream was now dead. As were all other dreams. The only one he had left danced before him, laughing as she bowed to him in a graceful denouement.

"Let's go to Spain," he said suddenly, setting the guitar aside.

Jett climbed onto his lap, straddling and kissing him. The floaty red material brushed his skin in a sensual tease. "You mean it?"

He did. But his heart had been speaking much faster than his brain could race to stop it. And suddenly Savin couldn't hold it all in any longer. He kissed Jett deeply, longingly, tempering his need to take her swiftly and wildly. He wanted to know her beyond the intimacy they'd shared. He needed to know her soul deep. Could he have that?

"I wish we could get married." He spilled out his heart. "I wish I could get you pregnant, over and over, and we'd raise a brood, living in a sweet little place out in the country. I wish for so much, Jett."

"Why can't we make those wishes come true? I'm in."

"You are? You know that's not possible. As long as the Other lives inside me…"

Jett met his protest with another kiss. This one burned against his mouth in the sweetest way. He wanted her to mark him so he would forever taste her on his lips and on his tongue and in his heart. She already lived there, deep inside him, and had carved out a niche much deeper than any wicked, demonic former queen ever could.

Jett he wanted to keep inside him. To never lose.

Was he giving up too easily? Perhaps he should give CJ those few extra days he requested? If it would see him and Jett fulfilling the wild wishes of his—

A knock at his front door startled Jett to stand upright, alert. Savin wasn't expecting anyone. It could be CJ or Ed. But neither made it a habit of visiting.

When he stood, Jett put up her hand to stay him.

"What is it?" he asked. Inside him, the demoness clenched at his spine and twisted. Savin winced, clutching his gut at the strange need to fold over on himself. "It's vile," he gasped. "A demon?"

"We'll not open that door," Jett said firmly. "Are all your wards up?"

He'd forgotten to put them back up after coming in with the food. And he'd been leaving them low since learning they weakened Jett. He shook his head.

"You've got to pull them up and strengthen them," she said.

"But they'll hurt you."

"I'll survive. But you won't if we don't keep whatever is out there out."

Jett stood by as Savin grabbed one of the demonic devices from the bedroom. He set to twisting the dials and brass knobs that would turn up the juice, so to speak, on his house wards. With every twist, she felt the repulsive vibrations tweak at her nervous system. It tightened her jaw. Her fingers curled into fists. But she breathed through it and summoned her queen to rise above it. She stood inside the protective wards, so they could do no more than keep her inside. Yet she wouldn't be able to help Savin in any way.

"Done," Savin finally announced. "Shit, Jett, you're in pain."

He bowed over her where she sat on the floor, back against the couch and hands splayed beside her. He caressed her head and studied her gaze. Such gentility in her protector. She loved him. Truly, she always had. And she wanted what he desired, to marry him and have children and live out on a quiet little country cottage.

But it seemed the only way to solve the problem was for one or the other of them to sacrifice. Only one would be left standing.

"I'll take care of this." He dashed for the door, and, reciting a demonic litany, he thrust forward the device as he opened the door.

Insectile skittering clawed the outer walls, and a screech resounded in Jett's ears. That had hurt whatever demon had vocalized, she knew that much. When she smelled flames and her darkness lifted at the scent, she followed the curiosity to stand and peer around the corner. Savin stood with his arms together, sigils facing outward—and they flamed.

He was marvelous. Truly, a hero in every sense that appealed to her.

When he dropped his arms, the flames hissed out and Savin kicked the door shut. He turned, startling when he saw her right behind him. "Jett, you should be more careful."

"I don't fear you." She wrapped her arms around him and hugged him. "You are my protector. You're not hurt? From the flames?"

"Never. The fire slips over my skin without burning me. Don't know why, but that's how it works."

She had always felt so comfortable near flames. And now she had returned to another comforting fire.

"Kiss me," she whispered. "Touch me, Savin. Make me yours. Please."

He lifted her into his arms, and as he passed by the kitchen, she did not sense the intruders outside the door. The wards had repelled them. For now. Savin carried her into the bedroom and laid her on the bed. When she looked into his eyes, she did not notice the inner pain from the wards. She had but to maintain a connection with him.

His kiss fell upon her like redeeming sunlight. Hot and lingering, and oh, so welcome. The tickle of his beard over her skin softened her anxiety and teased up a smile against his mouth. She pushed her fingers into his hair and clung to him, keeping him there at her mouth. Wanting to breathe all her pain into him and, in turn, take his away from him.

"You are my flame," she said. "My comforting flame."

"I don't want to burn you."

"Oh, yes, you must. Burn me with your heat, Savin. I need to feel you deep and hot within me."

Savin's wide hand strayed down her shoulder and to her breast. The less-than-gentle squeeze of her nipple shocked a vibrant pleasure thrill through her. Arching her back, Jett lured her lover down onto her and into her arms. He bowed his head and licked a trail down her chin, shoving down the strappy sleeve of her dress.

Nudging aside the fabric, he claimed her nipple with his hot tongue.

He supped upon her and, in the process, teased her senses to ultra-alert. She felt beautiful, wanted. *Not a horned demon queen.* She felt as if she'd never revealed that side of herself to Savin. She felt…loved.

Dragging her dress down as he followed with his tongue, Savin skated over her skin, lower and lower, circled her belly button, then tugged to get the dress below her hips.

"Yes, kiss me there," she said. Her senses soared with every delicious trace of his tongue.

His fingers wrapped about her hip as he lowered his mouth to kiss her mons and nuzzle into her hairs. The anticipation of welcoming him into her most intimate place made her spread her legs. But he lingered there, at the top of her thigh, his breath hushing hotly, and his mouth kissing here, then there, then moving lower and aside until, finally, she felt him enter her with his tongue.

Jett gripped the sheets. Her head tilted back into the pillow. Her nipples, tight and hard, cooled in the evening air. He dashed tastes and touches and suckles everywhere about her pussy. His wicked touch felt so right. She had not to command or request his submission. She might be queen, but this man was the champion she had always desired would ride in on a white stallion to rescue her from the darkness of Daemonia.

A stallion would have perished in such a place. And her knight had instead waited for her to rescue herself. But now the real saving had begun. He could lift her soul to the surface, to plunge through the flames and touch the light with his gentle protection and willingness to love her.

Savin's hair spilled over her thigh. Jett reached to clutch at it as his ministrations focused on her swelling clit. It pulsed and ached and hummed. Her entire body answered with a tightening, pleading urge to jump. To fall once again over the edge.

And this time she fell into Savin's arms.

Chapter 29

In the morning, Savin felt the threat as deeply as Jett had. Her spine tingled with a pricking electricity. They both knew demons were in the area, perhaps even the building. They were looking for her. Daemonia had sent scouts to retrieve their missing queen.

Would they know she had destroyed Drav? Despite his claims to royalty, he'd seemed insignificant. Else why had the legion not insisted he remain at court? She had done away with him out of defense, but Jett suspected Drav would not be missed by any in Daemonia.

But had the scouts she now sensed come for her or Fuum? It was possible they sensed the demon within Savin. Either way, if they succeeded in breaching Savin's wards, the results would not be pretty. So when Savin had to run out, this time he increased the efficacy of the wards, locking Jett inside with a powerful shield.

She rubbed her arms and pulled up her legs on the couch where she sat, feeling as though she were hiding and not standing up to the threat, as any queen should. This was not her. She was stronger.

If she could fight off those lurking, would that success show others she was a force not to be threatened?

She glanced to the front door. She could walk outside. As simple as that. To keep Savin safe.

Savin hung up on CJ. The dark witch reported finding something interesting in the Archives. Not the thing necessary to keep both Savin and Jett safe, but he felt he was getting close.

Uh-huh. Close. Like that was going to help matters.

Savin strode down the sidewalk, following the eerie sensation that clued him a demon was near. Not a corporeal one. He couldn't see it, but it was close enough he could reach out and grab it, he felt sure. Grabbing wasn't possible with the incorporeal kind. They tended to seek humans to inhabit. And while Savin could reckon them, the reckoning wasn't something he could whip out like a magical spell and—*poof*—the demon was sent back to Daemonia.

He needed a few minutes, at the very least, to summon a connection to the Place of All Demons. Knowing he didn't want to let the thing run free, yet also knowing he couldn't call attention to himself on this busy, tourist-filled street, Savin quietly put his forearms together to connect the demonic magic he possessed and began to chant under his breath while keeping the demon's aura in range.

He walked swiftly, roughly shouldering someone out of the way. They angrily called after him, but he couldn't pause for politeness. The incorporeal demon turned a corner. Savin hurried and rounded the corner and...bumped into a pregnant woman holding her stomach. She moaned and winced.

"I'm sorry, mademoiselle."

"No worries," she said. "It was so sudden."

"Are you...in pain?" Was she going to give birth? She wasn't overly large, but by the manner in which she clutched her stomach, he could tell she was pregnant.

"I'm fine now. Must have been one of those Braxton Hicks. You barely brushed me, monsieur. No worries."

And yet, as Savin took his hand away from her arm, he felt it. The shiver of darkness that seemed to laugh at him. The incorporeal demon had found a host. Hell. Had it entered her baby?

She required an exorcism. It was the safest way to rid the human body of an incorporeal presence. But how to tell her that?

She started to walk away, and Savin searched his brain for a way to tell her what had just happened to her without having her flee from him thinking him insane. If he let her go, that poor child...

A car pulled up to the curb and she waved to the driver. A man leaned over and opened the passenger door.

"Wait!" Savin called, but the car rolled away. He fixed the license plate in his memory, then pulled out his phone and tapped the info in a note. He would need to find her if the rift was not closed.

He could stop the damned thing, which had likely come from Daemonia, by closing the rift. Because when he was closing it, all the escapees would be sucked back inside even if they did occupy a human host. The door would be slammed behind them, and all would be returned to normal.

As normal as this crazy realm could get.

He couldn't protect everyone. But how many more innocents would be taken over by demons? He'd never been taken to task for protecting the city from demons such as Ed did. But he could not stand idly by and allow this to continue.

"This has to stop."

Savin dialed up CJ. The connection crackled, and he only heard CJ say he was "still looking" before it cut out. The Archives was many stories below ground. Cell reception was always iffy there.

"Still looking," Savin muttered.

Not good enough to close the rift. But he did have a spell he'd tucked away in a drawer at home that would drag the bitch inside him out, kicking and screaming, and send her back from whence she had come.

One queen was as good as any other.

With a decisive nod, Savin dialed his mother.

"What's up, *mon cher*?"

"Hey, Maman, just wanted to call and tell you how much I love you."

Jett walked outside Savin's building and found a place on the sidewalk where passersby would not bump into her. Projecting a morsel of her influence outward, she ensured that they wouldn't notice her beyond yet another uninteresting tourist. And then she spread out her arms and closed her eyes. With all her senses, she sent out a message to any demons close enough to hear: *Beware. Do not challenge me.*

Suddenly she was gripped by the upper arm and hurriedly moved toward the building door. "What are you doing outside?"

"I couldn't sit idly by," she said to Savin. "I had to let them know they could not come near me without a fight."

"You risk being seen by humans."

"I am half human," Jett protested. She tugged her arm from Savin's grip as they entered the building lobby. "Or did you forget that?"

"No. I'm just— I'm worried for you."

"I can take care of myself. As I did with Drav. Besides, I influenced those in the area to only see what they expected." She pressed her hands akimbo and met his blue gaze. He was only concerned, but if she allowed him to be her knight, he would lose himself. And she didn't want that sacrifice. Savin was supposed to live. "Where were you?"

"Out for a walk. I saw something disturbing. A pregnant woman hosting an incorporeal demon. It's probably in her baby. Hell, Jett, we need to end this."

"You said *we*. Does that mean you are willing to work with me?"

He winced. "I don't know how you can help."

"I can communicate with those who have recently come from Daemonia."

"What about the ones after you? Let's go inside and talk about this." He glanced around them. "I can't risk anyone walking by hearing us." He pointed up the stairs and she started upward. "Please trust me, Jett."

At his front door she took his hands and kissed him. "I will trust you if you will trust me."

"I do, I swear to you," he said, closing the door behind him. He took a moment to reinforce the wards and

Jett hissed at the intrusion to her system. "Too strong?" Savin asked.

"No, I'm good." But not really. She wanted this to end as much as he did. Dealing with having to worry about her sheen and Savin's wards was driving her mad. This was no way to normal. "So what do we do now?"

"I'm heading to the rift later with Ed and CJ. And CJ is still searching for a spell to draw out Fuum." He thumped his chest. "You hear that, bitch?"

Of a sudden Savin's body thrust backward and his shoulders slammed into the wall. He cracked a smile at Jett. "She heard me."

"Don't cajole her," Jett said. "I need you in one piece if we're to…" Could she say it? She'd confessed she loved him. But how to surrender to something so untouchable as that normal life they both wanted.

"We'll have it." Savin pulled her into his embrace and kissed her. "I know exactly what you're afraid to say. But I'm not. I'm going to fix things for you, Jett." His phone buzzed with a call. He silenced the ringer and kissed her again. "Let me hold you."

But he didn't say, out loud, *One last time*.

The phone on the bedside stand buzzed, indicating a message. Savin ignored it and nuzzled his face against Jett's neck. Her hair felt like silk, her body like home. Was he doing the right thing?

"I want you to be happy," he whispered.

"I am." She was drifting into reverie, perhaps even sleep. They'd exhausted themselves with each other, and life was not more perfect than it was in this moment.

Fitting.

Holding her until he felt sure her breaths were now

those of sleep, Savin carefully slipped off the bed and pulled up his jeans. The skylight beamed in moonlight that illuminated the room with an eerie quiet. He wandered out into the living room and, slipping his hand in between the couch cushions, pulled out the vial and instructions CJ had given him the other day.

Sitting cross-legged on the floor, Savin set the items beside him and took a moment to look across the shadowed display of guitars on the wall before him. The diddley bow he used for musicomancy leaned against the end of the sofa. He owned a Rickenbacker that had been signed by Tom Petty. The Flying V had Ace Frehley's signature scrawled in black Sharpie across its silver-speckled body.

Good times, that. He'd miss music. But then again, how would he know what to miss if he was not even alive to think that?

With a decisive inhale and exhale, Savin opened the paper and read the spell. It involved drawing a circle about him, so he chanted the words as he drew that circle with his finger and then arched it up over his head to enclose his seated figure in a sort of cone that now glimmered with the activated magic.

Savin's skin prickled. The Other sat up at attention.

He hastened the ritual.

Reading the final words silently to fix them to memory, he uncapped the vial and tilted the sludgy ingredients down his throat. It tasted…not terrible. Then, bringing his palms together to unite the moth halves, he spoke the words…

…and the demon within him clawed for hold at his soul.

Chapter 30

Jett rolled over on the bed, awakened by the cell phone vibrating on the nightstand. Savin was not in the bed—he must have wandered into the bathroom. She grabbed the phone and read the text. The dark witch Certainly Jones reported: I've found an option. Coming over right now.

An option? For what?

Sitting up, she noted the bathroom door was open. He wasn't in there. Had he left? It was late, but not early-in-the-morning late. Must be around midnight. She'd dozed into such a blissful sleep after their lovemaking. There was no man she desired more than Savin, and when he kissed and touched her, he made her believe she could be whole again.

Human.

She shouldn't have challenged him so outside the

building. She didn't want to alienate him. They needed to work together. She needed him as much as she suspected he needed her.

A strange noise sounded from the living room. Scratching?

"Savin?"

Instinctually, she spread her senses through the air, mining for demonic presence. Nothing.

Sliding off the bed, Jett grabbed the T-shirt Savin had been wearing earlier and pulled it on. It smelled like him, rugged and wild. But as she wandered into the living room, her footsteps quickened to race to Savin's side. His pores emitted a thick red smoke that coalesced in the air above his prone figure.

Jett screamed and shook him. He murmured something. She saw the paper on the floor with spell sigils drawn on it and the empty vial that reeked of foul things. "What have you done?"

Of a sudden the red smoke sharpened and began to form. Jett's heart dropped because now her senses felt the demonic presence. And she knew who this was. The former queen, Fuum. The one demon who had destroyed her life, and Savin's as well, had been freed and was taking shape.

An insistent knock on the front door was followed by a man's call to let him in. Jett sprang up. It must be the dark witch. She started for the front door, but an arm lashed out and caught her across the neck. Jett's feet left the floor and she tumbled backward, landing painfully on hands and butt.

"CJ, she's out!" Jett called. "I can't get to the door."

"You have fouled everything," the now-solid form of Fuum growled at Jett. She stood tall and regal, her long midnight blue hair flowing out as if blown by the wind. Her black flesh hugged tight to her skeletal bone structure, and the bits of red mist surrounded her like fabric from her shoulders to her knees. "I will not go back!"

"Nor will I!" Finding her strength, Jett stood. An eye to Savin on the floor showed her he did not move, and she worried he might be dying. Edamite Thrash had said that the demon within him could not be removed without his death. "What have you done to him?"

"I've kept him alive and well all this time." The bitch grinned a shark's smile.

The front door slammed inward, and the dark witch stumbled inside.

With a flick of her finger, the demoness pinned CJ to the wall. "This does not concern you, witch."

"Shit, he performed the releasement spell," CJ said. "Savin?"

"He's there on the floor," Jett said. "Is he going to die?"

"Of course he is," the demoness said. "He no longer has me to keep him alive. Men. They never know how much they need us women until it's too late."

"With you out of this realm, he can live," CJ called. The witch recited some Latin, and that allowed him to peel himself away from the wall.

"I'm not going anywhere..." The demoness hovered in the center of the living room, then tilted her look directly at Jett. "Without taking Drav's progeny with me."

"Oh, he's dead," Jett challenged. "Not that you'd care."

Fuum lifted a brow. "I don't. The idiot served me one purpose. But I do care that you are not where you belong."

Knowing what was coming, Jett released her sheen. Horns curled out and back over her ears. Her skin tightened and the sigils glowed as her skin darkened. She drew up her protective wards just as she felt Fuum hit her hard.

"Keep her busy!" CJ called. He plunged to the floor beside Savin.

"Gladly," Jett said.

She pushed at Fuum and managed to shove her away from her. The demoness's back hit the wooden support beam and she yowled. Releasing all the magic she could summon, Jett directed it toward Fuum. The old queen matched her. And Jett realized she was not so powerful as she had been in Daemonia. Truly, she was losing her demon. Yet Fuum could only match her. She had not so much strength, either.

How easy it had been to destroy that which annoyed her while sitting on the throne. And to rip out a man's heart. But she did not want to kill Fuum. She had to keep her alive so Savin could send her back to Daemonia.

The witch knelt over Savin, reciting a spell. He dusted him with ash and salt. Dragging his gaze over the guitars on the wall, CJ asked, "Which is the one you use to perform musicomancy?" Savin did not respond. The witch slapped his face and joggled him, stirring Savin from the depths of death. "Which one!"

"Single...string..."

With a snap of CJ's fingers, the diddley bow flew across the room and landed in the witch's grip.

Jett felt the demoness's tendrils digging into her, seeking a space where her defenses might crumble. Her strength was growing; she must be feeding off Jett's magic. And Jett's energy was quickly depleting. She wouldn't be able to hold her off much longer.

She saw the witch hold the diddley bow over Savin, and her lover lifted a hand to strum the string. A sudden, nerve-biting tone filled the room. The demoness was whipped away from Jett while Jett was also flung away. Her shoulders hit the wall hard, and she dropped to the floor in a sprawl.

"Continue!" CJ commanded the weak reckoner on the floor. "Let me help you up."

CJ managed to pull Savin upright and prop his back against the couch while the demoness dove for the diddley bow. Her fingers burned into the wooden body.

With a spoken hex, CJ caused the demoness to recoil, but only momentarily. She lunged for the witch, gripping his hair and pulling him away from Savin.

The reckoner leaned against the couch, immobile, yet his eyes were open. And when they met Jett's gaze, she pleaded silently with him; she wanted him to know how much she loved him, that he meant the world to her. That she forgave him for not being able to save her when they were kids.

"I love you!" she shouted.

The reckoner dragged the diddley bow to his lap. Head tilted back against the couch, he plucked a few discordant notes, then a few more. The demoness dropped the dark witch, who rolled to his back and shuffled away against the wall to sit near Jett.

Savin's playing lured the demoness to him. Her form was at once solid and then wispy red smoke that hovered over him, her face fully formed, moving but inches from his.

Jett's body cringed at the sound, but the clasp of CJ's

hand about her wrist grounded her. "Don't listen," he said. "Listen only to me. I will speak quiet words of strength." He began to whisper and Jett turned her focus from Savin's music.

Meanwhile, Fuum floated toward Savin, lured by the music. She bent, placing her face close to his as if to draw in his scent or position herself to lash out a wicked tongue to taste.

And then Savin whispered to the demoness, "Kiss me…"

"My lover." Fuum pressed her mouth to Savin's.

The reckoner plucked out a trill of notes and, seeming to gain strength from the kiss, segued into a riff that took a life of its own and formed harmony at the same time. The instrument wailed at the demon and she coiled away from her contact with Savin and into a twist of yowling pain.

CJ clutched Jett's hand and began to chant louder. She felt his magic enter her. He was keeping her here, so she surrendered to his dark magic.

A shimmery rift opened before them. The red queen screamed. Arms flailing and curses flying, she was sucked in through the rift, which then flashed and closed up.

CJ dropped Jett's hand. "It's done. I've got to go."

She grabbed his wrist. "Where?"

"To the rift at the edge of town. I'll call Ed. We can seal it now that the queen has been sent back. But I have to hurry before she again escapes. You take care of Savin."

"Will he die?"

"No. He…shouldn't." The witch winced. "He needs

you now, Jett. Give him the strength that he once got from the incorporeal queen. Give it all to him."

With that, Certainly marched out of the place, closing the door behind him.

Jett crawled over to the couch, where Savin held the diddley bow clutched in his embrace. She stroked the hair from his face and gently pried the instrument from his hands.

Softly, she kissed his forehead and then his mouth.

"I'm not sure how to do this," she said, "but whatever I have is yours. Take it all from me, Savin."

Breaths came slowly. A monumental effort. Savin had mustered up the energy to strum the expulsion spell on the diddley bow. He was vaguely aware that the Other was now gone. The queen called Fuum. No longer inside him. And he felt…empty.

Savin tried to lift a hand to clutch at Jett's hair, but his extremities felt leaden. She straddled him. The weight of her lightness buoyed him. The sweetest kiss landed on his forehead. And then that softness touched his mouth. Like a redeeming elixir, she gave to him that which he'd never thought imaginable.

Freedom.

He was now free of the demon who had lived within him for twenty years. Because he had found Jett and had been forced to face the decision to give up his life to expel the demon inside him. Which he had done. And with every breath, he felt his life slipping away.

"Don't leave me, Savin," she whispered against his mouth. "We have our whole lives ahead of us. I need you here. In this mortal realm. By my side. Your hand in mine." She clasped his heavy hand and he wasn't able to curl his fingers. "Just try, Savin. For me? Please, don't die. CJ said…I must give you my strength. I'm not sure how. But I'm going to try this."

The press of her palms, one against his forehead, the other over his heart, felt like a zap from a life-saving emergency device. Savin's body jolted, but the movement rocked his rib cage and he moaned. Was this how it had felt when she ripped out her father's heart?

Again, he was jolted. She was doing something to him. He wasn't sure what it was. But she could take his heart. It belonged to her. When he opened his eyes, he didn't see the black-haired beauty whom he had likely loved since he was a child. He saw red eyes and blue hair and horns that glinted like specularite.

Jett. His Jett. In all her demonic glory. He loved her so much he wanted to tell her, but his tongue would not move.

This time when he felt the jolt, it was followed by the intrusion of sharp, pricking tendrils that seemed to poke in through his every pore. Heat gushed through his system. It glowed red behind his eyes and flickered like flames. The vibrations he felt when a demon was near were pronounced, only tenfold. Jett chanted a demonic phrase that sounded deep and earthen and older than the stars. Her throaty hums vibrated in his bones. They entwined, their souls.

"Your get-out-of-death-free card!" Jett declared.

She grabbed his wrists and pressed his palms together, and Savin smiled as he was thankful he'd told her about this. Would it work? Jett held his palms together tightly. His palms heated and flames formed. Jett swore but did not let go of his hands.

It felt as if the sides of his hands fused together, burning, yet without flames. The moth wings fluttered and peeled away from his skin to take flight.

Savin gasped in a choking breath as if he were rising from the depths of a molten lava pool. Had she done the same after falling over the cliff?

"Stay with me," Jett said in a voice that defied him to stay. To not make the leap. To be brave enough to stand at her side and face whatever the future would push at them.

The moth landed on his chest, right over his heart, and then it danced off and into the darkness.

"Yes," he murmured. The vibrations began to undulate and his muscles twitched. He could lift his hand and landed it at Jett's hip. And the flash behind his eyes brightened like the sun. He sat up abruptly. She slid down his legs, observing him with those eyes that were swiftly growing brown.

"Jett, I love you," he said.

She held up her hand and he slapped his other hand into hers. And her energy, her vita, flowed up his arm and into his heart. He watched her hair drip away the blue color and shine richly onyx. And just as he reached to touch the horn that curled over her ear, it dropped away from her skull and, glittering madly, diffused and scattered to dust as it spilled over his leg and the floor.

Jett hushed out a heavy exhale and bowed her head against his shoulder. Her body relaxed against his and she curled up her legs. He embraced her and kissed her forehead. He wasn't going to die this day.

Chapter 31

Days later

The life force Jett infused into Savin saved him from death. And in that moment, he in turn had taken from her all that was demonic, and she became as human as she had been that day long ago when fate lured them to the edge of the lavender field. Which wasn't entirely human, thanks to her paternity.

They confirmed these things with the help of Certainly Jones, who read their auras. But as well, now when Savin looked into Jett's eyes, all he saw was her. The woman he loved, sans red gloss to her brown irises.

Jett, on the other hand, wasn't ready to completely mark herself off as human. She had lived in Daemonia for a long time. The entitlement that had come to her by sitting the throne lingered. And while she would never

wish for the return of horns, she sensed there were tendrils within her that would ever remind her of those
dark days. She didn't say that to Savin. He didn't need to
know a bit of the queen yet lingered. In her blood would
always flow Drav's legacy. Like it or not.

With the rift sealed, the city of Paris returned to as
normal as it could be with the paranormal species walking its streets and existing alongside humans. Demons
would always be a part of the population. And the smart
ones knew how to survive and blend in. Ed Thrash continued to police his kind. And Savin was ever on call for
another reckoning.

He would not give up his job. Because the call to
reckon demons had not changed. And yet now he didn't
feel it was so much a curse as a privilege to be able to
keep his fellow humans safe from the dangers they must
never know lurked so close.

The day was bright and Jett laughed as sunshine hit
her face. Savin clasped her hand and led her toward the
cemetery, where they both felt comfortable. It was their
place now. It didn't remind them of death and misery,
but rather, it honored the parts of themselves they'd allowed to pass on.

Skipping down a narrow stone lane ahead of him, Jett
glanced over her shoulder. Her smile was so bright. And
that blue dress with the flowers all over it was like summer in the autumn. He couldn't imagine being happier.

Actually, he could. If all went well.

Jett stopped at the sarcophagus that they favored for
afternoon picnics and sat on the edge, waiting for him
to catch up to her. As he arrived before her, Savin knelt
on one knee and took Jett's hand. Her look told him she

had no idea what he was up to, and it pleased him that he could surprise her.

He wanted to fill her life with only the best surprises from now on. For good or for ill, he would be there for her.

"I love you, Jett," he said.

"I love you, too. Why are you kneeling?"

"It's what a guy is supposed to do."

"What do you mean— Oh." Her eyes glinted. "Really?"

"I've done a lot of growing up over the years, but I think I've done the most the past days you've been back in my life. And I've kissed you, so…I can finally ask you the important question."

Jett pressed her fingers to her lips, beaming.

"Will you marry me?"

She plunged forward to wrap her arms about him, and Savin stood, taking her with him as her legs hooked behind his hips. Their kiss was filled with wonder and joy. Heartbeats fluttered and raced. And finally, their future looked bright.

* * * * *

I hope you enjoyed this story.
The paranormal romance stories I have written for
Nocturne are set in my world of Beautiful Creatures.
Some of the secondary characters have their
own stories that can be found at your favorite
online retailer.

Certainly Jones's story is
This Wicked Magic

Edamite Thrash's story is
Captivating the Witch

Ethan Pierce's story is
An American Witch in Paris